HEAVEN'S GATE

BY
ALAN HOSKINS

"Who Wants to Live Forever?"
Queen

Part One

PROLOGUE

The story I'm about to reveal is not one of fiction and not one of fact. Created from actual events, gathered together from what I know to be correct. The dialogue, well, I may have reconstructed for dramatic purposes. But I hope to stay true to the content of the conversations and the details assembling this bizarre tale.

My journey of adventure and mystery begins one September day.

1

I had reached the point of no return. I could not go on living like this anymore. Existing on a concoction of pills and fake promises, waiting for my life to deteriorate into some kind of horrific nightmare. Death had become more attractive than life. I was a policeman, and a good one, fit, active, with a future, a career and now what? It had all gone.

The decision was easy, ruthless, selfish, maybe? but simple. I was going to end my life and nothing would change my mind.

We were both so nervous that day, Grace and I, waiting for Jack to arrive. The girls, my two daughters, weren't around. They were at their Grandmothers. They couldn't be around to hear what I had in mind.

"Jack's here!" I shout.

Grace was in the kitchen preparing lunch. She walks into the lounge, looking worried.

"How are you feeling?" I ask.

"As good as I can be," she replies, then kisses me on the cheek.

Grace, my wife, has been fantastic and the girls too. I'm not sure they initially understood the seriousness of my disease, I don't think I did, but we all do now. I've been diagnosed with Motor Neurone Disease (MND). The strain I have is called ALS, Amyotrophic Lateral Sclerosis, the most common form of MND. Characterised by weakness and wasting in the limbs. Life expectancy, two to five years.

"Has he got a new car?" she asks, looking out of the lounge window.

I stand, my arms ache as I lift myself from the chair, my feet shoot bullets of pain through the tendons of my legs as they take the weight of my body.

"I think he has," I reply, feeling slightly jealous.

We both watch him get out of his shiny, new silver BMW. He sees us looking at him, smiles, then waves. He looks good. He's tall, handsome, successful and a good friend.

I live or used to live, in a little bit of England called Pennington Terrace in leafy Wimbledon, London. Jack and his family lived in the house next door to us. One too many affairs, by my friend, put an end to that. They got divorced, sold the house and moved away. That was a sad day. We loved having them living next door. Their kids were friends with ours, barbecues in the summer, all ruined, just because he couldn't keep it in his pants. However, we kept in touch, and I'm pleased we did. He's a surgeon, a good one. One of those that fly out to war zones, I don't know how he does it, I couldn't. Helping people is his life, and I want him to help me.

Grace makes her way to the door, opening it as he arrives.

"Hi, Jack," she says.

"Hi, Grace," I hear him reply.

"I like the beard."

"Thank you, where's John?"

"I'm in here!" I shout as he enters, "Flash bastard, is that a new car?"

He smiles, walks over to me, ruffles my hair, then kisses my forehead.

"You're only jealous!" he replies.

"Too right, I am."

We laugh.

"Is the kettle on?" Jack asks, then turns to look at Grace, a wry smile appears across his face.

"I could live in that bloody kitchen," she chuckles. "I'll put it on now," she then makes her way into the kitchen.

"Thanks, Grace. So, how have you been? Are you okay?" Jack says, then takes a seat on the couch opposite me.

"Yeah, I'm great."

"John, do you want a drink?" Grace calls from the kitchen.

"Tea, please," I answer.

"Tea or coffee, Jack?"

"Tea, for me," he replies.

"Did you go out last night?" I ask.

"What?"

"You look tired."

"Thanks, you don't look so good yourself."

"Piss off! Well, were you?"

"I was out with Anna, we had a few drinks, and yeah, I'm feeling a bit rough."

"Anna?" I enquire.

"I've mentioned her before, haven't I?"

"Is she the nurse?"

"Yeah, that's right."

"Getting serious then?"

"Not me," Jack laughs.

Grace returns, carrying two mugs of tea, hands one to Jack and the other to me.

"Have you got it?" she asks, noticing my shaking hand holding the mug.

"Yeah," I reply, unconvincingly.

Grace then joins us, sitting next to Jack on the couch. Immediately the room descends into an awkward silence. Jack looks at me, noticing my facial expression change. I feel a nervous explosion happen within me. He turns to Grace.

"What's going on here?" he asks. "You've got me surrounded."

"Let's have lunch first," Grace suggests.

"Before what?" Jack asks, looking back at me, "Come on, what's going on?" he repeats.

"We were going to leave it 'till after lunch," I reply.

"Yes! We were," Grace interrupts.

"Leave what?" Jack asks again.

"I need to ask your advice about something," I answer.

"Go on then," he replies.

"Can we leave this 'till we've eaten? You said you would," she protests, looking at me.

"Never mind that. Tell me, what's going on?" Jack asks.

"Let's just get this over with," I look at Grace solemnly.

She reluctantly accepts my request.

"There's no easy way to say this but……," I pause, "It's my illness, you know I'm not gonna get better."

Jack looks at me, puzzled.

"Well, I'm… we're…" I pause again and look at Grace, then back at Jack, "Thinking of euthanasia."

Jack doesn't say a word, looks straight at me, then turns and faces Grace.

"What did he say?" he asks her calmly.

"I said, I'm thinking about killing myself, suicide, at an institution."

"What! You can't be serious?" Jack calls out, shocked at the news he's just heard.

"I'm serious. What do you know about it?"

"What do I know about what?"

"Euthanasia, travelling to Switzerland to die, or wherever."

"You've got to be joking?" Jack looks at Grace, "He's joking, isn't he?"

A tear appears then rolls down her cheek.

"Bloody hell, where did this idea come from?"

"It's the only way out," I reply.

"The way out? I can't believe you're saying this to me."

"We thought you could look into it for us," I say.

"Look into it for you. No way!" he replies. "I try to save lives, not the opposite. I won't be any part of it."

"Look, it's not an easy decision to make," I lied, "But, I can't carry on like this, I'm getting worse, every day is getting harder."

"Let me help you another way then," he pleads. "I'll do some research, pull some strings, try and get you seen by a specialist."

"I've seen specialists. They can't do anything."

"You don't know that. You can't give up."

"Don't give up, don't give up," I feel the anger, frustration rise to the surface.

I can't stop myself these days, and my emotions had become uncontrollable. I'd become an emotional wreck.

"You don't know what it's like, every day waking up, wondering what part of me isn't going to work today. I feel helpless, useless."

"New treatments are coming out all the time," he protests.

"New treatments? To keep me alive longer, live fucking longer… like I'm enjoying this so much that I want to live longer. I won't get better, and nothing can stop this happening."

"You don't know that."

"I do know. In two years, I'll be in a wheelchair. My muscles will have wasted away. I'll lose the use of my legs, my arms, everything. Even my jaw muscles will fail. Leaving me mute, being fed through a tube."

"Okay, stop," he interrupts.

"No, I won't stop! Listen to me! This disease isn't going away. I'm dying, slowly, horribly. Look at me, you can see that."

"I know it's going to be hard, but…," he replies.

"Hard. I'll tell you how hard it's going to be, sitting here wasting away in front of my wife and kids, it's brutal this disease. I can't do it! I won't do it!"

I wipe my nose across my sleeve; a tear traces a path down my cheek. Grace gets up, walks over to me, sits on the arm of the chair and hugs me.

I feel her warm breath on my temple. I take a deep breath.

"Sorry, Jack," I mumble, "I can't do this any more. I'm a father, a husband. I'm supposed to be able to look after my family, it's what I lived for, but now it's gone. I won't have it; I won't have my family remembering me this way."

"I understand that, but I just can't do it, I can't help you in that way," Jack says.

"And I can't live like this," I reply. "I've had my life; now my time is up, everybody needs to move on. I need to move on. Just look into it for me, that's all I'm asking. I want the best place, and only you can find this out for me."

"I can't do it, I don't believe in it," he repeats. "New drugs are coming out all the time; a cure could be just around the corner."

"It's not. If anyone should know that you should. I won't change my mind. Look at me."

"What about Lucy and Sadie? You haven't said anything to them, have you?" Jack asks.

"No, no, of course not, but they're finding it hard, seeing their dad like this," Grace says.

"Bloody hell, Grace. Are you really alright with this?" Jack asks.

"Of course, I'm not. I bloody love him, but I won't let John suffer any more than he has to. I won't let that happen."

"We talked about this a few months ago," I interject. "Before I was diagnosed. There was a program on telly; this man was dying. All he could do was lay in his bed all day and move his bloody eyelids. What life is that? We both said then that we wouldn't want to live like that, and we'd rather be dead."

"Everybody says that, but it's not real," Jack replies.

"No, but this is real now; it's happening to me."

"Please, Jack," Grace begs, "He's serious."

"We're serious," I say, taking hold of Grace's hand.

Jack shakes his head, "Let me do some research first, find out what help is out there."

"There is no help, believe me," I answer.

"Just let me look, check some things out, please."

"You won't find anything."

"Let me just try, please." He pleads.

I shake my head, considering his request, "It's no good," I answer.

"I need to check this out. You can't just ask me to look into euthanasia without, firstly, looking at all the options available."

"I know all the options. There aren't any."

"I don't though, let me look into it and if there isn't then...."

I wait for his answer.

"Then what?" I ask.

"Give me a few days....to check things out. That's all I'm asking."

"Let him check John," Grace says, "You know we need his help."

I shake my head, thinking about how to respond. I know I have very few alternatives available to me.

"Go on then, you can try," I answer, after a few tense moments, "But, you'd better be quick. I'm serious about this, Jack. After Christmas, I'm gone. I'll do this with or without your help."

"Thank you," he answers, relief obvious in his reaction.

We sat briefly in silence.

"Grace, can I have a beer please?" I ask.

"Do you want one?" she asks Jack.

"I didn't, but I do now," he replies.

Grace leaves the room.

"There's that place in Switzerland, or that other place in Cuba," I say.

"Fucking Cuba! Shut up!" he whispers, despair apparent in his voice.

"Wherever? Find out for me, Jack, please. I need something. There's nothing anyone can do to help me now."

There's a pause. "Please," I say again.

Jack shakes his head. "I just don't know."

"Help me, Jack."

"I've said, I'll look into it," he answers, annoyed, "I won't be pressured into killing my best mate, though I could kill you now." Jack looks straight at me with a stern look.

"I'd let you do it," I reply.

Jack shakes his head again.

Grace returns from the kitchen, holding two bottles of lager, which she hands to us.

"Do you need a glass?" she asks Jack.

"No, thanks," he replies and takes a large drink from the bottle.

"Cheers," I say, raising my bottle.

Jack ignores my request.

Grace comes back and sits down next to Jack, holding a glass of white wine.

"I can't believe you've let him talk you into this," Jack says to Grace.

"What choice do I have. It's hard seeing him like this," she says.

"I know, but…," Jack replies.

"You don't know," she interrupts. "There's been bad days, awful days. Days you haven't seen, the kids don't know how to act around him. They can see how sad he is."

I raise my hand to wipe a tear from my eye; it's hard for me to hear Grace say those words and I feel guilty.

"I can't keep living like this," I say.

"Just don't do anything without speaking to me first, okay," Jack says, looking at me, a frown contracting on his brow. He turns towards Grace. "Okay, Grace?"

"Yes," she mumbles.

A buzzing noise can be heard coming from the kitchen.

"That's the chicken, it's ready," Grace says, then stands abruptly and heads for the kitchen. "You're still staying for lunch, aren't you, Jack?"

"I don't feel like it now," he replies.

"Come on; it's ready now. I won't mention it again," I say.

Jack looks at me, then Grace, "You better bloody not. If you do, I'm leaving."

"I won't."

We pause for a moment; Grace disappears into the kitchen.

"You do know what you're asking is a heavy burden to put on someone. Taking a life is not something you can demand." Jack looks at me, sternly.

"I'm not asking you to do it, just to get me the information I need. I trust you."

We sit in silence.

"Jack," I say eventually.

"Stop, stop. Please don't mention it or I'm going, I mean it," he answers, fatigue present in his words.

"I wasn't going to," I answer.

"Really?" he asks.

"Yes, really."

"What then?"

"This Anna, are you going to marry her? Because, you better do it quickly, I could do with a good wedding."

"Piss off!" he replies.

2

Jack washes his hands, then places them beneath the dryer. It's been a couple of days since our talk. He had just finished a six-hour surgery, complications meant that a regular operation had ended up taking most of the day. Exhausted, he looks up, checks his reflection, then picks up his Hugo Boss, leather, laptop bag and makes his way to the hospital café. He buys a blackberry muffin and a soya milk latte, then takes a seat at an empty table. He reaches down into his bag and pulls out his MacBook Pro laptop, places it on to the table and switches it on. It connects to the hospital Wi-Fi. He begins to type, Motor Neurone Disease suicide, into the Google search box. A list of results appears, he clicks on the first:

A company director dying from motor neurone disease has taken to his Facebook page to reveal when he is planning to end his life in a Swiss euthanasia clinic. John Sims, 52, has told his business connections he would end his life at an assisted-dying organisation in Switzerland after he was diagnosed with motor neurone disease. The former Oxford University graduate, who lives in Manchester, even told people when his funeral would take place and the reason why he planned to take his life. He posted: "Recently I have been diagnosed with aggressive Motor Neurone Disease (MND). As I was driven home, I had already decided what I would gladly have to do when my time was upon me."

Jack stops reading and flicks back to the list of results:

- A pensioner with a terminal illness, Motor Neurone Disease, committed suicide after watching a TV program on euthanasia

- Motor Neurone Disease sufferer wants voluntary euthanasia legalised.

- Motor Neurone Disease Patient: why I want to die.

Disturbed by his findings, he closes the computer, then takes a mouthful of his coffee.

He feels a hand on his shoulder and looks up.

"Hi, Tom," Jack says.

"Hi, Jack, mind if I sit with you?"

"Not at all, sit down," he replies, then makes space on the table for his friend to place his tray.

Tom is tall and thin with a bald head. Jack has known him since his days at university. He has established himself as a very respected surgeon in his own right, specialising in heart surgery.

"So, how're things?" Tom asks as he starts to open his pre-packed sandwich.

"Good thanks, and you?"

"Busy with work. You didn't tell me how much time lecturing would take up, it's bloody never-ending."

Tom had recently taken over from Jack lecturing at the local university. Jack's trips to war-torn lands, working for the red cross, had taken up too much of his time and his life. Forcing him to quit lecturing, at least for this year.

"I know, I thought you knew?" Jack answers.

"I know now," he says.

"Are you not enjoying it then?"

"No, I am, it's just a lot of work," Tom answers then takes a bite of his sandwich.

A group of junior doctors laugh loudly behind them, Tom and Jack stop talking and turn around, wondering what's happening. Jack recognises one of the pack, she is pretty, twenty-something, with long dark hair. She leans across the table, and her jeans are pulled tight against her well-exercised bottom. Jack watches her take a bottle of water from her friend, turning to take a drink she notices the two men looking at her. She waves at Jack. He smiles back and raises his coffee cup in recognition, then turns back around to see Tom grinning at him.

"Who's that then?" Tom asks.

"She's one of the junior doctors that's been in my surgery this week. Gemma.. I think she's called.. Gemma Collins."

"And?" Tom enquires.

"And…" Jack smirks, "She's so impressed with my skills, she'd like to find out what other attributes I have."

"Some personal, one to one training?" Tom laughs.

"If only! I don't stand a chance with her. I'm too old and definitely not with that lot around."

Tom looks beyond Jack to the table of Doctors.

"That used to be us back in the day," he says.

"Seems a long time ago now."

"Hey, you're looking good; you've still got your hair, not like me." He runs his hand over his bald head.

Jack smiles.

"Did I hear, right? Have you just returned from Syria?" Tom asks.

"I have indeed," Jack answers with an air of sadness.

"How was that?"

"Bloody terrible, lots of kids with horrific injuries. I wasn't prepared for the devastation out there. I thought I'd seen everything."

"You wouldn't advise going then?"

"No, the opposite. Good doctors are desperately needed. Why do you ask?"

"I'm thinking of going, maybe next year."

"I can give you the name of my contact, if you're serious?"

"I'll let you know. See how my life is in a few months."

"Did I hear you've just won an award?" Jack asks.

"I have," Tom answers, a broad smile appears on his face. "It's bit embarrassing. It's not just my award, it's the research departments, but with me being the head, I guess I'm the one who had to make the speech."

"What was it for again? White blood cell research?"

"It's interesting; we've discovered something that could be quite exciting, a real breakthrough. If we can get funding to move it to the next stage."

"Could it help with Motor Neurone Disease?"

"Motor Neurone? No, I don't think so? Why do you ask?"

"My friend, John, has been diagnosed with it. I think you met him once at a barbecue I had a couple of summers ago. He was my neighbour, when I lived in Wimbledon."

"Is he the policeman?"

"Yeah, that's him."

"He's not very old, hasn't he got young kids?"

"Yeah, it's dreadful news."

"How's he coping?"

"Not very well," Jack answers.

Tom notices his worried look.

"What is it?" he asks.

"He's thinking about euthanasia."

Jack looks straight at Tom, waiting for a reaction, but he doesn't seem shocked.

"I hear that all the time in those cases. It's hard for the patients to live with." Tom answers.

"You know about MND then?"

"I've done some work on the disease, but it was only in conjunction with another piece of research that we were doing. It wasn't specific to MND."

"Am I wrong? In hoping that I might find something out there to help him."

"There's no harm investigating."

"You don't think I'm wasting my time?"

"There might be something? I haven't heard of any great breakthroughs in that area, but I'd like to think that the future was bright for all diseases. How quickly these things develop, though, who knows?”

“I said I'd look into it for him.”

“Good luck.”

“No, not just treatments.”

“Then what?”

“Euthanasia.”

“Euthanasia! I don't know if that's a good idea.”

Now Tom looks shocked.

“What can I do? I need to find something that could give him hope, but if I can't….”

Tom doesn't reply.

“Can you think of any hospitals anywhere? specialising in MND? Anybody I could speak to?” Jack asks again.

“Leave it with me; I'll ask my colleagues. I think you should try and change his mind though,” Tom says.

“I'm trying.”

“Keep trying. From what I know. Once that seed is sown, it grows quickly.”

Tom's phone begins to vibrate on the table top. Tom checks who's calling.

“Sorry, I just need to take this.” Tom answers, then begins to talk on the phone.

Jack drinks his last mouthful of coffee, then turns again to look at the group of junior doctors behind him. More doctors have joined the group. They quickly rearrange the tables to accommodate the ever-growing pack. Gemma notices his interest and smiles at him again. Jack smiles back, confidently. She says something to the group, then begins to walk over to him. Tom finishes his phone call.

“Sorry Jack, I'm going to have to go," Tom says.

"No problem; give me a call sometime."

"I will. We'll go for a drink."

"Definitely, and please, if you can help me in any way with the MND."

"Leave it with me but speak to him, change his mind."

"I will." Jack answers.

"Dr Carlisle." The two men turn to see Gemma standing before them.

"Hi, Gemma," Jack replies.

"Sorry to interrupt, I was just wondering if I could ask your advice?" she says.

"Yes, of course, please, sit down," Jack says.

Tom begins to collect his things.

"You can sit here. I have to go." He says and Gemma sits down.

"I'll be in touch, Jack," Tom says.

"Hopefully, with some good news," Jack replies.

Tom crosses his fingers then glances at Gemma then back at Jack. A sly grin appears on his face.

"See you soon," he says, then walks off across the room.

Jack and Gemma watch him walk away.

"So, what was it you wanted to ask me?" Jack says, turning to face her.

3

That evening Jack is alone at his home, sitting at his desk. Numerous files are stacked on top of the antique, oak, surface. He picks up the wine glass next to him, drinks down the last of the Argentinian Malbec, stands and walks into his kitchen. He pours himself another glass of wine and returns to his desk. He checks his watch, 9:55 PM, he contemplates an early night. His phone vibrates in his pocket. He puts his wine down and pulls out his phone.

"Hi, Tom." He answers.

"Hi, Jack, sorry to call this late."

"It's not late. I was getting ready to go out."

Tom laughs. "I better be quick then, don't want to spoil your evening."

Jack smiles to himself. "Go ahead. What's up?"

"I was thinking about our conversation this afternoon, and… I may have found somewhere that might be of interest to you?"

"What? Really? Brilliant! Where is it?"

"Well, don't get too excited; it may be a long shot."

"Go ahead."

"I have this student in my class."

"You have lots of students."

"Not like this one."

"What does that mean?"

"She's not the usual exchange student."

"Exchange student? Where's she from?"

"She's here on a placement from a research hospital based in Romania. I've just been going over some of her work, that's what brought it to my attention."

"Romania!" Jack interjects.

"I know, it's even stranger than that, her being here is all very top secret. The university had to sign a confidentiality clause for her to come here."

"And you're telling me? Why?"

"I'm not sure why that is? But you didn't hear any of this from me, alright?"

"My lips are sealed," Jack says, chuckling, "Carry on."

"Anyway, the hospital that sent her here has had a great deal of success in the research and development of new drugs."

"What drugs? To do with MND?"

"Not specifically, but it looks to me like their research department is investigating everything."

"Everything? That doesn't make sense. How do you know?"

"I did a little investigating of my own when I first heard about Cristina's post."

"Cristina? That's your students name?"

"Yes, Cristina Albu. I didn't find much, but what I did find out was very impressive. The array of medicines attributed to the hospital's research facility, well, it's unheard of."

"Like what?"

"All sorts; blood disorders, heart problems, lungs, liver, you name it, this place has researched it."

"It's unusual for an institution to vary it's research so much, why would they do that?"

"I'm not sure; maybe they're still unsure of which direction to take."

"But why so secret?"

"A bit of a mystery really, maybe some of their techniques aren't so accepted these days. They tend to release all of their research through affiliated universities, distancing themselves from the results."

"Why would they do that? Surely they're missing out on funding doing it that way?"

"Maybe they don't need the money?"

"How many hospitals do you know that don't need the money?" Jack laughs.

"None. It's bizarre alright."

"And what techniques are they using? I'm guessing they're using animals then?"

"Maybe, but I checked out a drug that they were responsible for producing, Melotrax. Have you heard of it?"

"No, what's it used for?"

"It's used to regulate blood flow around the body; many patients with heart conditions are benefitting from this drug."

"Maybe I should know about the drug then? However, if it's such a triumph, why don't they embrace their success?"

"Again, I'm not sure, but if you look at the research, they've disclosed - before the drug was released - clinical trials were used to develop the drug."

"Clinical trials? Are they testing drugs on patients?"

"Yes, it seems so."

"That's not unusual, standard procedure for new drugs, nothing new there."

"Maybe, but not before the drug was officially registered."

"What are you suggesting? That they're using patients as guinea pigs?"

"I can't say for sure, but it looks like it."

"That's not possible; they'd be closed down if that was the case."

"I'm presuming that's why it's so secret and why it's located in Romania. Nobody knows about it."

"They can't be."

"If the patients they're testing the drugs on, aren't in the best of health, then…."

"Then what?"

"The drugs either relieve their symptoms or…."

Tom pauses

"Kills them?" Jack interrupts.

"Yes, it does look that way."

"Bloody hell, so why are you telling me this?"

"You did say your friend was intent on dying."

"He is."

"Then maybe you could convince him to enrol in one of these clinical trials."

"What? At a top-secret hospital based in Romania? He wouldn't go for it. I'm not sure I'm happy with it."

"It's probably not as brutal as I'm describing. If you could get John on a research program of any kind, at least then his death might help others, you never know, it may even help him?"

"It's all a bit….."

"Mad? Crazy?" Tom jokes.

"Yeah."

"I agree, it's a long shot, but what have you got to lose? Motor Neurone Disease needs this type of research. He could help develop drugs for the future."

"And how do you know they're running any clinical trials on MND. At this top-secret hospital?"

"I don't. I thought you could meet with my student and discuss it. Hopefully, she could tell you more about the research done there."

"I'm not sure?" Jack ponders.

"I wouldn't have phoned you if I didn't think there might be something in it. It's a one-off this place. I'd at least meet with her."

"I suppose it wouldn't do any harm for me to meet her." Jack falls silent. "Go on then, give me her number, and I'll call her."

"It might not be as easy as that."

"Why?"

"Due to this confidentiality clause we've signed, I don't think you phoning her up and asking her questions about her facility, is a good idea."

"Then what?"

"Well, I thought you could take one of my lectures."

"Oh yeah!" Jack laughs. "All this so you can skive off work!" He hears Tom laughing with him.

"I need to get out of a few lectures, to catch up on some other work. You'd be doing me a big favour and it gives you the opportunity to meet with her in an official capacity. Everybody wins."

"You've got it all worked out."

"I'll go ahead and organise it then?"

"Yeah, go on then."

"Great! I also get the impression she'd like to meet you."

"Meet with me? Why do you say that?"

"I think she thought you were still lecturing at the university."

"Really? Why do you say that?"

"After my first lecture, the one you used to take, she came up to me and asked me where you were. I think she was expecting to see you taking the stage, not me."

"And what did you say to that?"

"Just that I'd taken over from you and you were taking time out from lecturing. She didn't look happy. They just turned and stormed out after I told them."

"Them? Is there more than one student?"

"There's two of them, but Ivan's not a student."

"Ivan, who's he?"

"Well, that's another strange thing."

"What? Can it get any stranger?"

"It can; I'm not sure what he's doing here. Or, what his connection is with Cristina. He's just here and with her at every lecture."

"Is he her boyfriend?"

"No, definitely not her boyfriend; they don't hold hands, or even sit together. He always sits at the back of the lecture theatre staring."

"Staring?"

"Yeah, it freaked me out at first. But I've got used to it now."

"And he's not a student?"

"No, it looks to me like he's here just to keep an eye on her while she's over here studying."

"What? So, the university agreed to that?"

"I guess so. As I said, I'm not sure what's going on? Very strange? I've asked Steve about them."

"Steve?"

"Steve Robinson, the head, have you forgotten everyone already?" he laughs.

"Oh, yeah. What did Steve say?"

"He thought she might have a medical condition that requires immediate medical attention, and this guy is there to give it to her, if needed."

"Her doctor then?"

"Well, I suppose he could be. However, I wasn't convinced, I'm not sure Steve is. He doesn't look like a doctor."

"What does he look like?"

"Classic Hermon Munster lookalike, over six-foot-tall, broad shoulders, looks like he spends a lot of time at the gym. You wouldn't want to get in a fight with this fella."

"I'll try not to."

They both laugh.

"So, what do you think? I know it all sounds crazy, but it just might be something, something rather than nothing."

"Go on then, sort it for me. I need to meet this Cristina and Ivan. When do you need me to lecture?"

"Leave it with me. I'll try and sort it out tomorrow. Do you think you could cover my lecture on Thursday?"

"Let me just check."

Jack clicks his mouse and opens up the calendar on his computer.

"That should be fine," he says.

"Great. I'll ring as soon as I've sorted it."

"Thanks, Tom."

"No problem. I hope it leads somewhere. I'm eager to know what you can find out."

"Not sure about that, it's confidential," Jack answers.

"Ha, ha, piss off." Tom laughs. "I'll sort it tomorrow. Enjoy your night out."

"Night out?" Jack answers puzzled.

"I thought you were going out tonight?"

"That's right. I think my taxi has just arrived," he answers, chuckling.

"I better let you go then?"

"Thanks for this Tom."

"Not a problem. I'll call you tomorrow."

"Tom!" Jack quickly shouts down the phone.

"Yes," he replies.

"What's the name of the hospital? I'll try and do some research myself before I meet her."

"Good luck with that. Now, don't laugh, the hospitals called Heaven's Gate.

4

The week following my meeting with Jack, I had an appointment with my specialist Dr Robert. Grace and I arrived early that morning; I remember feeling good that day. My limbs ached, but no more than usual. The drugs I'd been, recently, prescribed seemingly were doing their job. It was also a weight off my mind telling Jack about my plans for the future. I'm not sure that was how Grace was feeling; she had been quiet; her mood had changed. Though we'd talked about euthanasia many times in the past few weeks, it had become real, and it was happening. I felt this too, but for me, it was liberating, knowing I was in charge of my destiny. Grace, I guess, was struggling.

The last few appointments had been pointless, soul-destroying. That morning, the fear had gone; there was nothing that Dr Robert could tell me that could upset me. I knew my future, and it made me strong.

Sitting in the waiting room, I looked around at the other patients. Some of the faces were now familiar to me; people I had seen many times, week after week. We'd never really spoken, just said hello. What did we have to in common, apart from our illness? I'd watch them struggling to stand, walk, talk. Their partners were looking tired, helpless, but trying hard to be positive.

I sat that morning with a sense of fulfilment. Part of me wanted to tell them, let everybody know what I had planned. Maybe we all could go to Switzerland, end this hell together, hire a coach. We'd surely get a group discount? They must have thought about it. Maybe they're thinking about it right now. Some seem like they've missed their chance, too ill to make that decision.

"Hi, John, Grace"

"Hello, David," Grace replies.

"Hi, David," I repeat. Things must be severe if you're on first name terms with your Doctor.

Dr David Robert is a highly regarded Neurologist, assigned to my care. He's an older man. Maybe sixty, wearing a white coat over a sky-blue shirt. I concentrate on his tie as he speaks to us. Is that a dog or a cat, embroidered into the silk tie? I ignore his welcoming words. We were at the hospital to get the results of some tests I had done a couple of weeks previous. I forget what they were for, and I didn't care.

"This way, please," he says.

Grace stands and then turns to help me.

"I'm okay," I say to her abruptly. She frowns at me then spins around and follows the Doctor. Guilt engulfs me again, I'm tired of this. The Doctor leads us down the brightly lit corridor to his office. We enter, he closes the door behind us, and we sit down. Dr Robert then sits at his desk opposite us, he casually opens the file in front of him, takes a moment to read the first few lines, then looks across at us.

"How have you been?" he asks.

"He's been good, haven't you, John?" Grace says enthusiastically.

I'm always amazed at how she can be so upbeat in these situations. I think her nerves must make her that way. I feel a deep sense of love for her. I don't know how she does it.

"I've been good, thanks," I repeat.

"And how are the cramps?" he enquires.

"Not any worse," I respond.

"Is the physio helping?" he asks.

Grace looks at me; her eyes say it all. The previous week I had been to the physiotherapy department at the hospital and ended up shouting at the young guy who was trying his best to stretch my legs. I have my excuses. It had been a long day, and we were late getting in for my appointment. I was feeling terrible. We ended up leaving after about fifteen minutes. Grace didn't speak to me for the rest of that day.

"I think so," I reply. Grace says nothing.

"Excellent I know those sessions can be quite demanding, but it's important to keep up the treatment." Dr Robert replies, then returns to his notes.

"He knows what I did." I think to myself.

"I can see from these tests that your symptoms have plateaued at this time." He then says.

"Is that a good sign?" Grace asks.

"Yes, it suggests that the progression of your disease may not be as quick as first thought."

"Great news," Grace says, smiling at me. I guess we have to go through this act in front of the Doctor.

"Yeah, great news," I reply, sarcasm obvious in my tone.

The rest of the meeting goes as predicted; the Doctor pushes and pulls my limbs. I feel sore and helpless during this. The Doctor continually says how well I'm doing. I'm tempted to tell him to fuck off, but I don't.

"Have you thought any more about an Advance Decision?" the Doctor asks, as we get ready to leave.

We sit silently; this had been brought up previously. But we, for one reason or another, had done nothing about it.

An Advance Decision, or an advanced directive, is where you make your treatment preferences known in advance in case you can't communicate your decisions later because you're too ill. A lot of MND sufferers make this Advanced Decision because, in the latter stages of the disease, many patients lose the ability to speak. Issues that may be covered by an advance decision include:

Do you want to be treated at home, in a hospice, or a hospital?

The types of medication you agree to take in that situation.

Whether you'd be willing to consider a feeding tube if you were no longer able to swallow food and liquid.

If you have a respiratory failure (loss of lung function) in the latter stages of Motor Neurone Disease, do you wish to be resuscitated by artificial means? Such as having a permanent breathing tube inserted into your throat (known as a tracheostomy).

Do you want to donate any of your organs after your death to the hospital, (the brain and spinal cord of people with MND can be essential for ongoing research into the condition)?

"I know this is a difficult thing to consider," says Dr Robert breaking the silence, "But, John, we must know how you would like to be treated if you are not able to communicate with us."

He looks directly at me. I'm tempted to tell him,

"I won't need anyone's help, because I won't fucking be here!"

"We'll discuss it this week, I promise," I reply. I hold Grace's hand

"Good," the Doctor says.

5

Jack removes his spectacles, rubs his eyes, and checks the time; 9.30 PM. In front of him are case notes for the patients he will see tomorrow. He takes a sip of coffee, then bends down and picks up his bag, unzips the side pocket, and takes out a small note pad, placing it onto the desk. 'Heaven's Gate' are the only words written on the page. He moves the computer mouse, enters his password, then writes Heaven's Gate into the Google search box. The results stream down the page.

Heaven's Gate (film)- Wikipedia

Heaven's Gate is a 1980 American epic Western film written and directed by Michael Cimino. Loosely based on the Johnson County War, it portrays a fictional

He remembers that film when it was released. He reads on,

"It is generally considered, one of the biggest box office bombs of all time, and in some circles has been considered to be one of the worst films ever made."

He smiles to himself and remembers now why he never bothered to go and see it. The rest of the results are all similar; all about the film. He re-types HEAVEN'S GATE ROMANIA and clicks search. He reads the results; nothing about the hospital appears. He changes his search again, HEAVEN'S GATE RESEARCH CENTRE ROMANIA. Still nothing. He takes another drink of coffee and stares at the screen. "It must be there somewhere," he thinks to himself. He then types Romanian translation into Google and opens up a translation site. He types in the words Heaven's Gate and hits translate

Poarta Raiului appears. He copies the result, then pastes this into Google. The results appear on the screen, all in Romanian. Jack notices one of the images, a castle or fortress is displayed, perched at the top of a mountain; it looks incredible. He clicks on the image. Its grandeur now fills the screen. He reads the words beneath the image; Rasnov Fortress, Transylvania.

"Transylvania," he thinks to himself. He clicks on the image, and it takes him to a Romanian travel website. He reads the description.

'Rasnov Fortress is located on a rocky hilltop, in the Carpathian Mountains, 200m above the town of Rasnov in Romania. It is 15 km southwest of Brasov and also about 15 km from Bran Castle'.

"Bloody Bran Castle?" Jack smiles at his discovery.

'The fortress is on the Bran Pass, a trade route connecting Wallachia with Transylvania. Saxons first settled in Transylvania in the 11th century, and the Saxon town of Rasnov was founded in 1225. Archaeological research has revealed the existence of fortification traces on the site since prehistoric and Dacian times (a province of the Roman Empire from 106 to 274–275 AD). Following the first Tartar invasion of 1241, a series of fortresses were constructed by the Teutonic Knights to defend the people. Rasnov Fortress is one of these peasant fortresses. The Teutonic Knights were a German medieval military order, formed to aid Christians on their pilgrimages to the holy land and to establish Hospitals. Mainly made up of volunteers and mercenaries, they would pledge allegiance to the cause, and defend with their lives, the people inside the fortress. It is said that, in case of capture, the knights had their tongues removed, so that they could not communicate the secrets held within the walls of the fortress.

This castle differs from some in the area, in that it was meant to be a place of refuge for the commoners, not an army stronghold. Inside the fortress, a working village still exists, with a school, chapel, and various craft shops. The chapel is thought to be one of the oldest buildings within the fortress walls, and is unusual, in the fact that it encompasses a large furnace, used for local cremations. The building is still in use, so out of bounds to tourists. The chapel is commonly known as Heaven's Gate'.

"So that's Heaven's Gate?" He wonders then continues to read.

'The first written record for the fortress is from 1331, and when the Tartars invaded in 1335, Rasnov Fortress was already strong enough to offer resistance. The castle has an upper and lower section, with polygonal perimeter walls reaching an average height of five metres. The east side is the most heavily fortified, and the walls on both that side as well as the northwest side are doubled.

The defences include nine towers, two bastions, and a drawbridge. As Turkey and Austria battled over Transylvania, arms were stockpiled in the defence corridors within the walls. In March of 1612, Rasnov Fortress was besieged by Gabriel Bathory (a Prince of Transylvania), and surrendered in April after the secret route to their water supply was found. Bathory's forces settled into the fortress and held off two attempts to win it back by joint forces from the towns of Brasov and Rasnov. The following year a ransom was paid, and Bathory and his troops left.

With the location of their water supply no longer a secret, the need for a well inside the fortress became more evident. With the castle atop a calcareous mountain, however, it meant digging down 146m through solid rock. Work on the well began in 1623 and took 17 years to complete. Two Turkish prisoners, who were promised their freedom once the well was finished, are reported to have dug out the well, but with their freedom never granted, they were rumoured to have been burned in secret, and their ashes scattered from the top of the fortress. The well provided an extra layer of security as it meant the people didn't have to travel outside the fortress walls for water. The last siege of Rasnov Fortress took place in 1690 during the previous Turkish invasion of Transylvania. It was damaged by fire in 1718 and rebuilt the following year. The next significant damage occurred as the result of an earthquake in 1802. The last use of the fortress as a refuge was during the revolutions of 1821 and 1848 when Romanian refugees and revolutionaries resided here. Although much of the fortress has been renovated over the past one hundred and fifty years, it still has many of the original features. Descendants of those, from the time of the Teutonic Knights, still reside within the walls. The fortress can be reached by walking up the steep winding road that leads to the entrance of the fortress. The views from the top of the fortress are astounding, looking across the village of Rasnov, and further on to the Carpathian Mountains'.

Jack pauses and takes another drink of coffee.

History lesson completed, but no mention of a hospital. Jack considers his findings. Bran Castle? Vampires? Transylvania? It all sounds too weird.

He types into the Google search box Rasnov Fortress.

Result after result, explain in similar ways, the history of the fortress, but no mention of a hospital or research facility. He types Heaven's Gate Chapel Rasnov fortress. More descriptions of the chapel appear, but no images are available. One image that does appear is an old black and white photo, claiming to be one of the earliest photos taken inside the fortress, dating from around 1855. It shows a grim image of life inside the fortress. A handful of people stand posing in the street, thin, without smiles on their faces, ragged old clothes hang on their bodies. It reminds Jack of a scene from a concentration camp, not a village. In the background stands a thickset man, larger in build than the villagers, who holds centre stage, he stands upright holding a gun.

Jack's phone vibrates; Anna calling. He closes the page on his screen and answers.

"Hi, Anna."

"Hi, where are you? still at work?"

"I'm afraid so, why?"

"I was thinking about driving to yours."

"Are you okay?" he asks.

"I'm fine. It's been a long day, and I could do with a glass of wine and a cuddle."

"A glass of wine and a cuddle sounds good."

"What time will you be finishing?" she asks.

"Right now. I think I've had enough for one day. Give me half an hour to get home."

6

The Black Dog Bar is situated no more than half a mile away from the hospital. It stands proud at the end of two terraced rows of houses; most of the homes in the area are now rented out to nurses and junior doctors, who frequent the Black Dog most days and nights. Jack, currently single again, has begun to use the facilities on offer far to often than he'd like to admit.

It's Saturday night, and Jack has just entered the establishment. He has arranged to meet his friend Michael, 'Mickey', Richardson, an old acquaintance, who like Jack, is now divorced. The two friends meet quite regularly, to discuss ex-wives, football and women. Jack is early; the time is half-past eight; they are scheduled to meet at nine o'clock. The room is quite full. Music plays loudly from the tiny speakers embedded in the ceiling. Jack doesn't recognise the song. Laughter from surrounding tables adds to the cacophony of noise. Jack wonders why he arranged to meet here.

He makes his way to the bar, a group of women stand in his way, blocking his ability to get served.

"Bloody hell, I don't need this," he thinks to himself. While he waits to buy his drink, he takes his phone from his pocket. There's a message from Anna.

'Hi Jack, hope you've had a good day - not sure what I'm doing tonight - Daniella is coming round for a drink, then we might go out later - let me know if you're out and we'll meet up! Call me!!! Xxx

He reads the text, then places his phone back in his pocket.

"Hi Jack," a voice says.

He looks up, the women who were standing in front of him have been served and are walking away from the bar.

"What would you like to drink?" the barmaid asks.

"Hi, Miss Julie," he replies, smiling. "A pint of…." He pauses and looks at the real ale beers on offer. "I think I'll have a pint of Golden Mary, please."

She smiles and walks away to get his drink. He watches her behind the bar. She is probably twenty-five; he likes her; everybody likes her. They have spoken a few times, flirted a bit, but nothing more. He feels a hand on his shoulder.

"Now that's good timing," Mickey says with a broad grin on his face.

"Hi Mickey, what would you like? A pint?"

"Great, thanks. What are you having?" he asks

"The Golden Mary."

"Sounds good, I'll have one of those thanks."

Julie returns with Jack's drink.

"Sorry, could I have another one please," he asks. She smiles then returns minutes later with another drink.

They walk around the bar to a quieter area, placing their drinks onto an unoccupied, dark wood, round, tall table.

"So how was your week?" Jack asks Mickey.

Mickey begins to answer. While he talks, Jack notices Gemma, the junior Doctor, walking into the bar. She is with a group of four or five women, all about her age, dressed to kill, all of them looking gorgeous. She notices Jack, smiles and waves at him. Jack raises his glass in acknowledgement. Mickey realises Jack has stopped listening and looks over his shoulder to see what has taken Jacks interest.

"Who's that?" Mickey asks.

"Gemma, she's a junior doctor from work."

"Is she now?" he answers, with a smile.

"She was present at one of my surgeries this week."

"She's lovely," Mickey says.

"I know," Jack replies, then walks over to Gemma, leaving Mickey to stand on his own.

"Hi," Jack says, as he walks up to her.

"Hi," she replies. All her friends stop talking and look up at him.

"Evening ladies," he says.

"Evening, Dr Carlisle," one of the women replies. Jack looks at her but doesn't recognise her.

"I've made an appointment to see you on Tuesday, is that still okay?" Gemma asks.

"Yeah, that's fine, I'll look forward to it. Can I get you a drink?" he asks. Gemma is wearing a small denim jacket, undone, showing a flowery, tight-fitting, scooped neck dress, not too short, but short enough to show off her athletic legs.

"Thank you, white wine, please," she replies. "Who are you with?" she asks, looking across at Mickey.

"My friend, Michael. I'll get you that drink," Jack says, then makes his way to the bar. He waits to be served. After what seems like an age, he eventually reaches the bar and orders the white wine. He pays for the drink, then feels a tap on his shoulder. He turns around. Anna stands in front of him.

"That's good timing. Is that wine for me?" she asks, smiling.

"Hi, Anna." He answers, surprised to see her.

"It's for that lady over there with Mickey," he says, gesturing with the wine glass. Mickey has made his way across the room and is standing with Gemma.

"And why are you buying Mickey's girlfriend a drink?" she enquires suspiciously.

"She's one of the junior doctors from work,"

"So why the drink?"

"Be rude not to," a false grin appears, "Would you like a drink? I'll get you one."

"It's okay, I'll get my own."

"No, I'll get you one, I'll just give this to Gemma."

"To Gemma?"

She pauses.

"It's okay, Daniella is at the bar, she's got me one."

"Okay, I'll be back in a minute," he says, then makes his way over to Mickey and Gemma. Anna watches him walk over to them. Jack hands Gemma her drink and says something to her. She laughs out loud.

Daniella hands a large glass of white wine to Anna. She notices Anna's frustration.

"What's wrong?" She asks.

"Nothing," she replies.

The two women notice an empty table, quickly they rush over to claim their prize. Moments later, Jack arrives at their table.

"May I join you?" he asks.

"What's wrong? has Gemma had a better offer?" Anna asks sarcastically.

"What? Yeah, I think she has. I'll leave them to it," he replies, then he kisses Anna on the lips. She glares back at him. He smiles, sits down and takes a drink of his pint.

"Are you going to introduce me?" Jack asks.

"This is Daniella, I'm sure you two have met before," Anna replies.

"I don't know if we have," Jack replies, holding out his hand.

"I was at your barbeque. When was it? June or July," she answers, leaning over the table, and shaking Jack's hand. Her accent is strong, making her sound assertive and sharp. Jack is unsure of her nationality.

"Ahh, yes, I remember," he smiles, not remembering her at all. Daniella is tall, slim, with classic angular Eastern European features. Her hair is dark and long, framing her beautiful features.

"I must go to the loo," Anna announces, then stands up. Jack shuffles his chair to let her get past him.

"Don't you go buying any other girls drinks while I'm gone, okay," she says, then kisses him on the lips, smiles and walks off towards the toilet.

"So where is your accent from? Poland?" Jack asks.

"No, Romania," she answers.

"Romania, that's a coincidence. I'm just doing some research on a hospital in Romania."

"A hospital. Why? Which one?" she asks.

"It's a research facility, but I'm not sure where it is yet."

"You're not sure where it is? How come?"

"No, it's kind of top secret. I really shouldn't be telling you about it," he says, smiling. Daniella looks back blankly at him, not getting the joke.

"How did you find out about it then? Do you know its name?"

"A friend of mine told me about it. I think it's called Heaven's Gate."

Jack notices Daniella's expression change.

"What's wrong? Have you heard of it?" He asks.

"Do not go there," she answers sternly.

"What? Why not?" He asks.

"That place is evil."

"Evil." Jack laughs, "That's a bit strong, isn't it? It's a hospital, not a prison. Are you thinking of the same place as I am?"

"I know where you mean," she interrupts. "Do not go there. There is nothing good to be found."

"Why do you say that?" Jack asks, realising she's serious.

She doesn't answer.

"Come on. You can't say something like that, then not tell me what you know."

"I will not say," she replies.

"Come on, tell me. Evil is an unusual description for a hospital, please, explain yourself."

"There is an old Romanian saying; Cu cheia de aur se deschide poarta raiului."

"What does that mean?"

"A golden key opens any gate, but not that of heaven."

"And what does that mean?" Jack asks, looking confused.

"What you seek is not the gateway to heaven."

"Well it might not be the gateway to heaven, but it might be the gateway to a better life, for a friend of mine."

"Cine sapă groapa altuia, cade singur în ea," Daniella says, accentuating the words.

"And what does that mean?" Jack asks.

"He who digs a pit for others will fall in it himself."

At that moment, Anna returns.

"This all looks very serious, what are you two talking about?" She asks.

"Daniella is just giving me a lesson in Romanian proverbs," Jack replies, standing up. Anna looks confused and makes her way past Jack and sits down.

"The lesson is over," Daniella announces.

7

Since my last appointment, I have felt my breathing begin to shorten. My chest feels tight. I know this is the muscle controlling my diaphragm, beginning to weaken. I will eventually lose the ability to breathe on my own. I'll need an oxygen mask to force air into my lungs, and then, finally, I will lose my voice. As the Doctor had suggested, it is at this time that I should make plans for an advanced decision. Grace and I have not talked about making these plans, I was slightly surprised that she hadn't mentioned it, but maybe she knew she was wasting her time. I am not frightened of dying; I am not scared of being incapacitated. I just don't want to be incapacitated, would you? It's not the same thing as being frightened. I understand that Grace wants to keep me as long as possible, because she loves me, and it's difficult to accept, to say goodbye before nature does it for me. But I am not a child, I am a man, and I have been making decisions all of my adult life, and this is another decision I am going to make.

Every day now, I feel my body weakening, betraying me. I can't work anymore. I can't drive, and I will eventually need help to shower and dress and go to the toilet. This is humiliating, that's what all this is, a feeling of helplessness. I am a man, and this is no way for a man to live or die.

All I have achieved is now history. I have always had a positive outlook on life and have tried my hardest to live life to the full. During my career in the police, I met many people who wanted to take their own lives. I talked with them, tried my hardest to change their minds, but now it is me who has those thoughts. I know there are many patients with this disease, who don't want to die. They have achieved something I can't, come to terms with their illness. Maybe treating themselves to a holiday of a lifetime is enough for them. I applaud them for that. But that is not me. I cannot do that. I am not that person. I have done what I need to do. Another holiday? Well, what will that give me? More memories of a time when I was able to walk, do things for myself. I don't need them.

A wave of melancholy flows over me when I think that I will never see my kids finish school, go to college, get married, see my grandkids. That feeling is one I wish nobody to experience. I have cried night after night thinking about that. I cannot go on. I will not get better. There is no cure. If I had cancer, I would have hope, up to the last minute. That hope is not there with my illness. Once the treatment I am on has ended, and it cannot help me anymore, I will be given morphine and reduced to a dumb mute. I will sit in my chair and watch as people scurry around me, cry in front of me, hold my hand, say how they loved me, talk about me. If I were single, no family, I would be dead now, I would have taken my life months ago.

A few years ago, when the kids were small, we had a dog, Sandy she was called. A lovely golden retriever, we thought she'd last for years, but then she got Ill. I think she was five years old, still young. We took her to the vets and feared the worst. She had kidney disease. The vet told us we could prolong her life with medication, but she could not be cured. So, did we? No, we didn't. We said our last goodbyes and the dog was humanely put to sleep.

Now, I know we're not dogs, or cats, or mice, or rabbits, but there is a time to live and a time to die. Right now, it is my time to die. We accept this for our pets, but not for our friends and family. Why? We would not keep a pet alive just for our selfish needs, but we will try our best to sustain life for a human being, even though we know the outcome, and the person will not survive longer than two years. I will not live longer than two years. I know there are people out there who need protecting. They might not be of sound mind and so that decision, to take their own life, must be taken out of their hands. But I am of sound mind.

I have been reading a lot about assisted suicide. At this time, in Britain, it is an offence to help someone to die, punishable by up to fourteen years in prison. In Europe assisted suicide is legal in the Netherlands, Belgium, Luxembourg and Switzerland. Switzerland is the most publicised of all the countries, as they are willing to take patients outside of Switzerland. There has been much written about the clinics over there offering an assisted death. Before my illness, I would have condemned those people travelling there to die. I now know how they must have been feeling, making that decision to end your own life, respectably.

In Switzerland, you die in the morning. I guess it's more convenient? To be considered for assisted suicide, you have to have a terminal illness, you must be of sound mind, and you have to have been thinking about it for a long time. I meet all the criteria. The drug they use to kill you is similar to an anaesthetic. A quarter dose of the medicine is enough to put you under for an operation. The dose that they give you, to kill you, is thirty times this and they are confident that you will feel nothing when you die. You'll drift off into a deep sleep then, within 4 minutes, the heart stops, and you are dead.

I can't wait.

8

The time is 1.30 PM. Jack drives into the university car park. He finds a space, parks his car, takes his briefcase from the boot and walks into the grand reception area of the university. It's the first time he's been inside this building since term broke up last year. Tom has arranged for him to lecture, from two 'til four, that afternoon. He stands and gazes around the hallway, students and lecturers walk past him. He doesn't recognise anybody, so he walks over to the reception desk. The receptionist has her head bowed down, writing something on a form in front of her.

"Hello, Claire," he says, the woman looks up from her work. A broad smile appears immediately.

"Hi, Jack." She replies, then gets up from her seat, leans across the counter and hugs him. He wraps his arms around her and kisses her on the cheek.

"You look gorgeous," Jack says. Claire's cheeks begin to show a faded pink sheen.

"I like your beard," she replies, giving his chin a quick scratch. She sits down.

"Have you missed me?" he asks.

"I have, I used to enjoy our little conversations. Most of the lecturers are so stuffy. You're lucky if you get a hello from them."

"Perhaps, we should organise a morning conversation then," Jack answers, with a sly smile.

"Mr Carlisle, what are you suggesting?" she blushes her cheeks now a rosy red colour.

Jack laughs.

"Has Tom organised a pass for me? I'm lecturing for him this afternoon."

"He has."

She wheels her chair away from her desk and opens a drawer, in a filing cabinet behind her; pulling out a purple lanyard with a white identification pass on it. She hands it to Jack. He looks at it; VISITOR printed across the front in bold black letters.

"Where's my old pass?" he asks.

"It's in the bin, gone forever," she replies.

"How quickly people forget," he says.

"I haven't forgotten you, Jack,"

"Thank you," he says and puts the pass around his neck.

"Is this going to be a regular visit?" she enquires.

"Not sure yet. I suppose it depends on how well today goes."

"I'm sure you'll be fine."

"Fingers crossed." Jack crosses his fingers and shows them to Claire. He checks his watch.

"Must fly, don't want to be late on my first day."

"It was nice to see you again."

"And you," he replies, "I'll try and see you before I leave, later."

"I hope so," she says excitedly.

Jack walks away, climbs the stairs, then enters the university staff room. It's quiet, he scans the room for Tom, then gets out his phone and calls him.

"Hi, Tom, I'm in the staff room, where are you?" he asks, gazing around the room as he talks. A lecturer, who's sitting in the far corner of the room, notices him and waves. Jack raises his hand in acknowledgement.

"Hi, Jack. I won't be long, give me two minutes," Tom replies.

"Okay, see you soon." He hangs up and walks over to the man who waved.

"Hi, David." He puts out his hand.

The man gets up from his chair and shakes Jack's hand.

"How are you?" he enquires.

"Good, good."

"What do we owe the pleasure?" he asks.

"Just a favour for a friend."

"A friend?"

"Tom. I think he's getting a bit snowed under, so I said I'd help out."

"Yeah, he's a busy man, and we're glad to have him." David looks over Jack's shoulder, "He's here now,"

Jack spins round to see tom walking up to them.

"Jack, David," says Tom, shaking both their hands.

"Are you ready?" Tom asks.

"As I'll ever be," Jack replies.

"Come on then, let's get going."

"Good to see you, David," Jack says.

"Nice to see you too, Jack. Give me a call, and we'll have a drink sometime."

"I will do," Jack replies.

The two men then leave the staff room and walk out into the corridor.

"Do you know if Cristina's going to be here today?" Jack asks.

"I'd be surprised if she wasn't."

"Why do you say that?"

"She came to see me at my office and asked if it would be possible for me to arrange a meeting with you. After today's lecture."

"Meet with me? Why?"

"I wondered that too. It turns out your reputation even spreads out to the far-flung reaches of Romania."

"Really?"

"Well, I guess so. She said she was interested in a paper you had written, last year on Rhesus disease."

"Rhesus disease? I'm not sure there was anything groundbreaking in that paper."

"Well, something impressed her."

"How did she know I'd be lecturing today?"

"New university rules. Any change of lecturer, you now need to inform the students. They're paying the fees, so I guess they need to know what they're paying for."

"Well then, that's great. I can't wait."

They continue down the corridor and enter the lecture theatre through the grey, swinging double doors. Jack makes his way to the desk, positioned at the foot of the lecture theatre. He places his briefcase on to the heavily patented dark wood surface.

"It's like I've never been away," Jack says to Tom.

"Good, I'll get off then. Call me when you're done, and I'll come and meet you."

"Okay, thanks, see you later."

"Good luck," Tom replies, shaking Jacks hand.

Students start to file in through the doors at the top of the lecture theatre, chatter and laughter ring around the hall. The room begins to fill up fast. Jack recognises a couple of students from last year and acknowledges their presence. He quickly scans the room for someone who could be Cristina, an Eastern European looking woman. There are two girls already seated, but they are talking with friends and do not seem interested in him. He sits down and gets out his notes. He has prepared a detailed debate on the use of new medicines in the battle against heart disease and their testing structure. He scans through the opening facts on the paper, trying to find a suitable opening line for his lecture. Out of the corner of his eye, he notices somebody walking towards his desk. He looks up. A beautiful woman stands before him. She's dressed casually in jeans, a white and blue horizontal striped t-shirt and a black leather jacket. She has shoulder-length, blonde hair, and is probably in her mid to late twenties.

"Hello," Jack says, standing up and holding out his hand.

"Hello," she replies, her accent has similar tones to Daniella's.

"It's nice to meet you. My name is Cristina." She shakes Jack's hand.

"Nice to meet you too, Cristina. My, your hands are cold, you need to get warmed up," he says.

"It's a cold day today," she replies.

"I know, it's freezing out there."

Behind her, Jack notices a tall, broad-shouldered man, wearing a similar outfit to Cristina. Black leather jacket, black t-shirt and jeans. He looks straight at Jack, his face stern and severe. He has short, blond hair, and a chiselled chin. He reminds Jack of Ivan Drago, the character played by Dolph Lungren, in Rocky four.

"Hello," Jack says to him. He just stares at Jack.

"And this is?" he asks Cristina.

"His name is Ivan," Cristina replies.

"Nice to meet you, Ivan," Jack says and holds out his hand again. Ivan continues to glare at him for a moment before taking hold of his hand. Ivan's grip is firm, solid. Jack feels the pressure around his fingers.

"My, you have a strong grip," Jack says, trying to make light of the situation. "You look like you work out a bit, are you a student here too?"

Ivan doesn't answer.

"He is not a student," Cristina replies, "He is here with me, to observe my studying."

"To make sure you're not partying too much?" Jack jokes.

"Something like that," she replies, without smiling.

"Would it be okay to meet with you after the lecture?" she asks.

"Yes, that would be fine. What is it you would like to discuss?"

"I was interested in the research you did on Rhesus disease. The paper you wrote was fascinating."

"Tom, Mr Rooney, mentioned something about that. I'd love to answer any of the questions you have later."

"Thank you." She replies.

"And I would like to ask you a few questions too if I could?"

"You would?" She looks confused. "About what?"

"About the hospital, you work for, Heaven's Gate. I think that's what it's called?"

"Heaven's Gate," she replies.

"Yes, am I correct in thinking that's what it's called. I was struggling to find any information on it."

"Why were you looking?" she asks, sternly.

"No reason. Tom, Mr Rooney, just mentioned you were from a respected hospital in Romania. I hadn't heard of it, so I just thought I'd find out a bit more about it."

"And what else did Tom, Mr Rooney, say?" she asks.

"Not much." Jack feels a slight tension in the air.

"Then, I'll look forward to our meeting later," she says.

"I will, too," he replies.

Jack watches her walk away and takes her seat in the third row. Ivan continues to walk to the top of the auditorium and sits in an aisle seat on the back row. Jack watches him as he searches the room, inspecting the last few students entering the theatre. Ivan's eyes turn to meet with Jacks. He stares at him. Jack feels uncomfortable and turns his attention back to his notes.

He collects his thoughts, stands, and begins to talk.

9

I never wanted to go, I love my kids, but I just knew I shouldn't go. My daughter Sadie was in a school performance of the Sound of Music. She loves drama, dancing, gymnastics. She's a right little performer. Always singing around the house, or at least she used to sing around the house. Lately, she's been much quieter, I know why.

The day had started horribly for me. I felt tired, emotional. I knew the moment I opened my eyes; something was wrong. I ached all over. I hadn't slept well. I manoeuvred myself to the edge of the bed and sat there, contemplating my situation. It's hard to deal with, your mortality. My legs were hurting, and I could feel that my muscles were becoming weaker. It's scary, terrifying, the uncertainty of it all.

"John breakfast is ready," Grace calls from downstairs. I don't reply.

"John, are you okay?" I hear Grace call again, concern apparent in her voice.

"Yes, I'll be down in a minute!" I shout.

The past few days had been great. Grace and I don't talk about my death; it's something that is there, we know it, but we don't talk about it. She's accepted it, at least I think she has, what choice has she. I get the feeling she would like my disease to progress rapidly. So that my decision to end my life would be taken out of my hands. I would like my condition to progress quickly, but it doesn't work that way. It creeps and crawls its way around my body; every so often it lets me know it's still there, inside me, controlling me.

"John!" Grace calls again.

"What?!"

"Are you ok?"

"Yeah, I'm coming now," I shout.

"Bloody hell. Just leave me alone," I think to myself.

I get myself together, breathe deeply, stand and make my way into the en-suite. I look at my reflection in the mirror. It must be two days since I've looked at myself properly, my self-esteem non-existent. I see every line, every grey hair. I'm becoming fatter. A double chin appearing, "It's the drugs," they tell me. I'm going to put on weight, great! It just adds to my misery, my ongoing battle with depression. Yes, my depression, selfish as it is, I wallow in my self-pity, why shouldn't I? I leave the room and make my way downstairs and walk into the kitchen. The girls are sitting at the table, uniforms on ready for school. I kiss them both on the head, and walk towards Grace, she has her back to me, washing up some dishes. I put my arms around her and kiss the back of her neck. She twists her head to look at me.

"How are you feeling?" she asks.

"I'm fine, just a bit sore," I reply. I walk back over to the table and pick up a slice of toast; I take a bite; it's cold and hard.

"Has that toast gone cold? I can put some more in if it has?" she says.

"Thank you, but I'm not hungry," I reply. I take a seat next to the girls and look across at them. They keep their heads down, unsure of my mood. Grace brings me over a cup of tea. I take a sip and place the cup on the table.

"What's happening at school today? Anything good?" I ask them.

"It's my play tonight, dad," Sadie replies.

"Do I have to go?" Lucy asks.

"Yes," Grace replies.

Lucy looks at Sadie and mouths, "I hate you."

Sadie smiles and takes a mouthful of cereal.

I feel like Lucy. I'd like to say," I'll stay at home with you, Lucy," but I can't, and I feel terrible for thinking it.

A few hours later we're in the car. Grace is driving, heading to the show. Lucy is sitting in the backseat sulking, having been told again that she's going. Sadie is already there. I turn around to look at her.

"Enjoying yourself?" I ask.

"No," she replies, arms crossed, staring out of the window.

We drive up to the school; the car park looks full.

"There doesn't look like there's a space, we might have to park on the street," I say.

"There's a disabled space there," Grace notices.

I'm now the proud owner of a blue badge. I hate it. I say nothing. She drives up and parks right outside the school, in the disabled bay. She looks at me, knowing I don't like it. I'm tired, and I say nothing. We all get out of the car. I use my stick to rest on, as I close the door.

"Hi, John," I hear a voice. It's Stephen, one of Sadie's friend's dads.

"Hi, Steve," I reply. I'm getting used to the sorry looks people have on their faces. I turn and hold out my hand for Lucy to hold. She thinks for a moment, angry with me for making her come tonight, then takes hold of my hand. We walk into the school. The hall is half full, parents searching for the best seats.

"Where should we sit?" Grace asks.

"Not the front," I reply, "Try and get an aisle seat."

We walk down the centre of the hall, seats either side of us. We see two seats, but not three together.

"Grace," a voice shouts from the seats. "Sit here, we'll move up," the woman says. The whole line stands and shuffles along. I hate their pity.

"Thank you," Grace replies. I sit on the aisle seat; Lucy sits in the middle between Grace and me. Grace looks in her bag and hands Lucy a bag of sweets.

"Do you want a drink?" she asks her.

"No," she replies and starts eating her sweets.

I look around, I nod and smile at the faces I know. I feel a tap on my arm.

"Mum wants you," Lucy says.

"How are you feeling?" Grace asks. I put my thumb up and smile, and she smiles back.

The lights go out, and the show starts. I search the faces of the kids on stage. I can't see Sadie then she appears, running on from the wings. I'm so proud. I could cry. One of the children slips on stage and chuckles can be heard from the audience. I'm engrossed in Sadie, not watching anybody else. The first half of the play flies over, the audience breaks into rapturous applause, and the house lights come on. I look across at Grace, a big smile on my face. She smiles back at me.

"Can I have ice cream?" Lucy asks.

"Yes," I reply.

"Do you want me to go?" Grace asks.

"No, I'll go," I reply, struggling up to my feet, forcing all my weight on to my walking stick. My leg has gone stiff during the performance. I stand, stretch, and steady myself.

"Do you want to come with me, Lucy? I'm not sure what flavours they have."

Lucy stands and holds my free hand, and we walk out of the hall. A table has been set up in the school entrance, selling drinks, coffees, sweets, and ice cream, all profits going towards the schools Drama Club. I know this, as there is a massive handmade poster displayed on the wall behind the table. We stand in line. There are about six people before us in the queue; my leg hurts.

"Go and have a look at what they have," I say to Lucy. She walks down the side of the queue and peers at the ice creams.

"Hi, John, how are you doing?" Adam, another dad from school, is stood behind me, holding his son's hand, I think his son is called George.

"I'm fine," I reply

"You're looking well," he says.

"Well, I've been better," I say. I want to tell him to piss off. Lucy comes to my rescue.

"Chocolate," she says.

"Great," I reply and turn my back on Adam. We shuffle slowly towards the table. Eventually, we get there. The woman in front of me has been there for a few minutes, checking which sweets are gluten-free, or peanut-free, or fucking something else free. I feel like telling her to piss off and bring your own sweets if you're that bothered. She leaves, and I breathe a sigh of relief. I buy the chocolate ice cream for Lucy and two bags of jelly babies. We make it back to our seats just as the lights to go down.

"Where have you been?" Grace asks.

"The queue was terrible. Here, I got you these," and I hand her a bag of jelly babies. She smiles. I open my bag, take out a sweet and settle in for the second half. I enjoy the second half as much as the first. Whistles and shouts greet the final curtain call. For a few moments, I feel lost in joy, my illness a mere memory. I wipe my eyes. Everybody stands up to clap, I put all my weight on my stick, forcing myself up to join them. Then my chair is knocked from behind me. I feel my knee bend, my stick leaves my hand, shooting across the room, and I fall to the ground. A pain shoots through my wrist as I try to halt my fall, bending my wrist back on contact with the wooden hall floor. I cry out. Everybody around me quickly stops clapping. I look up. Faces surround me.

"Are you alright?" A voice asks. I don't reply.

"Is he hurt?" A different voice. My wrist hurts.

"Are you able to stand?" Another voice. "Pass me that chair," the voice says.

I feel myself being lifted and placed into the chair.

"John," Grace says.

"I think I might have hurt my wrist," I reply, looking at her.

"Should we get an Ambulance?" she asks.

"No, just get me home," I reply. I feel a hand on my shoulder. I'm guessing it's the man who helped me up, but I don't know him,

"Are you alright?" He asks.

"Yes, thank you," I reply.

People start to move all around me, collecting their children and leaving the hall. I feel their eyes staring at me.

"I'll just get Sadie?" Grace says.

I look up at her and nod, then look across at Lucy. Her face red, tears in her eyes. I put out my hand to hold hers. Then pull her towards me. I kiss her, and she sits on my knee. "I'm not hurt, Lucy" I whisper, putting my arm around her.

"I'll be fine."

10

Thank you," Cristina says, as Jack places a cup of coffee in front of her. He then sits down in the seat opposite.

"He can join us if he wants?" Jack says, looking over to where Ivan is standing at the entrance to the university café, surveying the room.

"He is fine where he is," she replies.

"Is he looking for somebody?" Jack says as Ivan's eyes scan the room. "Is someone else coming?"

"No, why do you ask?"

"He just looks like he's waiting for someone?"

"There's nobody else arriving," she replies firmly, then stands up and removes her jacket. His eyes admire her slim and athletic figure.

"How are you enjoying being in England?" Jack asks as she sits down.

"It's great. I love it here."

"You've been to England before?"

"Yes."

"Studying or on holiday?"

"I think you would call it, mixing business and pleasure," she answers, then smiles.

"Do you have a boyfriend here then? I notice you're not married."

"I have lots of friends here, boys and girls."

"Lucky you," he replies, the edge of his mouth slowly curling into a smile. "And how are you finding the English weather?"

"Your weather does not bother me," she replies, then takes a sip of her coffee. "It gets much colder in Romania."

"I'm sure it does. So why did you choose this university to study?"

"It is a beautiful building, and it has an impressive research department."

"Is there a particular area you are interested in?"

"Circulatory problems interest me. This university has an impressive record when it comes to research in that field."

"And is that something that your hospital is also interested in developing?"

"It is."

"So that is why you are here? To learn?"

"Yes, and other things."

"What other things are they?" Jack asks. Cristina contemplates her response.

"Why did you want to meet with me?" Jack asks.

"You wrote an interesting paper on Rhesus disease. We found it particularly informative."

"My paper on Rhesus disease," Jack repeats with an unmistakable tone of bewilderment.

"Yes, I know someone who has a similar disease."

"A similar disease. I didn't know there was a similar disease. What's it called?"

"We are still investigating the exact cause of the disease. There is no name yet."

"No name. What are the symptoms?"

"As in Rhesus disease, the pregnant woman's blood attacks the foetus in her womb. But the reasons why are not yet clear."

"And how does my paper help?"

"Parts of your research correlates quite closely with the work we've been doing at my hospital. We found it quite exciting that someone else discovered a similar connection."

"A connection. I'm sorry, I don't understand, how can there be a connection with my paper and a disease I've never heard of?" Jack takes a sip of his coffee.

"It was not so much the content, but the way you wrote the research."

"I'm still confused. There was nothing in that paper that's going to change the world. I'm not sure I received a single piece of correspondence about it."

"Your understanding of the circulatory system is remarkable. The conclusions you came to, the techniques you used. There were many aspects of your research that could be refined."

"Remarkable? Refined? You must explain that to me."

"We will."

"And who are we?"

"The doctors, my superiors, at Heaven's Gate. We would like to discuss your findings with you."

"You would?" He answers, surprised.

"Yes."

"Forgive me, but I don't understand what was so groundbreaking in that paper, to cause a hospital, based in Romania, to send someone to talk to me."

"The paper is not the only interesting piece of work you have done."

"What do you mean?"

"Mr Carlisle, you are a surgeon at the pinnacle of your career; you have surgery in two hospitals; your research is respected around the world. The work you do with the Red Cross is, on its own, impressive."

"It sounds like you know everything about me, and I know absolutely nothing about you. Or your Heaven's Gate."

"You will…" Cristina pauses, then picks up her coffee and takes a sip, "In time."

"In time?" Jack questions,

"Our relationship is only beginning."

"It is?" Jack looks surprised, "I searched Heaven's Gate yesterday, online."

"And what did you find?" She interrupts.

"Nothing, it's as though the hospital doesn't exist."

"Good, there is a reason for that."

"Go on," Jack replies, fascinated by her answer.

"The research we perform at Heaven's Gate is…." She pauses.

"What?" Jack asks.

"Confidential."

"Confidential, what does that mean?"

"It means that we keep the research at our facility very discreet. It enables us to work without being disturbed."

"Disturbed."

"Yes."

"And what kind of research would that be?"

"All will become clear when you speak with my superiors."

"When I speak with your superiors?" he repeats. "Why would I want to do that? I thought it was you who wanted to meet with me."

"I do, but my superiors would also like to meet with you."

"Why? To talk about my paper on Rhesus Disease? Surely an email would have done, or a phone call?" Jack waits for her to answer. Cristina takes another sip of coffee. "You can't have come all this way just to praise me about that paper?"

"That and other aspects of your career."

"What aspects?"

"When we have gained your trust. We can answer any questions you have."

"When you have gained my trust? This is bizarre. I have no idea what you are talking about."

"Mr Carlisle, I can see you are confused. I think we should end this meeting now. I will speak with my superiors and contact you soon."

"Your superiors."

"Yes." Cristina places her coffee cup on the table, moves her chair back and stands up. She takes her jacket from the back of her chair and puts it on."

"Wait, where are you going? You can't just leave it like that." Jack gets to his feet quickly and grabs hold of Cristina's arm.

"Let go of me, now," Cristina demands.

"Not until you tell me what's going on?" He replies.

Before Cristina has a chance to answer, a hand grabs hold of Jacks arm, and with some force, it is pulled and twisted behind his back. A sharp pain rushes through him, causing him to cry out.

"Ivan!" Cristina shouts, "Let him go!"

Jack feels the grip on him relax, and his arm drops to his side. He turns to face his assailant, rubbing his arm. Ivan stands before him. He looks at Jack then at Cristina.

"I am sorry about that, are you ok?" She asks.

"Yeah, I'm fine" he replies, feeling annoyed and embarrassed. "What the fucks going on?" he asks sternly, holding his gaze with Ivan.

"We will be in touch, Mr Carlisle."

"I can't wait," Jack answers, sarcastically. The two men still locked in eye contact.

"Goodbye Mr Carlisle," Cristina then motions to Ivan, he looks beyond Jack's shoulder, then back at Jack.

"Ivan, come on, it's time to leave," Cristina says, then makes her way to the café exit. Ivan takes one last look at Jack before following her.

Jack watches them leave, sits down and rubs his arm.

11

"Can you put the hood up?" I shout at Jack.

"What?" He replies.

I'm sitting in Jack's car. We're on our way to the Rose and Crown for lunch, Jack's treat. The roof is down on his new BMW. A cold wind swirls violently around my head. Prince, When Doves Cry, is playing loudly on the car stereo.

"I love this track!" Jack announces, ignoring my request.

"I hate him!" I reply, "Fucking turn it off, put some Queen on!"

"They're shit!" he shouts, smiling. I know he's joking, everybody likes Queen.

The Rose and Crown used to be our usual haunt before my diagnosis. It's been months since I've been there. Jack phoned and asked if I'd like to go for lunch and then to see Chelsea play at home, he thought that it might cheer me up. I hadn't seen or heard from him in days. I'd sent a few texts, without reply. I was beginning to think he'd run out on me, didn't want any part of my proposed death. I wouldn't blame him if he had. His phone call that day was a welcome relief. The past few days had been demanding, the night of the school play hung heavy on my mind. Grace had driven the kids and me straight up to A&E after my fall. My wrist was only sprained, not broken, unlike my pride. The following day I found it hard to get out of bed. Engulfed in self-loathing, I refused food and any approach to make me feel better. They had no choice but to leave me there, in the darkness, wallowing in my self-pity. I'm sure Grace felt as helpless as I did. I'm not proud of how I acted; Depression is a selfish occupation. I had never thought more about dying, every minute of every day. How could I do it? Pills, hanging, jump in front of a train, they all have their problems, but I couldn't shake it. It crawled around my mind like an insect, irritating me, burrowing deeper and deeper. Death was the only light at the end of the tunnel. The black dog had me well and truly trapped within its sharp jaws; there was no escape.

"What happened?" Jack shouts at me.

"What?" I answer, he turns down the radio.

"Your wrist, what happened?"

My wrist now wrapped in a cream cotton bandage.

"I fell," I reply. His facial expression changes, he doesn't believe me. "What do you think happened? Do you think I'd slit my wrist?"

"Maybe."

"I'd do a better job than that if I had," I reply. Jack just shakes his head and turns his attention back to the road ahead.

"Did Grace call you?" I ask him. He ignores me. "Jack, did Grace call you?"

He turns to look at me, "Yes."

"I thought so."

"Don't be annoyed with her. She's worried about you."

"I'm not annoyed. I knew there had to be a reason why you called."

"What does that mean?" He asks. I ignore him. I don't want to say anything I shouldn't. Not yet, anyway.

I knew today would be another opportunity for me to speak with him. I had to pick my moment carefully; I didn't want to ruin the day, but I had to know what he had found out if anything. Grace told me not to mention it, "Just enjoy the afternoon," she said. But I knew I couldn't do that.

I look at him while he drives. He's dressed in a black Ralf Lauren polo shirt, blue chinos and a slim fitting silver grey duck-down jacket. He's a good looking man, I forget how old he is, but he must be forty-five at least. You wouldn't think it though, he looks ten years younger and stinks of success. I was dressed in, well, I couldn't tell you. I didn't care about how I looked anymore.

We arrive at the Pub. Jack swings the BMW into the car park.

"It's full," I say, "We'll have to park on the road."

The nose of a car slowly appears from the line of stationary vehicles, Jack notices it.

"Not quite," he replies, smiling. The car pulls away, and Jack drives straight into the vacant space.

"You're fucking blessed," I declare loudly. He just laughs at me.

We enter the crowded pub. I feel anxious as we stand at the entrance, waiting to be seated. I hope nobody recognises me; I don't want to talk to anyone. Jack walks over to the barmaid. My mind drifts to better days in this building, nights playing pool, drinking, laughing. A wave of melancholy flows over me.

"They have a table," Jack announces, on his return. I snap out of my miserable thoughts.

"Of course they do."

"What?" he looks confused.

"You, you're fucking blessed."

"Yeah, I am," he replies, laughing. "Come on."

I follow him. We make our way to a small square dark wood table and sit down opposite each other. He looks across at me.

"What's up? Are you feeling alright?" he asks

"Yeah, yeah," I reply, he notices my anxiety.

The waitress appears quickly.

"There's a thirty-minute wait for food, is that ok?" she asks.

Jack looks at me.

"That's fine," I reply.

"Can we order some drinks?" Jack asks.

I order a pint of real ale, Jack asks for a pint of lime and soda. The waitress leaves announcing she'll be back shortly to take our food order.

"You know I'm gonna get pissed and emotional?" I declare.

A broad grin appears on his face, "What's new there?" he says. We both begin to look at the menu. Minutes later, the waitress returns with our drinks.

"Are you ready to order?" She asks.

"I am, beef and ale pie for me please," I answer. Jack continues to look at the menu. I pick up my drink and swallow down half of it.

"Sounds good, I think I'll have the same," he says, then glares at me. "Steady on, John. We've got all afternoon. I'm not carrying you home drunk."

"Don't worry. I'm not gonna get drunk, well, not that drunk." I reply, trying to appease the situation.

"You're the one who's going to get in trouble. Grace won't be happy."

"I'll just blame you!" I say, picking up my glass and taking another drink., "Cheers!"

"Cheers!" he replies, reluctantly. "So, how have you been?"

"I thought Grace told you."

"What? That you had been a miserable bastard."

"Yeah, that's about right."

"What's changed?" he asks.

"That's the problem. Nothing has changed."

"Well, maybe a nice day out is just what the doctor ordered."

"It just might be, thanks for this."

"I just hope Chelsea win. They've been playing shit lately."

"They have," I pause, take a mouthful of ale, and look directly at Jack.

"What?" He asks, reading my mind.

"I'm under orders not to mention it."

"Then don't," he replies bluntly.

"What's the saying? We might as well talk about the elephant in the room."

"It's a big fucking elephant," he retorts.

"Let's just get it out of the way now, so it doesn't spoil the rest of the afternoon."

"I've got a better idea. Let's just not say a fucking word about it. Then it won't."

"Come on. You must have known I would bring it up."

"I hoped you'd changed your mind."

"That won't happen, Jack. The decisions made, with or without your help." I pause. "I take it, from your silence, that you've done nothing."

"I've asked colleagues for their advice."

"And what did they say?" I ask, he doesn't reply. I watch him take a sip of his drink. "They told you, there's nothing, nothing anyone can do. Didn't they?"

"I'm not giving up just yet."

"Giving up on what? Me?"

"Yes, you."

"There's no help for me out there. You know that now. I need a different kind of assistance."

"There might be something."

"There isn't," I answer, I watch him nervously move in his chair. "Come on, Jack, you're an intelligent man, be honest with me. I know I can't be treated."

"Just don't give up yet." He says.

"Why? Why shouldn't I just give up?" I ask, he doesn't answer. "Go on, give me a reason."

He looks away. I notice his apprehension.

"What is it? Come on, say something."

He turns to face me. He looks nervous.

"Look, Jack, if you don't want to help me, then that's ok. It's wrong of me to put that much pressure on you. I'm sorry."

"Don't be sorry. I know you're feeling depressed. I want to help to give you some hope."

"But you can't." I interrupt.

"Just leave it with me, I'm working on something."

"What?"

"I can't tell you yet. It's a bit too soon."

"Can't tell me what?"

"Let's just say I'm looking into something."

"Looking into what?"

"I can't say right now, I don't know much," Jack sits back in his chair.

"Well, tell me what you know," I observe the expression on his face. I'm unsure of what he is about to say.

"Look, it's early days," he pauses.

"Go on, tell me."

"There's nothing to tell yet."

"Come on, Jack, fucking hell, just tell me. What have you found? I've got no time for games."

He places his drink on the table, leans towards me. "I might have found a hospital you could go to."

"To do what? End my life?" I ask, surprised. I feel my heart rate begin to rise with excitement.

"No, not to die. Well, hopefully, not. It's a research hospital."

I sit back in my chair, disheartened by his revelation.

"I'm not joining some fucking research program. I'm on that now. All that hospital does is try different pills on me. They haven't got a clue, no one has."

"This place is different. They could help."

"How?"

"Just leave it with me for a couple of days, I need to find out more about it first."

"You're wasting your time and mine."

"Maybe not. I'm meeting with someone from the hospital tonight. I'll know more then."

"Tonight?"

"Yeah, after the game."

"Who are you meeting?"

"It's complicated."

"It's complicated. My life's complicated. You're not making any sense."

"I know, but I haven't got much to tell you yet. All I know is what my friend has told me."

"And who's your friend?"

"Tom, he's a surgeon friend of mine, he lectures at the University."

"And what does he know?"

"He told me about a hospital that has a very well respected research facility. They have achieved an outstanding success rate in developing new drugs."

"New drugs for MND?" I ask.

"He's not sure."

"I bet he's not sure. I've tried all the new drugs out there. I should fucking rattle when I walk. The number of pills I take in a day."

"These drugs would be brand new, not available to the general public."

"What? I don't understand."

"This hospital, it isn't what you might call, an ordinary hospital. The research they do there, well, it's confidential."

"Confidential? What does that mean?" I ask.

"I don't know yet. I still need to find that out."

"What makes you think they can help me? And how can they help me?"

"I'll know more after tonight."

"They can't help, I've looked at everything, there's nothing out there."

"Not yet, but there might be something in the future, and you could help develop that drug."

"What are you talking about?"

"New drugs, still in development. They need patients to try them, to see if they work, to see what side effects there might be. You could help develop these new drugs."

"I still don't see how this is going to help me. I don't want to go on any more drug tests. I've had enough of that, nothing works."

"John, seriously, your participation in a research programme could be invaluable. Who knows what they might discover. It might not help you right now, but maybe patients in the future can benefit from your involvement in something like this. Now, how does that sound? You selfish fucker."

I sit back, reflecting on Jacks words. I'd never thought about being on a research programme, why would I? I didn't know it existed.

"What kind of research? What drugs?"

"I don't know. That's what I need to find out."

"And this person your meeting, tonight, is he a doctor?"

"She, and yes, kind of."

"Kind of. What does that mean?"

"She's over here training. She's in Tom's class at the university. That's how he found out about Heaven's Gate."

"What did you call it, Heaven's Gate?" I say, surprised.

"I know it's a strange name for a hospital, but trust me, it's a special place."

"Where is it anyway?" I ask, Jack smiles.

"It's not far, just a plane ride away."

"A plane ride away!" I repeat, "Where is it?"

"Romania," he answers.

I laugh out loud, "Romania! Your joking, aren't you? Who knows what they get up to over there. They could bloody torture me."

"I hope they do," he says, smiling.

"Romania? Grace is going to love that."

"Don't say anything to Grace yet, not 'til I've found out a bit more about it."

"I won't. I'll let you tell her."

"It's supposed to be a lovely country," Jack says, "Think of it as a little holiday."

"A holiday, I could use one of them."

"Then you're up for it if I can sort it?"

I pause, thinking, "Maybe?"

"Maybe? come on, what other options are there?" Jack stares at me, "None, you've told me that a million times."

"Find out more. Then get back to me."

"But you're interested?"

"What options do I have?"

"None." Jack laughs

12

"Eleven pounds fifty please mate."

Jack opens the taxi door and steps out onto the pavement. He searches in his pocket for his wallet, picks out a five and a ten-pound note, then hands it to the driver.

"Keep the change," he announces, the driver accepts and drives away.

The time is 7:55 PM. The table was booked for eight o'clock. A simple text from Cristina that morning read-

Hello Dr Carlisle

I have taken the liberty of booking a table tonight at San Remo, on English Street, at 8 o'clock. I hope you can make it. Maybe we can continue our discussion from the other night.

Cristina

Surprised, but delighted to receive her text, Jack agreed to the meeting. He looks up at the sign above the window. San Remo is written in a blue neon 80's font. The glow from the sign lights up the autumn darkness and throws a shadow across the face of a man leaning against the wall outside the restaurant. Jack recognises the now familiar figure. Ivan stands centurion like, to one side of the doorway. He's wearing a large black padded parka coat.

"Good evening Ivan, is Cristina inside?" Jack asks as he walks towards the restaurant.

Ivan nods his head, then pulls open the glass door.

"Thank you, are you going to joining us?" he asks.

Ivan slowly moves his head from side to side.

"Well, you're welcome to. It's cold out here." Jack says. He doesn't reply; Jack enters the restaurant, leaving Ivan behind him.

It's a busy Saturday night. Jack looks around the room but cannot see Cristina.

"Evening sir, do you have a reservation?" A young waitress stands in front of him.

"I do, I think my date has already arrived?" he replies

"What name is the reservation booked under? I'll check for you."

"Mr Carlisle. Jack Carlisle,"

"Ahh, yes, she has just arrived. Please follow me." The waitress then spins on her heels and walks into the restraint.

"Hello," Jack says as he approaches Cristina. She looks up from her menu.

"Hello," she replies.

Jack sits down opposite her, then takes a moment to admire her appearance.

"May I say you look lovely tonight," he says.

"Thank you."

She's wearing a halter neck black dress, and her hair is tied up tightly. Apart from the ruby red lipstick, she is looking naturally beautiful.

The waitress hands Jack a menu.

"I'll be back soon to take your order," she declares, the leaves them alone.

Jack scans the menu, an awkward silence prevails.

"Your text this morning was a nice surprise." He says, disturbing the peace.

"I'm just pleased you could make it."

"How could I refuse?" he replies.

"Can I get you something to drink?" They lookup. A waiter is standing beside them.

"Would you like some wine?" Jack asks her.

"Yes."

"What do you prefer? Red or white?"

"Red, please."

Jack quickly scans the wine list,

"I think we'll have a bottle of the Saint Emilion, and some water, please."

"Good choice. I will get that for you now." The waiter replies then walks away.

"I hope you don't mind me ordering, but the Saint Emillion is very good."

"I'm sure it is" she replies.

They both then return to their menus.

"I've heard the steak here are very good," Jack says. "Are you a meat-eater?"

"Yes. If that's your recommendation, then I think I know what I'm having."

"I might have to join you," he says, then takes another quick look at the menu, before closing it and placing it on to the table.

"Two steaks it is!" Jack announces. She copies him and closes her menu.

Jack looks across at Cristina, then turns his attention beyond her shoulder, to the silhouette of Ivan standing outside.

"At least I can keep my eye on him from here," Jack says, then points at the window.

Cristina doesn't turn around. "What do you mean?" she asks.

"I can see him approaching if he decides to attack me again."

"He won't," she replies firmly. "I'm sorry that happened."

"That's alright, no harm done. What is he anyway? Your bodyguard?"

The waiter returns to the table, disturbing their conversation.

"Would you like to taste the wine, sir?" He asks Jack.

"Yes, please," he replies. The waiter delicately pours wine into the bowl of his glass. Jack takes a mouthful of wine.

"Gorgeous."

The waiter then fills both glasses and leaves.

"So, is he?" Jack asks again.

"He is my friend. That is all."

"Boyfriend?" He asks.

"No," she answers sharply.

"Excuse me, are you ready to order?" The waitress asks, notepad in hand.

"Are you ready?" Jack asks Cristina.

"Yes, I'll have the steak please."

"May I recommend our specially prepared forty-two-day, dry-aged sirloin steak?" the waiter replies.

"Sounds fantastic." She replies.

"And how would you like that cooked?" The waiter asks.

"Rare, please."

"Rare?" Jack says, surprised.

"If the meat is good? Then it should be left fresh."

Jack ponders her response.

"And for you, sir?"

"I think I'll have the same and rare. Thank you."

The waitress then walks away. Jack picks up his glass.

"Cheers!" He says, Cristina repeats the salute and picks up her glass. They both take a drink of wine.

"So, what's going on?"

"What do you mean?"

"I mean. Why do you want to see me? Why do your superiors want to meet me?"

"As I said, at our last meeting, I wanted to discuss your research on Rhesus disease."

"That doesn't make any sense. If I hadn't organized to take that lecture for Tom, we would never have met. Then what would you have done then?"

"That was an unforeseen error on our part."

"What was?"

"We did not know you were going to retire from lecturing. I was expecting to be in your class."

"Why?"

"I was looking forward to meeting you, working with you, getting to know you."

"Getting to know me."

"We need to be certain that we have the right person."

"The right person?" Jack queries, "For what?"

"May we have our meal first?" She asks.

"No," Jack replies abruptly, picking up his glass and taking a drink of wine.

"I hoped we could enjoy our meal first."

"And I hoped you would explain yourself first."

Cristina considers her response. Jack observes her dilemma.

"Just tell me." He demands.

Cristina looks nervously at Jack, then moves her chair away from the table, bends down and picks up her handbag. She searches inside, takes out a white sealed envelope and slides it across the table. Placing it in front of Jack.

"What's this?"

"It's a letter from my superiors. Inviting you to Heaven's Gate."

"I can't wait to find out, what's in here" Jack answers, picking up the envelope and placing his finger inside. He tears a corner open.

"Please, do not open it now," Cristina says, then places her hand on top of his. Halting his progress.

"What? Why not?"

"I do not know what is in the letter, so I cannot answer your questions. Any questions you have can only be answered by my superior's."

Jack looks at the envelope; His name, printed, on the front in a simple black font

"You're seriously asking me to ignore this letter."

"Just while I'm here, open it later, please."

"I ask you for answers, and you give me more questions."

"Everything will be explained to you in good time."

"What's everything? I'm not sure I can wait." Jack inspects the envelope. "What can you tell me?"

"I'm sorry, but nothing."

"Nothing, come on! A woman is sent from Romania just to hand me a letter. Your superiors aren't that naïve. They must have known I would ask questions."

"I'm sure all your questions will be answered, just not by me."

"Not by you. Come off it. I don't believe you. You must know something."

"I'm sorry I cannot help you."

"So, when they sent you, your superiors. What did they say? Just hand him this letter," Jack holds it by the torn corner, "Then walk away. Did they think I'd be okay with that?"

"Not quite. I am also here to make sure your journey is arranged to your satisfaction."

"My journey. I don't understand. Why didn't they just post this to me? Or even send me an email? It doesn't make any sense."

"We do not operate in that way. You deserve more respect than that. We like to be," she pauses "More personal."

"I wouldn't call this personal. I'd call it ridiculous."

"I'm sorry you feel like that. We did not mean to cause you any offence. We have the utmost respect for you and your work."

Jack fills his wine glass, then takes a drink.

"Am I really to believe all this? How do I know your hospital even exists? Where is it exactly?"

"Dr Carlisle. I can promise you the hospital exists."

"Where is it?" he repeats.

"Rasnov, it is near Rasnov in Romania."

"I looked, there's no hospital in Rasnov. The only Heaven's Gate I could find was a crypt, or chapel, built into the walls of an ancient fortress." Jack watches Cristina closely. Her expression changes.

"What is it?" he asks.

"Poarta Raiului" she replies.

"Yeah, that was it. Written above the door of the chapel. It translated to Heaven's Gate."

"Not quite. It says, the gateway to heaven. The chapel is the oldest building within the walls of the fortress."

"The oldest building. There are others?"

"Yes," she replies, reluctantly.

Jack ponders his next question. "Is the hospital also within the walls of the fortress?"

Cristina turns her gaze away from Jack.

"Tell me." He orders a response, irritated by her actions.

Cristina picks up her wine and takes a drink. "Yes," she answers.

"Excuse me," they both lookup. A waitress stands before them holding two plates of food.

13

It had been days, weeks since I'd felt that good. You could almost say that I was happy. The afternoon with Jack had been great, Chelsea won and for the first time, in a long time, I had hope in my heart. I knew it was a long shot, a shot in the dark, but it was something. I needed something.

I opened the door of Jack's car and rolled out onto the pavement. He positioned himself above me and laughed.

"Are you okay?" he asked, then grabbed hold of my coat and pulled me to my feet.

"Never been better," I replied, wiping my jeans.

"I think that might change when Grace sees you like this."

"She'll be fine."

"Well, I'm not gonna hang around to find out. I've got an appointment with a doctor to get ready for."

"John." We both look in the direction of the voice. Grace is standing at the door of my house.

"Hiya, gorgeous," I reply.

"Are you drunk?" she shouts.

I look at Jack, "You'd better go," I tell him.

"I'm off then. I'll be in touch soon," he says, waves at Grace then disappears into his car. I watch him drive into the distance; Grace joins me on the pavement, I turn to look at her.

"Your beautiful," I say, then kiss her hard on the mouth; my tongue entwined with hers. She pulls away.

"John! You are drunk, stop it." She says.

"I want to go to bed."

"What?" she answers, surprised by my suggestion. The afternoon had also brought my libido back. I thought that feeling had burned in the flames from hell. I pull her towards me and kiss her again. My hands clench her buttocks.

"John," she says, embarrassed, "Not here."

"Come on, then, lead me to the bedroom."

"The kids are still up. They're having their dinner."

"Later then."

"I'll hold you to that," she says, with a sly smile. Then takes hold of my hand and leads me into the house. I stumble through the lounge and enter the kitchen. The kids are sitting at the table eating.

Sadie looks up from her meal, "Hi dad," she says.

Lucy has her back to me; she turns and studies me. I lean against the kitchen cabinets to steady myself.

"Are you drunk?" Lucy asks. I laugh.

"A little," I reply, then pull out the chair beside Sadie, and join them at the table. I steal a chip from Sadie's plate.

"Hey, dad!" she says, annoyed.

"Do you want anything to eat?" Grace asks

"Have you eaten?" I ask.

"No, not yet. I was waiting for you."

"Should we get a curry then?"

"A curry?" She looks surprised. It had been a long time since we'd ordered a curry on a Saturday night.

"Yeah, do you fancy one?" I ask

"I do," she smiles.

14

Cristina slices through the steak in front of her. Blood streams from the raw meat, circulating her plate. She takes her first mouthful.

"What do you think?" Jack asks, watching her chew her food.

"Very good," she replies, wiping her mouth, then taking a drink of wine. They sit quietly enjoying their food. Jack contemplates his next move. The envelope now safely placed in Jack's inside pocket.

"Heaven's Gate," Jack announces.

"Yes," she replies, looking up from her meal.

"That's a strange name to call a hospital."

"Why do you say that?"

"You don't think it is?"

"No, it's beautiful."

"Beautiful! I wouldn't call it that. It sounds like a place you would go to, to die."

"In Romania, we are not afraid of death."

"Maybe not. But being treated in a hospital named Heaven's Gate. Well, it wouldn't fill me with confidence."

"I can assure you, Dr Carlisle, that the patients at Heaven's Gate are very well looked after. We have some of the world's most experienced surgeons working there."

"You do? Who?" Jack asks. Cristina pauses before answering.

"I am not at liberty to say right now. But you will be introduced to everybody on your arrival."

"On my arrival," Jack repeats, "You're very confident I will accept the invitation?"

"I see no reason why you wouldn't."

"What?" Jack laughs. "A beautiful woman travels across Europe with her bodyguard, to hand me a letter, inviting me to meet her superiors. At a secret hospital in Romania. Am I supposed to take this seriously?"

"Yes," she replies confidently. "I am sure everything will be explained to you."

Jack taps his jacket pocket, "I know, it's all in the letter. You haven't told me what your role is at the hospital. Are you a junior doctor there?"

"Yes, and no."

"You're not one for giving a straight answer, are you? What does that mean?"

"I work at the hospital, but I have lived there all my life. My home, my village, is situated within the fortress walls."

"It is?"

"Yes. It has been there for hundreds of years."

"How long has Heaven's Gate been a part of the fortress?"

"It has been an integral part of our lives for a long time now."

"The hospital is there just for your village. How can it survive, catering just for your village?"

"You misunderstand me. It is there for everyone, but we are proud of its existence."

"So, the hospital does take patients from outside your village?"

"Yes."

"Very ill ones?"

"Now I am confused, what do you mean?" she answers.

"There is a thought, that a hospital is a place where patients go to be involved in clinical trials; and this is why the hospital is so secret."

"And who thinks that?"

"Me. I'm struggling to understand what other reasons there could be, for a hospital to be secret."

"Many facilities are offering clinical trials, that is not unusual."

"Then, the methods you are using at Heaven's Gate must be unusual."

"What are you suggesting?"

"That you are using patients, to test unauthorised drugs." Jack states. He scrutinises her reaction, hoping to discover a fault in Cristina's cold response.

"The treatments we offer…" she takes a moment to consider her answer, "You might say are unusual, but they are not unethical."

"Can you tell me what treatments you practice?"

"I am sure, on your arrival at Heaven's Gate. That your questions will be answered."

"I bloody hope so," Jack sits back in his chair. His mind was racing with thoughts of how he can involve me in Heaven's Gate. "And this work, this research. What areas are you working on?"

"We have many fields in development."

"Are any of them investigating Motor Neurone Disease?"

Cristina looks surprised by his question.

"No, not that I know of. Why do you ask?"

"I have a friend who has the disease."

"It is not something I understand. I am sorry."

"I'm not sure anybody understands the condition. You said, not that you know of. Does that mean you could be investigating?"

"No," she answers decisively.

"But you just said…"

"I know what I just said," she interrupts, "We cannot treat your friend, I am sorry."

"I didn't ask."

"Dr Carlisle, I understand why you would try to help your friend. But we at Heaven's Gate cannot help him."

"But, you just said you didn't know, and if you don't know, then maybe I really should speak to your superiors."

"The answer will be the same as mine."

"It might not be."

"It will."

"If they want to speak to me, then I have my own set of demands."

"You have a set of demands?"

"If it means I can help my friend. If it means I can get him involved in one of the clinical trials. Then yes, I have my demands."

"The invitation is just for you."

"Well, we'll have to see about that," Jack replies while carving his steak, a broad grin appearing on his face.

15

We lay side by side, exhausted. I breathe deeply, filling my lungs with warm air.

"Are you alright?" Grace asks. I turn my head and look at her.

"Never felt better," I reply, squeezing my arm under her back. She puts her arm around my chest; her leg stretches over mine, and she pulls herself close to me, kissing me on the cheek.

"I love you," she whispers.

"I love you too." I kiss her lips, then take a moment to admire her beauty. I notice her expression. I know that look. She wants to know what's going on but is too nervous to ask.

The evening had been great, different. I'd put the kids to bed, read Sadie a story, the first time in months. She hugged me before I said goodnight.

"I love you, dad," she said. I nearly cried.

Then Grace and I went to bed.

"You want to know what's going on, don't you?"

"I'd like to if that's alright?" she says nervously, not wanting to spoil the mood.

"Jack has an idea."

"What kind of idea?"

"It's a long shot. I've not to get too excited about it."

"Go on."

"He thinks he might have found a hospital that will take me on a research program."

"A research program," She repeats, surprised. "I thought you weren't going to take any more drugs?"

"I'm not, or I wasn't, but this is different."

"How?"

"I didn't quite understand what he was saying, but I think it's a drug-testing program, for drugs not yet approved the government."

"I don't understand either. Would you be like a human guinea pig?"

I laugh, "yeah, that's what I thought."

"And is it?"

"I guess it is."

Grace pulls her arm from under me, and manoeuvres herself on top of me, straddling my waist. She looks down on me intently. I look up at her, admiring her breasts. I lift myself and kiss one of her nipples.

"And what do you think about that?" She asks, pushing my head away from her chest. I drop back down onto the bed.

"I don't know. I told him to fuck off at first. Then he said it could do some good. I could do some good."

"You could how?"

"These new drugs need testing on patients. It can speed up the development of the drugs. They might not help me directly, but for other MND sufferers in the future. Well, this kind of research could help them."

"But they can't help you?"

"Unlikely, Jack said it was a win, win situation for me."

"What does that mean?"

"If the drugs work, then I get my life back."

"And if they don't?" Grace asks.

I pull a sad face, "Then I get my wish."

"John!" she protests.

I stretch my arms up and pull her down on top of me. I kiss her, then hold her close to me.

"What if there are side effects?" she whispers in my ear. I feel her warm breath on my cheek.

"How bad could they be?" I answer.

"Where is this hospital? How come Dr Robert hasn't mentioned it?"

"I don't think he knows about it, to be honest."

"What? Why not?" Grace turns to face me. I roll over on my side and smile at her

"What is it?" she asks again.

"It's in Romania."

"Romania! John, you can't be serious."

"I know it's a crazy idea."

"Crazy! It's bloody ridiculous. They could be doing anything out there."

"Look, Jack has still got to organise it yet. He's having a meeting with someone from the hospital tonight. Hopefully I'll, we'll know more then."

"John, you can't be serious."

"I need something, Grace. This just might be it. I feel good about it. I had nothing, now I've got something."

"It's ridiculous. I don't like it."

"Let's just wait and see what Jack comes back with. He wouldn't organise this if it meant I was going to die. You know how he feels about it. He must think this hospital can offer something. He thinks it's the best chance I've got. I trust him, Grace, you should too. He'll look after me."

"He better bloody had!" she replies, and I kiss her again.

16

Jack turns the key in the lock, pushes open the door and steps into his home. The evening had ended amicably, they finished their meals, Jack tried another line of questioning, but to no avail. Cristina's reluctance to answer any more questions forced Jack to end the evening early and head back home, to read the letter.

"Goodnight, Ivan," he announced, as he passed him on his exit. As expected, there was no reply from the erroneous figure.

Jack walks through his lounge, turning on lamps as he passes them, making his way through to the kitchen. Pours himself a large glass of wine, checks his watch, 10 PM. Then walks back into the living room and sits down, placing the glass on to the coffee table in front of him. His hand reaches inside his jacket and pulls out the letter.

"Now then, what surprises are in here?" He wonders as he tears open the envelope and begins to read.

Dear Mr Carlisle,

I hope I find you in good health.

My name is Doctor Otto Schneider, and I am governor here at Heaven's Gate. My colleagues and I would like to offer you the opportunity to visit our facility here in Rasnov, Romania.

Though our approach may seem very strange to you, I can assure you that we are very serious about our invitation. As you may be aware, the research that we perform at our hospital, is highly confidential. Which means we have to take certain precautions before inviting anyone within our walls. With this in mind, we hope we have your discretion and respect.

We have monitored your career for some time now and are very impressed with your work. I am sure you have many questions you want to ask us, and there are many we would like to ask you.

I will try my best to answer them all on your arrival. Cristina will arrange all the necessary travel arrangements.

Please contact her when you are available to visit.

Thank you for your time, and we look forward to meeting you soon.

Yours Sincerely

Dr Otto Schneider

Jack stares at the letter, unsure of how to interpret the writing on the page. He takes a sip of his wine, stands and walks over to his computer. He sits and begins to type.

Dr Otto Schneider

The search results appear on the screen.

Dr Otto Schneider, acclaimed surgeon, surprises the medical world by retiring at age forty-eight.

Jack continues to read,

On August 4th 1992, Dr Otto Schneider surprised his friends and colleagues by announcing his retirement. Dr Schneider, a leading surgeon in the field of heart and blood diseases and a pioneer of keyhole surgery, said his decision was due to family issues.

Jack quickly scans the text. Awards and commendations become commonplace throughout his career. He has an impressive resume. There is nothing, in any of the results, about where he is working now.

"Well, Google, you may not know where he is, but I do," Jack thinks to himself.

He picks up the letter and rereads its contents. There is no address, phone number or email.

"These people don't want to be found," he ponders, then types:

Rasnov Fortress

Into the Google search engine.

Dramatic images of the impressive building are displayed across the top of the screen. Jack clicks on an image and reads the short paragraph explaining its existence. Written mainly to entice tourists, there is no mention of a hospital. A sentence catches his attention.

Within the fortress walls, a thriving village exists, it's inhabitants could be related to an early race of people now extinct called Gepids.

Jack quickly types,

Gepids Rasnov fortress.

The results are displayed; they have their own Wikipedia page. He clicks on the link and reads.

The Gepids were the "Most shadowy of all the major Germanic peoples of the migration period", Neither Tacitus nor Ptolemy mentioned them in their detailed lists of the "barbarians", suggesting that the Gepids emerged only in the 3rd century AD. The first sporadic references to them, which were recorded in the late 3rd century, show that they lived north of the frontier of the Roman Empire. All information of the Gepids' origins came from "malicious and convoluted Gothic legends" recorded in Jordanes' Getica after 550. They settled along the northern shore of the Baltic Sea on an island at the mouth of the Vistula River, called "Gepedoius", or the Gepids' fruitful meadows, as written by Jordanes,(Jordanes was a sixth-century Roman Bureaucrat, who turned his hand to history later in life)

Modern historians debate whether the part of Jordanes' work which described the migration from Scandza, was written at least partially on the basis of Gothic oral history or it was an "Ahistorical fabrication" Jordanes' passage in his Getica is the following:

Should you ask how the [Goths] and Gepidae are kinsmen, I can tell you in a few words. You surely remember that in the beginning, I said the Goths went forth from the bosom of the island of Scandza with Berig, their king, sailing in only three ships toward the hither shore of Ocean, namely to Gothiscandza. One of these three ships proved to be slower than the others, as is usually the case, and thus is said to have given the tribe their name, for in their language gepanta means slow. Hence it came to pass that gradually, and by corruption, the name Gepidae was coined for them by way of reproach. For undoubtedly, they too trace their origin from the stock of the Goths, but because, as I have said, gepanta means something slow and stolid, the word Gepidae arose as a gratuitous name of reproach.

Their persecution over the following years forced the Gepids to retreat within the walls of the Rasnov Citadel. A fortress built high in the mountains, above Rasnov. It is not known if they eventually fled the walls of the citadel, or just starved within the walls, but no remains of the historic tribe were ever found.

Jack types.

Rasnov Romania

Rasnov (pronounced Ryshnov) is a small town in Transylvania and is home to the spectacular Rasnov citadel. The citadel was built around twelve forty-one, as part of a defence system for the Transylvanian villages exposed to outside invasions. Sitting atop a crag one hundred and fifty meters high, the fortification several times served as a refuge for Rasnov inhabitants. A decisive aspect for building the citadel on the actual location was the route of the invading armies, which were coming from the Bran pass and were passing through Râ□nov, on their way to Burzenland. The only chance of survival for the inhabitants of the area, inclusively from Cristian and Ghimbav, was the refuge inside the citadel. Compelled to stay there for decades, the people of Râ□nov and the nearby villages turned the fortification into a dwelling.

Jack returns to the images of the fortress and begins to scroll through photos. A picture he has seen before appears, an old black and white photo, believed to be the earliest known taken inside the citadel, circa 1942. Jack studies the picture, a group of villagers stand motionless. Dressed in ragged clothing, gaunt with solemn faces. The scene is reminiscent of that taken at the concentration camps in world war two. He uses the computer to zoom in, scanning the faces of the men and women. A chill suddenly runs down his spine, he pauses, unsure of his discovery, feeling his chest tighten. He sits back in bewilderment, then zooms in to one of the faces in the picture, then shakes his head.

"Bloody hell, it's Cristina!"

17

The condensation streams down the shower cubicle door, aiding my view of Grace. I sit quietly, perched on the toilet, watching her. I feel great. It's early morning. I check my watch, six thirty-five. Grace always gets up at half past, so she can get ready before the kids get up. She turns the shower off and slides open the door,

"Ohhh!!! John! You scared the life out of me," she cries out, surprised to see me.

I smile and hand her a towel. She begins to dry herself. I watch her. She's beautiful.

"What are you doing?" she asks, confused by my attention.

"Just looking," I reply, then stand and kiss her my hand strays between her legs, I hear her breath deeply.

"I love you."

"I love you too," she replies. I kiss her again. "But I've got to get ready and get the kids up," she interrupts. I move my hand from between her legs.

"I'll get the kids up," I say.

"Are you sure?"

"Of course," I reply, leaving her to get ready.

I slowly push open Sadie's door. I can see she's fast asleep, carefully I creep over to her, then sit carefully down onto her bed. I begin to stroke her hair. She looks beautiful.

"Sadie," I whisper, her eyes open. She blinks quickly, her eyes adjusting to the light.

"Dad."

"Morning gorgeous, time to get up."

"Where's mum?"

"Downstairs making breakfast, come on, time to get up."

"No," she replies, then turns away from me, pulling the duvet tight up to her chin.

I smile to myself, "Five minutes," I say then rub her hair. I leave her in bed and walk into Lucy's room, she's already awake, sat up in bed.

"Morning, are you okay?" I ask

"Yeah, I heard mum in the shower, it woke me up."

I sit next to her, "cuddle," I ask. She throws her arms around me, and I hold her tight. I kiss her forehead.

"What do you want for breakfast?" I ask, she thinks for a moment,

"Rice Krispies."

"Okay, I'll tell mum," then stand and make my way to her door.

"Are you going to take us to school?" she calls out, I turn to look at her.

"Do you want me to?"

"yeah."

"Okay then, I will. Love you," I reply.

"Love you too, dad."

I leave her room and make my way downstairs. I hold the bannister tightly as I descend, but I feel different, strong. I meet Grace as I take the final step.

"Kids are up," I say

"What? Even Sadie."

"Well, nearly all the kids are up."

"Do you want some tea?" she asks.

"That would be lovely, thank you. Lucy wants Rice Krispies. I don't know what Sadie wants." She walks away from me. I grab her arm,

"What?" she asks, turning to look at me. I kiss her again.

"Everything's going to be okay," I say

"I hope so," she replies, then kisses me.

18

Jack opens his eyes. His phone vibrates on the bedside table beside him. He doesn't move, concentrating his gaze on the ceiling above him, his eyes adjusting to the morning light. Turning onto his side, he leans over and picks up his phone. Missed call, from Anna.

"Fuck!" the realisation of where he is supposed to be hits him. He checks the time, 9.30 AM The phone begins to vibrate in his hand, Anna calling again. He answers,

"Where are you?" Anna shouts down the phone.

"Sorry, Anna, I'll be there in half an hour."

"The fucking train leaves in five minutes."

"Okay, okay, we'll get the next one. There must be loads of trains to Brighton. Get a coffee. I'll be there soon."

"Not this time Jack, I'm going on my own, goodbye. Bastard!"

She hangs up,

"Shit!" Jack says.

They had arranged to travel to Brighton, to meet with Anna's Friend Daniella. She teaches art, and one of her ex-students was having a gallery opening.

"She's going to be famous," Anna had declared.

Jack sits up in bed, looks around the room, then at the letter sat on the table beside him. He places his glasses on his nose, picks up the letter, and rereads it.

"Heaven's Gate," he ponders, then remembers his conversation with Daniella, at The Black Dog. Her reaction confounds him.

"What was her problem?" he feels the need to speak with her; he has to go to Brighton and meet with her again.

His phone vibrates into life next to him. Quickly he picks it up.

"Half an hour. There's a train at ten-fifteen," Anna barks down the line.

"Anna," he says relieved, "I'll be there."

"Hurry up!" she answers, then hangs up.

He places the letter back on to the table, pulls the covers aside, jumps out of bed and heads towards the en-suite. He quickly showers, gets dressed and makes his way downstairs. Grabbing his car keys and jacket, he leaves immediately.

Jack checks his watch as he enters the station foyer, five-past ten. He sees Anna sitting at a small aluminium table drinking coffee. She looks up and sees him approaching.

"Hi, gorgeous," he says, kissing her on the cheek.

"Piss off. You're lucky I didn't get on that train,"

"I'm sorry I didn't sleep very well."

"Where were you last night? Weren't you with John yesterday?" she asks

"Yes," he pauses, "And no, I'll tell you about it later. I need a coffee; do you want another one?"

"No, I'm fine thanks. What do you mean, you'll tell me about it later?"

"I'll just get a cappuccino first, when's the train due?"

Anna checks her watch, "Soon."

"Do we need to buy tickets?"

"No," She says, pulling two tickets from her pocket.

"You owe me," she says, holding the tickets high.

"You're a star. I'll buy lunch."

"Too right, you will," she answers, placing the tickets back in her pocket.

Jack kisses her on the lips, then makes his way to the kiosk to buy his coffee.

"So, where were you?" Anna asks, as the train quakes into life and moves away from the station platform. Jack takes a drink of his coffee then turns to look at her.

"I had a meeting last night."

"Who with, John?"

"No, but it was about John."

"What was about John?"

"The meeting. I met with a student of Tom's."

"Tom, who's Tom?" she interrupts.

"Tom Rooney, you know him. He works at the hospital, took over from me at the university."

"Go on." She says cautiously.

"Well, he has this student in his class, from a hospital that's based in Romania."

"Romania." She interrupts again.

"Yes, the hospital she works at."

"She." Anna interrupts again.

"Yes, she's called Cristina and, according to Tom, her hospital has an amazing research department. He thinks they may be able to help John."

"Really, how?"

"Hopefully, by getting him on a clinical trial. I know it's a long shot, like I said to John, the trial might not save him, but it could help sufferers in the future."

"You've told John?"

"Yeah, he's excited by it."

"And the meeting went well? With this Cristina woman."

"I think it did."

"When does he start this trial then?"

"Not sure, she needs to contact her superiors."

"Superiors."

"That's what she calls her boss. Hopefully, I'll find out soon. John still isn't coping very well. He had a fall, at his kids' school play. I think he's more depressed than ever."

"I'm not surprised."

"If this works out, it just might give him a little bit of hope. He needs something."

Anna gets out her phone, "What's the name of the hospital? I'll google it now."

"You won't find it, the work they do there is very confidential. I wouldn't have known about it if it wasn't for Tom."

"What do they do out there that's so, confidential."

"I've still to find out. It sounds an interesting place, though."

"Sounds weird."

Jack laughs, puts his arm around her then kisses her on the cheek.

"Yeah, I know."

19

The taxi pulls up outside Beckstones Art Gallery. Jack pays the driver, and they both step out on to the pavement; a cold sea breeze engulfs them.

"God, it's freezing. Let's get inside quick," Anna says.

The two of them rush towards the gallery entrance and disappear inside. Dazzling LED ceiling lights illuminate the room. The white walls amplify the glow. A young man, dressed in a white shirt and black tie, walks up to them. He's holding a silver tray, and on it, flutes of champagne.

"Would you like a drink Madame?" he asks.

"Thank you," Anna replies, taking a glass from the tray.

"And for you, sir?" he enquires.

"Thank you very much," Jack replies.

They stand at the entrance, drinks in their hands, observing the room. People walk around, enjoying the art, mutterings fill the air.

"Do you know any of these people?" Jack asks.

Anna takes a moment to answer, "I don't think so, no," she replies.

"There's Daniella," Anna says, then waves at her. Daniella walks over to them.

"Hi, Anna," Daniella says, then kisses Anna on both cheeks, "thanks for coming." She looks at Jack.

"Hi," Jack says.

"Hi, Jack." They kiss on both cheeks.

"What do you think?" Daniella asks.

"It's very impressive," Anna Answers. "Who are all these people?"

"Mainly friends and family, but I know a couple of agents are here from London," Daniella replies

"Agents. Who's the artist?" Jack asks

"She's there," Daniella points over to a young woman, dressed in blue denim dungarees, a white t-shirt and oxblood Dr Marten boots. Her hair is bright pink and wrapped in a glittery headscarf.

"She's lovely," Daniella says, "I'll introduce you later. There's a real buzz around her work."

"Maybe I should buy a painting then?" Jack replies

"Maybe you should," Daniella replies. "Have a look around. The prices are on the little cards next to the paintings, we've sold some already. They're the ones with the little red dots against them."

"You've sold some already?" Jack asks, surprised.

"Like I said. Her work is good."

"Have you sold that one?" Jack points at a grand picture, hanging on the wall, at the far end of the room.

"No not yet, not sure anybody here has a home big enough for that one, we're hoping someone turns up from one of the hotels around here?"

"I like it," Jack says.

"It won't fit in your house!" Anna laughs.

"It might. Come on, let's have a look." Jack says, then walks towards the painting.

"We'll see you in a while," Anna says to Daniella, "Hopefully I'll get him to buy one."

"Okay." She replies.

The two of them wander around the room, arm in arm. Jack stops in front of one of the paintings.

"I like this one," he says.

The picture depicts a woman lying on a large wrought iron bed. Some of the covers have fallen from her, revealing her naked body.

"Is that because her tits are showing?" Anna questions.

"It is not, don't you like it?"

"Not really."

"Why? It's moody and calming." Jack takes out his spectacles from his inside pocket and places them on this nose. He stoops closer to read the card on the wall.

"Sleeping in Summer. By Charlotte Green," he mutters to himself.

"It's six-fifty," he says.

"Six hundred and fifty pounds! Are you going to buy it?" Anna asks, surprised.

"I think I might." Jack turns around and looks for Daniella. He catches her eye and beckons her over.

"Daniella, can you put one of your dots on this one please?"

"I can," she exclaims, then turns to look around the room.

"Charlotte," she calls out to the artist, who quickly walks over to them.

"Yes." She says on her arrival.

"This is Anna and Jack, friends of mine, and I think they're about to buy one of your paintings."

"This one?" she says, as a broad smile covers her face.

"Yes, I like it," Jack interrupts.

"Thank you. The woman is my friend Mary. I painted it when we shared a flat."

"Well, I think she, the painting, I mean," he looks at Charlotte and smiles, "Looks great."

"Quick get a red dot on it before he changes his mind," Daniella says. They all chuckle and Charlotte takes a sheet of red dots from her pocket and places one next to the title on the card,

"Sold!" she says and holds out her hand for Jack to shake.

"Sold," Jack repeats, shaking her hand.

"Do you mind if I take some details from you now?" Daniella asks Jack, "I'll get it delivered to you as soon as the show is over."

"No, not at all, let's get the deal done."

"Okay, follow me." Daniella walks over to a dark oak desk placed in the corner of the room.

"I won't be a minute," Jack says to Anna and leaves her to speak with Charlotte. Jack follows Daniella to her desk. The two of them sit down opposite each other. Daniella opens a large A4 sized invoice pad.

"Sorry about this, but I just need your address and card details, if I could?" Daniella says.

"No problem," Jack explains where to send the painting and pulls out his MasterCard to complete the purchase.

"Thank you," Daniella says when the deal is finalised.

"It's a great picture, I like it and if you're right - and she becomes famous - then I might just have bought myself a nice little investment."

"Fingers crossed," Daniella replies, then turns away to place the invoice book in the draw beside her.

"Do you mind if I ask you something?" Jack asks, Daniella looks across at him with a puzzled look.

"What is it?"

"Heaven's Gate? The hospital I mentioned the other night in the Black dog."

"What about it?" she replies sternly.

"You said it was evil, what did you mean by that? How can a hospital be evil?"

Daniella looks past Jack, into the room, then back at him, "I think it just took me by surprise, that you knew about that place."

"I was surprised you knew about it. The work they do there is highly confidential."

"Is that what they say?" She replies, sarcastically.

"Yes, how do you know of it?" Jack asks.

"I have family there."

"What? Where? At Heaven's Gate?"

"No, Rasnov. My family is from Rasnov."

"You grew up there?"

"No, we moved to Bucharest when I was a baby," she then hesitates. "Do not go there."

"Why? you're not going to tell me it's evil again are you?" Jack laughs

"I am not joking when I tell you the people who live there, are…." she pauses again.

"Are what?" Jack asks

"Different to us, me, you, Anna, all of us."

"How?"

"You would not believe me."

"Look, I have met someone from Heaven's Gate, she looked normal to me."

"She? You've met someone?" her tone changes, "Who? When?"

Jack hesitates, "It doesn't matter who she is, but she was - very much - like you and me."

"If she is from there, then she is cursed, that race is cursed. Do not say they are like me. They are nothing like me," anger now apparent in her words.

"Cursed? How? Why would you say that?"

Daniella takes a drink of her champagne,

"Do you want to know?" she asks.

"Yes, tell me."

"What has she told you?"

"Nothing yet."

"Whatever she tells you will be lies. She will not say what she is."

"And what is that?"

"She is descended from an ancient race of people called the Gepids?"

"I read about that last night."

"They were thought to be extinct. I wish they were."

"What?" Jack says, surprised.

"They were, are, an evil race. If it had not been for the fortress, we would have eliminated them from the earth forever."

"Now look," Jack says irritated, "Whatever your racist views are, I don't want to hear them."

"I am not racist."

"You could have fooled me. You're talking about genocide."

"They are not like us."

"Why? Because of the colour of their skin?"

"They are not human."

"You're ridiculous."

"Then go!" Daniella says harshly. "Go, I will not sit and have you laugh at what I know to be true."

"Jack, Daniella," they both turn, Anna is standing next to them, "What's going on? Is everything okay?"

"Yes, everything is fine," Jack replies.

"Tell me," Daniella interrupts, "Your friend, did she have someone with her? Guarding her?"

Jack doesn't answer, but looks at her with a look of resignation,

"She does, and has he spoken?" Daniella smiles, "No, he hasn't."

"Who?" Anna asks.

Daniella then walks from around the desk. "Be very careful, Jack, trust me."

"What are you talking about?" Anna Asks her.

"Jack has a new friend, I would watch her, if I was you," she replies, then turns to Jack.

"Thank you for buying the painting. I hope it brings you much joy. Now I must try and convince someone else." Daniella then walks away into the gallery

"What was all that about?" Anna asks, confused.

"No idea." Jack answers.

20

The late afternoon sun blazes through my lounge window. A shadow breaks through the beams of light. I look up from the TV, then hear a knock at the door.

"Grace, I think Jacks here?" I call out.

"That's good timing," she says, appearing at the kitchen door.

I look up. Her hands are covered in flour.

"What are you doing?" I ask

"Baking a cake for Janice. I thought you said he was coming at three?" she replies. We both look across at the clock, 2:45 PM.

"Bloody hell, I didn't realise the time," she says anxiously.

"You get cleaned up. I'll get the door." I force myself out of the chair to make my way towards the door.

"Hi Jack, come in."

"Hi John," he replies, then walks past me into the lounge. I follow him.

"Sit yourself down, do you want a cup of tea, coffee?"

"Tea please, where's Grace?"

"I'm here," she shouts, appearing at the kitchen door again. "I'm just cleaning up. I won't be a minute. Tea was it?"

"As long as it's no bother" Jack answers.

"No, I'm making one now."

"And for me," I say smiling at her, she smirks, then disappears back into the kitchen. I walk over to my chair, sit down and turn off the TV.

"How have you been?" Jack asks me

"I've been great thanks," I reply.

"Really?" he looks at me strangely.

"Yeah, I've been looking forward to my little holiday."

"Holiday?"

"To Romania," I reply. I notice his apprehension.

"What is it? Is it not happening now?" I fell my heart sink into despair.

"No, No, It's still on."

"Then what?"

"It just might take a little more time to organise, than I thought."

"Why? What's happened? What's gone wrong?"

"Nothing's gone wrong. I'm still sorting it, that's all," he says apologetically.

"And can you sort it?"

"I think so?"

"You think so? Bloody hell."

"What's happened?" we look up, Grace has entered the room. She's carrying two cups of tea.

"He can't get me in," I say to her. I was disillusioned by what I'd just heard.

"I didn't say that!" Jack says I look at him. Grace places the two cups down on to the coffee table in front of us.

"Wait, I'll just be a second," she says, then quickly returns to the kitchen.

"Sorry," I say quietly to Jack.

"It's not over," he says, shaking his head and picking up his tea. Grace takes her seat next to Jack.

"Go on then, what's happened?" she says. Jack turns to look at her.

"What's John told you?" he asks.

"Just that you've might have found a hospital for John," she pauses, "Oh, and it's in bloody Romania!" she doesn't smile.

"Well, all that is true."

"So, what's happened?" I ask again.

"I had a meeting on Saturday night – after the game - with a student from the hospital."

"A student," Grace asks

"Yeah, she's studying over here, a friend of mine put me in touch with her. Anyway, it turns out she wants me to go over there and observe the research carried out at her hospital."

"Are they offering you a job?" Grace asks

"I'm not sure, maybe?"

"And how does John fit into this? Are they working on a cure for MND there?" Grace asks.

"I'm not sure yet. I hope so."

"You hope so." Grace repeats, "You do know you've got John excited about this." She says sternly.

"Yes, I know. I'm excited about this."

"Why? You don't even know what they do out there." She says bluntly.

"Maybe not, but everything I do know is positive. Their success rate in developing new drugs is outstanding."

"But are they working on a drug for MND?" she asks.

"I need to find that out."

"What did the student say, when you asked her?" Grace interrupts.

"She said she didn't know everything that was going on at the hospital, and that they might be able to start something, depending on what facilities they have available."

"What? Just because you asked them to, they're going to start a research program." Grace persists.

"Maybe not just because I asked."

"Then what?" I ask.

"They want me to visit their facility. I get the impression that I might be able to influence them."

"And what if you can't?" Grace says abruptly. I can see she is starting to get annoyed.

"Well, I don't know that yet."

"What did she say about me? Did she say I could come with you?" I ask, then notice his expression change, "She told you I couldn't go, didn't she?"

"No, not exactly," he answers, nervously.

"What did she say?" Grace asks Jack pauses before answering.

"She was just unsure about you travelling with me. The invitation was just for me. She has to check with her superiors first."

"Her superiors!" Grace says, "And when will she know?"

"I said I'd call her in a couple of days."

I sit in my seat and watch him, I know he's lying.

"And what if they say no? What are you going to do? Sneak me in?" I ask.

"If I have to, yes," he answers.

"You are not!" Grace says, shocked at what she is hearing.

"It's not going to happen, is it Jack?" I ask solemnly.

"It is, I just need to figure it out," he replies. "Look, I've been invited to this hospital. They've sent someone across Europe, to ask me to visit personally. They're serious about getting me there."

"But not me," I interrupt him.

"Well if they want me, then they get you. That's my plan."

"Your plan! Your dealing with John's life here. You'll need more than a plan before I let you take him halfway across the world for nothing." Grace says.

"I'll make sure it's not for nothing. I wouldn't waste my time, or John's."

"You know nothing about this place. We know nothing. John googled it, and we couldn't find it. What kind of hospital is it anyway?" Grace protests.

"You won't find it."

"Why not?" Grace asks.

"The work they do out there…" he pauses, "Well, it's highly confidential."

"Why? What do they get up to over there?" She asks quickly.

"I don't know yet. I'm gonna go there, find out and hopefully get John on a clinical trial."

"And what kind of drugs will they give him? What if he has a reaction to them?"

"What? And it kills me." I interject, a smug look on my face.

"It's not funny, John!" Grace shouts.

"Let me have this meeting first. I'll know more then," Jack says.

"And when will that be? I can't wait forever, Jack."

"I know, I know," he answers.

"The clocks ticking," I say

"I know" he replies.

Jack then places his cup down and pulls his phone from his pocket. He stares at the screen.

"I just need to get this. It's Amy"

"Okay," I reply, Amy is his ex-wife. I watch him stand, then walk into the kitchen.

"This is a stupid idea," Grace says.

"What? Why?"

"Why? Travelling to Romania, to a hospital in the middle of bloody nowhere, it's ridiculous," Grace replies, shaking her head. Our conversation is interrupted, as we hear Jack's voice getting louder. He begins to shout at the phone.

"Fucking hell Amy. I've taken time off work," we hear him say, I look at Grace, and raise my eyebrows

"Yeah, whatever, fuck off!" Jack continues, then walks back into the lounge.

"Sorry about that," he apologises to us.

"Are you okay? What's happened?" I ask.

"Fucking Amy."

"What about fucking Amy?" I ask again.

"She's taking the kids away next week."

"And that's a bad thing," I wonder.

"It is yeah, I was supposed to have them next week. The kids are off school. I hardly see them as it is."

"Why has she done that then?" I say.

"She says, she's going away with friends. Some story about being offered a free room in a cottage they've booked. Someone's dropped out. She thinks it'll be good for the kids to get some fresh air."

"It might be?" I reply.

"Don't you bloody take her side," he shouts at me.

"Sorry," I pause, "So, you've got no plans for next week then."

Jack looks at me, "Not now."

"Then get in touch with them, do you think they can organise your trip for next week?"

"What? I don't know, probably."

"I'd rather know sooner than later Jack….whether they can do something or not."

I can see he's still engulfed with anger when he replies.

"Okay, I'll call them." He replies.

21

Jack takes a sip of his drink, then scans the room. He notices an empty table, walks over to it, sits down and checks his watch, 5:53 PM. He's arranged for the meeting to be at six o'clock, in the Black Dog.

"Hello," he says, greeting Cristina on her arrival. She's wearing skin-tight black jeans, a horizontal black and white striped t-shirt and blue denim jacket.

"Can I get you a drink?" he asks.

"Just a coke please."

"Ivan, can I get you anything?" Jack looks at him. Ivan shakes his head.

"He's okay," Cristina says.

"I won't be a minute, please take a seat."

He returns to the table with Cristina's drink and sits down.

"Thank you," Cristina says, then takes a sip of her coke. "I was surprised to get your message."

"You were?" Jack answers.

"Yes, so soon after our meeting."

"There's no time like the present." Jack smiles.

"Firstly" she begins, "I would like to thank you for accepting our invitation. It is our honour."

"You don't need to say that, is that what you've been told to say?"

Cristina smiles, "No, we… I… am very happy that you have accepted."

"Good, I'm happy too. I can't wait to get there. You've made it sound beautiful and intriguing."

"I don't think you will be disappointed."

"I hope not."

Cristina opens her bag and pulls out a bright blue Filofax. She opens it, then flicks through the diary pages, stopping on today's date.

"So, when would you like to visit?" she asks.

"Next week," he replies.

"Next week!" she says surprised.

"Is that a problem?" he asks.

"No, not at all. We just thought you might need some time to organise your diary."

"Let's just say I had an appointment cancelled."

"Well, we are pleased you can visit so soon. What day would you like to fly?"

"Is Monday or Tuesday, okay?" he asks.

"I'm sure it will be fine. I will check flight times for next week and get back to you. Let me know which flights suit you, and we will book the necessary tickets and transfers."

"How long does the flight take? Which airport will I fly into?" He asks.

"You will fly into Bucharest; the flight takes around three hours. From there, the journey to Rasnov is about two and a half hours. We will try our best to make your journey as comfortable as possible."

"And you will be travelling with me?"

"No."

"No!" Jack answers, surprised. "Why? Have you got another letter for someone else?"

"Not at all. I will be travelling back, but not by plane."

"Not by plane. Then what? Train?"

"Yes."

"Really. How long does that take?"

"I like trains," she answers, ignoring his question and placing the Filofax back into her bag.

"Are you scared of flying?"

"No."

"Then what?"

"I just prefer to travel by train. The experience is far more rewarding."

"So, I'll be travelling alone?"

"Yes, but we will have someone waiting for you in Bucharest, to take you to Rasnov."

Jack considers his options. Flying alone was not part of his plan. He needs to keep his relationship with Cristina active. She's his only connection with Heaven's Gate.

"Is everything okay?" she asks, noticing his hesitation.

"I just thought you'd be travelling with me."

"I'm sure you have travelled alone on many occasions."

"That is true, but I would feel happier arriving at Heaven's Gate with you by my side."

"I am sorry, but I cannot fly with you."

"Then I will travel with you."

Cristina stares at Jack, "What?"

"I'll get the train with you."

"Why? There is no need to travel with me. Your flights and transfers will all be taken care of. You will have somebody meet you in Romania who will take you Heaven's Gate. I will meet with you later in the week when I arrive."

"Maybe, but I would like to travel with you," he looks across at Ivan, "And of course you, Ivan."

Cristina looks at Ivan, then back at Jack.

"I will need to speak with my superiors," she says.

"Speak to them then, and can you ask them about John?"

"What about John?"

"Ask them if I can bring him with me."

"That is not possible."

"But I'd like you to ask."

"I know the answer will be no."

"Then I will have to think again about my decision."

"Please, Dr Carlisle, I understand your determination to help your friend. But, as I have said, there is nothing we can do for him at Heaven's Gate. I thought you understood the sensitive nature of our facility. It disappoints me that you would throw away this opportunity."

"I need to help my friend. If he doesn't go, I don't go."

There is a moment of silence, Cristina looks across at Ivan, he immediately stands.

"I am sorry you feel that way." Cristina says, then picks up her bag and stands up."

"Where are you going?" Jack asks nervously.

"There is nothing more for us to discuss."

"What? Wait." Jack stands, his plan to help me, quickly disappearing.

"You're leaving. What will your superiors say when you arrive back without me?"

"They will understand." She answers directly, then holds out her hand for Jack to shake.

Jack quickly realises he has pushed his luck too far.

"Okay, wait. What if, when I'm there, at Heaven's gate. I find out that you can help him. Will you organise for my friend to be flown out there as soon as possible so that he can start his treatment?"

"If that is agreed with my superiors. Then yes."

"Good, then I'll go."

"You have changed your mind?" she says, cautiously.

"Yes, if there's any chance I can help my friend. Then yes, I will visit Heaven's Gate."

"Would you like some time to think about your decision?"

"No, honestly, I'm happy to go."

"Then I am happy too. You will not be disappointed. And you are sure you don't want to fly."

"I am sure," Jack replies, "The journey will be much more enjoyable with you as company."

"Thank you. I will make the necessary arrangements and get back in touch."

Jack shakes Cristina's hand, then notices Anna entering the bar. Cristina notices his reaction and turns to see what has caught his attention. Behind Anna follows Daniella, Jack feels a wave of anger grow inside him. Anna waves, when she sees him and makes her way over to them.

"Hi," she says, then kisses him.

"Hi," Jack answers, "What are you doing here?" he asks.

"I've just come for a drink," she answers, then looks at Cristina and Ivan, "And who is this?" she says, holding out her hand.

Cristina pauses before reacting.

"Sorry," Jack says awkwardly, "Anna, this is Cristina, Cristina, Anna." They shake hands.

"And you are?" she asks confidently, holding out her hand to Ivan. Ivan just stares at her, motionless.

"His name is Ivan. He doesn't say much." Jack says, trying to lighten the situation.

"We will leave you with your friend. I will be in touch soon and thank you again."

Cristina and Ivan then make their way to the exit. Daniella stands at the bar, watching them as they pass her.

"What are you doing here?" Jack asks, annoyed.

"I came for moral support."

"And what's she doing here?" Jack looks across at Daniella.

"She wanted to come."

"I bet she did, fucking hell Anna, what have you told her?"

"Don't swear at me. I've said nothing. I don't know anything. You're the one who's been asking her questions." She snarls.

"She shouldn't be here."

"Well, we won't be then. Fuck you, Jack," Anna says, then spins around and storms out of the bar, saying something to Daniella as she passes her. Daniella glares at Jack, then follows Anna out of the bar.

22

I hear the door open; in response, I pull the duvet up close to my chin and breathe deeply. I know it's Grace, I move as she places herself down on the bed, she strokes my hair and a tear rolls down my cheek.

"John," she says quietly, "Come on, it's past lunchtime. Do you want something to eat?"

I just lie there silently, gathered in my cocoon.

"John," she says with more urgency, "Please, you've got to get up. You'll feel a lot better."

I close my eyes, she waits in silence, then stands and leaves the room. All the hope I had, had gone. I'd not heard from Jack in two days. I knew nothing would happen, it was a long shot, but it was my only shot. I was wallowing in despair, I couldn't go on like this, but I had a fear, a fear of what I was leaving behind. Suicide is not easy, people don't take that decision lightly, I wasn't taking it lightly, but I knew it was close. I could feel it looking at me right now, as I tried hard to stay hidden from its gaze. It was waiting for the moment, a moment of weakness, then it would take me.

Jack had just finished his lunch when he checked his phone and read the message from Grace.

Hi Jack, have you heard any more about the hospital visit? John is very depressed again. He thinks the opportunity has gone, has it? I know I wasn't pleased about the idea, but I realise now much it meant to him. I'm worried Jack, he's worse than ever. Can you let me know what's going on, soon? I'm afraid he's going to do something stupid. Thanks, Grace.

"Shit!" Jack thinks to himself, then places his phone on to the table, next to his travel itinerary. Cristina had carefully organised his journey to Heaven's Gate. London to Paris, then on to Munich, Budapest, eventually arriving in Rasnov, Romania and Heaven's Gate. He realises there's only one solution and switches on his computer.

I'm not sure what time it is when Grace re-enters the room. I hadn't eaten all day, ignoring her hourly requests for me too, "Eat something." I didn't want anything.

"John!" she shouts at me with some urgency. I lay motionless. The bedroom light illuminates the room. I open my eyes, blinking rapidly as my eyes adjust to the light.

"John, It's Jack on the phone."

I slowly turn on to my back. Grace is standing above me. She thrusts the phone towards me.

"Answer it then." She says, anxiously.

I take the phone from her.

"Hi Jack," I say sleepily.

"John?" I hear him say, not recognising my voice.

"Yeah, what is it?"

"Sorry I didn't recognise your voice there. Are you sitting down?" he asks

"Yeah, like always. Why?"

"Because I have some news,"

"What news?"

"It's taken a bit of time to plan, but it's all sorted."

"What is?"

"You're coming with me."

"What? Where, to Heaven's Gate?"

"Yes," he replies. I feel my heart begin to pound beneath my chest.

"How? Why? I mean, how did you get them to change their minds?"

"I'll tell you about it later. Are you in tonight?"

"Yeah, I'm in."

"Good, I'll be round about nine, give you time to get the kids in bed."

"When are we going?" I ask, then hear him laugh.

"Tomorrow," he replies

"Tomorrow!" I reply, then launch myself upright, looking straight at Grace.

"Is that okay?" he asks

"Yeah, yeah, definitely, sooner the better."

"Good, I hoped you'd say that. Okay, I'll be round soon,"

"See you later then. Bye," I hang up.

"What's going on?" Grace asks.

"Jack's got me into that hospital."

"He has?" Grace looks surprised.

"Yeah, he's coming round later tonight, about nine. He said it's all sorted."

"And when are you going?" she asks, knowing the answer.

"He said tomorrow."

"Tomorrow! bloody hell, John."

"What?"

"Tomorrow…. we haven't got anything organised."

"What's to organise? I just need a bag packed and I'm ready."

"What about me?" she asks

"I have to do this, Grace." I look at her. Her eyes begin to glaze with tears.

23

The TV is on, but I'm not watching. I just stare blankly at the screen, my mind racing, wondering what was about to happen? I check the time, eight fifty-five AM. I had made it out of bed, showered and shaved. I was disgusted with my reflection; how could I be like this? I had lost complete control of my emotions. I needed help, Jack's help. A knock on the door shatters my thoughts of sadness.

"Jack's here," I shout, then quickly force myself to my feet and make my way to the door.

"Hi," I say with a smile.

"Hi, John," Jack replies, then walks past me, into the house.

Grace stands in the middle of the lounge.

"Hi Jack," she says, reluctantly. Her sombre expression shows her true feelings.

"Hi, Grace," Jack says.

"Do you want a drink?" she asks.

"Yes, please, tea would be lovely."

"John, do you want one?" she asks

"Yes, please," I answer, we sit down. Jack has a blue cardboard folder in his hand.

"What's in there?" I ask, "The grand plan?"

"Yeah, you could say that."

"So, what is the plan?"

"Shouldn't we wait on Grace"?

"Yes, you should wait on Grace," she announces, standing at the door.

"Okay" I reply. We sit in silence, unsure of how to proceed.

"How did you organise it so quickly?" I ask.

"It was kind of now or never. Are you still okay about it?"

"Yeah, I can't wait to be honest, I thought it wasn't gonna happen."

"Well, don't get too excited."

"What? Why?" I ask worriedly.

Grace appears, places the drinks on to the coffee table, then returns to the kitchen. She emerges moments later, holding a large glass of white wine and takes her seat next to Jack.

"So, what's going on?" she asks, "John says you've got him into that hospital."

We both notice Jack's nervousness.

"It's not quite as easy as that."

"What?" I interrupt.

"There was a change in my travel arrangements."

"What do you mean?" I ask

"I thought I was going to fly out there, sort it, then fly back. But Cristina doesn't fly."

"Why is she scared of flying?" I ask

"Probably."

"Cristina?" Grace asks.

"Yes, she's the student that's been sent over here to invite me to Heaven's Gate."

"I don't like that name, Heaven's Gate. It's a stupid name for a hospital." Grace says, "And why do you have to travel with her, you and John could fly together without her."

"Yeah, why don't we just fly?" I ask

"I thought about that, but we need Cristina."

"Why?" I ask

"She's the only person I know from Heaven's Gate, and I'm beginning to build a relationship with her."

"Your sleeping with her?" Grace interrupts.

"No, I'm not!" Jack says, annoyed. "I'm forming a professional relationship with her. I think we'll need her when we get there. If we were to fly without her, then we'd land, I'd get taken to the hospital, and that's it. I'd have no more options. I don't know anybody else out there. I need her help. We need her help." He looks at Grace, "Professionally. Plus, I still need to find out more about Heaven's Gate."

"About the treatment, I'll be getting?" I ask, noticing his apprehension.

"What is it?" I ask, "What's wrong?" Jack pauses before answering.

"I haven't got you involved in anything yet."

"What!" Grace hollers, shocked, "Then why are you going?"

"Fucking hell Jack," I interrupt, "So, why are you here? you said we were leaving tomorrow."

"We are. I'm going to take you with me."

"Why?" Grace asks.

"So that when I get there, I can get him in straight away." He replies.

"Into what?" Grace asks.

"I don't know yet."

"You don't know yet!" Grace laughs, "You're not going, John!"

"Look!" Jack interrupts, "I think they will be able to help him."

"How?" Grace queries.

"I'll know more when I… we… get there."

"You're not going," Grace says, annoyed, "It's ridiculous."

"Grace, I wouldn't take him if I didn't think there was a chance. What's the worst that could happen? We get there. My plan backfires, they can't help him. So what? Then we come home."

"And it's as easy as that is it?" she says irritated by Jack's words. "You can't play with people's emotions like that, getting his hopes up, when there might be nothing for him. It's just not right."

"What other chance has he got?" Jack says

"I'm still here!" I shout, they both turn to look at me, "Grace, I know this is crazy. Jack, this is crazy. But I'm going. I have to go. There's nothing for me here."

"It's true," Jack says, looking at Grace, "I've checked, and checked again. I know what medication John is on, and that is the best that he can get here in England, maybe in the world. Nothing is going to stop John from getting worse. We've both seen the change in him over the past few weeks. His symptoms aren't going away." Jack pauses, "The last thing I want is a phone call from you telling me you've found John dead. After taking some pills, or worse." Grace looks shocked and upset. "I know this is hard, what you're going through, what you're both going through. But if I can give John a little hope, for a little while, then I'm happy with that."

"You might be happy with that, but what about John? What about me? You might have made yourself feel better, but it's us that have to pick up the pieces when he gets back. How is he going to feel then? When he has nothing. How's he going to live with that?"

"You mean, how are you going to live with that?" I say to Grace. She looks directly at me.

"Yes! How am I going to live with that? It's hard enough now."

"Okay, okay," Jack says calmly.

"Grace, I love you, but I just need a chance. I need something." I watch her as she wipes her nose. "You know how I've been this last couple of days. I know how I've been. I've been terrible. I know I have. I can't help it. I have nothing left."

"You've got the kids and me, you keep forgetting that."

"I know I do but…." I pause, an awkward silence surrounds us, "Please, Jack, carry on. What's the plan?"

"Are you okay?" Jack asks Grace, she picks up her glass of wine and takes a drink, her hand shaking.

"Yes," she replies.

Jack looks at me, then continues.

"I've organised your travel," he says, picking up the blue file.

"You've organised my travel?" I ask.

"Yes," Jack looks at me, "Like I said earlier, it's turning out to be slightly more complicated than I hoped."

"And what does that mean?" I ask bewildered.

"You have to travel alone."

"Travel alone!" Grace interrupts, "I don't think so, right, stop all this nonsense now. It's just ridiculous."

I ignore her, "I'm travelling on my own?" I ask calmly.

"Yes, well, not completely on your own. I'll be on the same trains as you, so I'll be there, just not sitting with you."

"Why?" I ask.

"Cristina doesn't know you're travelling with us," Jack states, then waits for the room to erupt. He is greeted with silence.

"She doesn't know I'm coming?" I repeat.

"No, she's happy for you to get treated once everything is agreed, but the invitation to visit the hospital is for me only. She's very serious about keeping Heaven's Gate as confidential as possible."

"I don't understand, isn't she going to be annoyed when you tell her. Smuggling your dying friend across Europe to infiltrate her secret hospital, might not go down to well."

"Maybe, but it'll be too late then, you'll be accepted on whatever they have to offer and available for treatment immediately."

I sit back in my seat, unsure of how to proceed, I look at Grace, her face pink with emotion.

"What's wrong?" Jack asks seriously.

"What's wrong?" Grace repeats sarcastically, "everything's wrong, can you not see that?"

"I know I've asked you to help me Jack, but this…"

"He's not strong enough to travel on his own, never mind everything else." Grace protests

"He won't be on his own. Like I've said, I'll be there, on the same trains, in the same hotels. I can be with him in minutes if he needs me."

"Ridiculous!" we both look at Grace, "This is ridiculous, how many times do I need to say it? You'll travel all that way for nothing John."

"You won't!" Jack protests, "I wouldn't put you through this if I didn't think there was a chance. It's an extraordinary facility, unusual in its operation, maybe? but if anywhere might be able to help you, Heaven's Gate can, I know it."

"And is there a chance?" I ask

"Yes, I'm sure of it" Jack looks at me then Grace,

"Go on then, open that folder," I ask.

Jack immediately picks up the blue folder and takes out a handful of A4 size printed sheets, "I have all your travel details here," he places them onto the coffee table in front of us. I lean forward to take a closer look. Grace acts ambivalent to the situation.

"I was sent my travel details last night, from Cristina, and I've managed to book your tickets on all the same trains as I'm on."

"I hope you've booked them. First-class?" I asked, trying hard to lighten the mood.

"I have."

"You have! are you joking?"

"No, I'm not joking, I'm not having my good mate slumming it, while I'm up in first class."

"How much did it all cost you?" I ask.

"It doesn't matter about the money, buy me a drink when we get there," Jack says, smiling at me. I smile back. Grace ignores his joke. Jack picks out one of the sheets and places it on to the coffee table.

"This is a map of the journey we'll be taking," he continues. I pick up the photocopied map in front of me. A blue line traces a path across Europe, from London to Brasov, Romania. I've never even heard of Brasov, Jack then picks up another sheet and hands it to me, taking the map from me and laying it on to the table. That's a summary of the journey we will be making; he then refers back to the plan and places his finger onto the city named London.

"You… we will travel from London to Paris on the Eurostar, it leaves St Pancras at nine twenty-four and gets into Paris at twelve forty-seven. Then, at Paris Gare du Nord, you need to transfer to Paris Gare Du L'est." Jack looks up at me, "I've organised a taxi, to pick you up and take you there. It's not far, maybe five or ten minutes." He pauses, "Are you okay so far?" he asks, I nod.

"From Gare du L'est we, travel on to Munich. The train leaves at thirteen fifty-five, so you've got time in Paris to get some lunch, if you wanted to, before boarding the train. It arrives in Munich at nineteen twenty-seven. Here we take a break."

"A break?" I ask.

"Yeah, we're going to spend the night in Munich. I've booked you a room at the same hotel as me, but you must be discreet when you get there. I don't want Cristina finding out about you in Munich. It's too soon."

"It's like a bloody spy film," I say.

"I'll come and see you, make sure you're okay when I get there," he says, smiling, "I might even buy you a drink?"

"Thanks, I think I'll need one," I reply.

"I've organised another cab to take you to the hotel from the station and pick you up in the morning to transfer you back to the station."

"Bloody hell Jack, how much is this costing you?"

"Too much," he replies with a grin.

"We then, in the morning, travel from Munich to Budapest. The train leaves at nine-thirty, so hopefully, you'll get a good night's sleep and some breakfast, before setting off. It arrives in Budapest at sixteen nineteen. Now, this is the fun bit." He states, I just look at him in bewilderment.

"We then catch another train from Budapest to Brasov, overnight, on a sleeper train."

"A sleeper train, bloody hell, this is a journey and a half, are you sure we couldn't just fly?"

"Cristina tried to convince me to fly again last night when she emailed the details over. She even included flight times with the train information. It just won't work without her, plus it's an adventure, isn't it?" He looks at me.

"Yeah, I guess it might be?" I reply. I'm excited, nervous, but something inside me is beating, life is beating, I feel the adrenaline rushing through me.

"At Brasov, I go on to Rasnov."

"You go? What about me?"

"I've booked you a hotel in Brasov. I'm being chauffeured straight to Heaven's Gate, from the station. I've got a room organised at the hospital. You can get settled into your hotel and…" he pauses

"And what?" I ask

"Just wait."

"Wait?"

"Do some sight-seeing, read a book, anything. I'll be in touch as soon as I can."

"Brasov? Rasnov?" I look at him, confused, "Are you sure?"

"Yes."

There's a silence from everybody. I look at the train journey, recheck the times.

"It sounds like a nice journey," I say and turn to look at Grace, she has tears in her eyes.

"I need to go," I say to her.

"I know," she replies, I take hold of her hand.

"You better look after him," Grace says to Jack.

"I will, you know I will," he replies. I pick up the sheets again and browse through them. I try to make some sense of what I have in front of me.

"Where are we staying in Munich?" I ask him.

"The Sofitel Munich, it looks lovely. I've checked it out online, it's in a perfect location, just down the road from the train station."

"And the sleeper train?" I ask

"Should be fun. You have your own private berth."

"Orient Express like?" I ask smiling

"Maybe, it looks nice."

"And do I stay undercover all the way?"

"Undercover? Probably best to, but definitely 'til we get on that sleeper train. Once we're on our way to Brasov, well, Cristina can't stop us then, can she?"

I feel a tear gather in my eye, then roll down my cheek.

"Thanks, Jack,"

"It's okay, are you okay?" he asks me, then turns to look at Grace, "And, are you okay?"

She doesn't answer. We can both see she's struggling with the idea, trying hard to hold back more tears.

"Yes, I am," I reply, "Grace?"

"No, not really, it's ridiculous," she replies.

"Look, this can be a good thing," Jack interjects, we both look at him.

"I'm not doing all this, so you can go there to die. I'm doing this, because there might, just might, be a chance that they can help you. Grace, I'm going to bring him back, he's not going to die under my watch. And when we're back, if it's not gone to plan, then I'll do what I can to make him, and you, as happy as you can be." Jack looks at Grace. She nods, reluctantly accepting the outcome.

"John, are you okay with it?"

"Yes."

"Good" he replies.

24

Jack plunges into his leather armchair and takes a large mouthful of whiskey. Exhausted by the day's developments, he lays his head back and closes his eyes. A calmness engulfs him. He feels himself drifting into sleep. Quickly he opens his eyes, blinks rapidly, stands and moves over to his desk. Photocopied sheets of paper lay randomly all over the patinated surface. He collects them together, shuffles them into some kind of order and places them into a plastic A4 wallet. The top page catches his attention, the old black and white photo of the villagers living inside the walls of the citadel. He pulls it out and examines the face of the woman in the picture carefully, she looks so much like Cristina, "it must be her mother," he wonders. He then places it back into the wallet. All he knows about Heaven's Gate is in his hands, "it's not much," he ponders, then places the wallet inside his Ted Baker messenger bag. He checks his passport is also there, before picking up the bag, his whiskey then climbs the stairs to his bedroom.

An empty suitcase lays open on his bed. He deliberates over what to pack. At that moment, a surge of apprehension flows through his body, a realisation of what he is about to commence. He takes another drink, forcing the unwelcome visitors from his mind. Lacking enthusiasm, he opens the chest of draws next to him, and takes out the top layer of t-shirts and places them into his case. His phone vibrates in his pocket, he pulls it out and reads the text.

Can I come round? X

It's from Anna.

Yes, you can help me pack x

He replies.

Okay, I'll be there soon x

He reads the reply, then places his phone on the bedside table. The phone vibrates again. He looks at the screen. An unknown caller is displayed, he answers,

"Hello,"

"Hello, am I speaking to Dr Carlisle?" A man replies.

"Yes, who is this?"

"Good evening, let me introduce myself. My name is Dr Otto Schneider."

"Dr Schneider!" Jack interrupts surprised by the announcement.

"I thought it was only right that I should give you a call before your journey begins," he continues, "And I would especially like to thank you for accepting our invitation to visit Heaven's Gate."

"How could I refuse? It's not every day that I'm approached by a beautiful woman who's been sent across Europe to hand me a letter."

"I know our methods are not commonplace in the medical world, but we have our reasons."

"Cristina has explained the confidentiality that is required. I'm interested to know why?"

"That question and many more will be answered on your arrival."

"I hope so," Jack interrupts bluntly.

"You will not regret your decision, we have an impressive facility here, and I am very much looking forward to meeting with you."

"I'm looking forward to meeting with you too," Jack replies, "The letter did not say why I had been selected, or what you want with me?"

"It did not seem right to put those details into a letter. I will explain all when you arrive."

"Is there nothing more you can tell me now?" He asks the line goes quiet.

"Hello, Dr Schneider," Jack says anxiously.

"I think it is better, I'll explain all when you arrive."

Jack chuckles to himself, "I thought you would say that."

"Well, I am sure you have much to organise, so I will wish you a good evening, and a safe journey tomorrow."

"Thank you,"

"May I say we were surprised you chose to travel by train."

"There was no way I was going to travel on my own. My only connection with Heaven's Gate is Cristina. I will be staying very close to her. That is, of course, if Ivan lets me?"

"He is a good man. He will make sure you arrive safely at Heaven's Gate."

"I'm sure he will."

"We have tried to make your journey as comfortable as possible. If there is anything that is not to your liking, please inform Cristina."

"I'm sure it will be fine. Thank you."

"Enjoy the journey, Dr Carlisle. I'll look forward to meeting you in a couple of days."

"And I will look forward to our meeting with great interest," Jack answers, sounding official.

"Thank you. Goodbye."

"Goodbye," Jack replies, the line goes dead. Jack stares at his phone, then hears his doorbell ring and walks back downstairs.

"Hello," he says, on opening the door.

"Hello," Anna replies.

"I'm glad you came over,"

"Good," she replies and throws her arms around him.

25

"Paris, Munich, Budapest, Brasov," I study the map. It reads like a student's summer trip around Europe, not the last hope of a dying man. I feel excited, nervous, but an air of melancholy hangs over me. I never wanted to be put in this position. I feel vulnerable, but what can I do? Life has dealt me this hand, and I have to play it.

Paris, I like Paris. Grace loves Paris. I proposed to her there. It nearly went very wrong. We were in our early twenties, just finished University. We travelled to France on the ferry, got the coach from Victoria. I had it all planned, proposing in Paris, the most romantic city in the world. I'd bought the ring. It was in my rucksack. The channel crossing was rough, Grace wasn't feeling too well, as we started our approach into Calais, the ship threw us violently from side to side.

"I need to lie down," Grace pleaded with me.

The PA system sprung into life, informing all passengers to return to their cars and coaches for departure. I took hold of Grace's hand and led her below deck to where the coach was parked.

"Come on, let's get on that coach. You can get some rest then." I told her. We were first to arrive at the closed doors of our coach. Grace was not looking good.

"John, I think I'm going to be sick again," she murmured, "I need to sit down."

There was a line of passengers beginning to grow behind me, waiting on the driver to open the door. After a few minutes, my patience was starting to wane.

"Where was the driver?" I wondered.

Grace was leaning on my shoulder, desperate to get into the coach. I tried the door handle, it moved, so I pulled open the door. It had been open all that time.

"Come on, Grace, we're in," I said, then led her and the other passengers onto the coach.

I settled Grace into the window seat, placed my coat over her and sat down beside her. She assumed the foetal position, hugging her knees and putting her head against the window. I close my eyes, relieved we've made it without her being sick. Moments later, I hear a commotion, shouting. It's the driver, he's animated, arms waving as he says something in French. I didn't know what he was saying. I didn't care. The couple sat in front of us then turned around to look at us.

"What's happened?" I ask them

"He's asking who opened the coach doors?"

"Oh!" I replied innocently and put up my hand.

"It was me," I declared. With that, the driver stopped shouting and bounded up the aisle to me. He then begins yelling at me, with more gesturing. Then he walks away.

I didn't understand a word he was saying, the two people in front of me were still looking at me.

"What was that all about?" I asked them.

The woman looked slightly embarrassed.

"He's saying that you broke into the coach, he says the doors were locked."

"But they weren't locked," I protest.

"He says that if anything is missing,"

"Missing?" I interrupt.

"Stolen," she continues, "Then you're to blame."

"What! Fuck that!" I stand and storm down towards the driver.

"Non, Non, Non!" I remember shouting, I didn't quite have the grasp of the French language, "I've done nothing!"

"The driver adjusts his rearview mirror, ignoring me, muttering to himself.

"Piss off then!" I hollered, as I turned to walk back. I remember all the faces on the coach staring at me. I was annoyed and embarrassed. Quickly I made it back to my seat.

"What's going on?" Grace asked.

"Nothing, you get some sleep."

The coach continued its journey to Paris. I tried my best to calm down and forget about what happened, happy in the knowledge that nothing had been taken as we, the passengers, all got on the coach at the same time and at least the couple in front of me knew I hadn't taken anything.

"Grace," I lightly shake her.

"Yeah," she replies, rubbing her eyes.

"Come on. We're here, how are you feeling?"

"I think I'm a bit better?" she says, smiling.

"Good."

Passengers begin to vacate the coach, the couple in front stand then turn to look at me. Have an excellent time, the woman says.

"And you," I reply, and then stand to get my rucksack. There is some kind of disturbance around me, and I turn to see the coach driver heading up the aisle towards me.

"You have stolen some money!" he declares with some viciousness.

"What? Piss off," I reply, and ignore him. I was throwing my rucksack on my back.

"Come on, Grace. We're getting off."

"What's going on?" she asks.

"Nothing," I say looking at her, then I turn to exit the coach. The driver blocks my route.

"Empty your bag," he asks sharply

"What?"

"Empty your bag," he repeats, then pulls the strap from my shoulder.

"Fuck off! what do you think you're doing?" I angrily protest.

I then realise what might be about to happen if I have to open my bag, then Grace will see the ring. I will have to propose right now, not the most romantic gesture.

"Who's had money stolen?" I ask aggressively.

"Him," the driver points to a dreadlocked hippy student, standing sheepishly, at the coach doors.

"What have you had stolen?" I shout at him.

"One hundred quid," he replies,

"Well, I haven't got it!" I shout.

"I know, I just need a claim form from the driver and then I'll go," he shouts back. I realise he's chancing his luck.

"Get the police," I say assertively, to the driver.

"What?" he replies.

"Get the gendarmes. Then I will open my sack."

"No, police!" The dreadlocked hippy shouts. We both turn to look at the student. "Just give me a fucking claim form, man," he continues.

"Get the police," I repeat, glaring at the driver. The driver looks at me.

"What's going on, John?" Grace asks again. She now has collected her things and is waiting to leave.

"That chancer says I've stolen a hundred quid from him."

"What?" she looks confused. I turn and look at the driver.

"Will you please just get the police?" I ask again.

"No, police" the dreadlocked hippy repeats, "I just want a claim form."

The driver looks at him, then at me, and understands what is going on.

"You can go," he says calmly.

"What?" I reply.

"You can go," he says, then walks away from me as if nothing has happened.

"No, fuck that!" I protest, "Get the police!" Grace has hold of my arm.

"Go!" the driver shouts at me.

"Come on, John," Grace pulls at my arm, "Leave it."

"Fucking wanker!" I shout at the dreadlocked hippy. He just smiles at me, then follows the driver. I hope he didn't get that form.

Two days later, I proposed to Grace, lying on the grass beneath the Eifel tower. She cried and said, yes. We ate cheese and bread, opened a cheap bottle of red wine and got drunk. It was one of the best days of my life. She laughed when I told her what could have happened.

"I still would have said yes," she said.

Grace sits down beside me.

"How are you feeling?" she asks.

"Come here," I say, she leans forward, and I kiss her.

"I love you."

"I love you too," she replies, "should I get the kids?" she asks.

"Yes," I reply, "do you know what you're going to say?" I ask her

"Yes," she replies confidently. She stands and walks to the bottom of the stairs,

"Girls," she shouts, no answer.

"GIRLS!" her voice raised.

"What?" I hear Lucy shout from her bedroom.

"Come down here. We've got something to tell you." There's a silence

"Girls!" she shouts again.

I hear their feet pound on the floor as they come down the stairs, my heart is beating fast with anticipation. They enter the room and sit down. Quickly they realise something serious is about to happen.

"What's going on?" Lucy asks.

"Lucy, come here," I say, and hold out my arms. She stands, takes a step towards me, and I pull her onto my knee. I can see she's already getting upset.

"There's no need to cry, this is good news," I tell her, then look over at Grace; she has Sadie on her knee, she's started crying too.

"Look, girls, we have something to tell you, but it's good news," I wipe Lucy's eyes and look at her.

"You know Jack? Doctor Jack?" I look at them, they nod.

"Well, he's found a hospital that's going to try and make me better."

"Are you going to get better dad?" Sadie asks.

"I hope so."

"Which hospital? the one in town?" Lucy asks.

"Not quite," I reply, "It's in another country."

"Where?" Lucy asks

"Germany," I reply.

Grace and I had decided that Romania just didn't sound as good as Germany and seeing as this was supposed to be top secret, it made sense.

"Germany?" Lucy repeats.

"Where's that?" Sadie asks.

"In Europe, idiot!" Lucy responds.

"Yes, in Europe," I confirm. "So, you won't see me for at least a couple of weeks."

"When are you going?" Lucy asks I look at her.

"Tomorrow."

"Tomorrow!" she starts crying and holds me tight. I cuddle her, holding her close to me. I can feel my eyes filling up. I look at Grace. She is mirroring my actions with Sadie. I can hear her crying, her face buried in Grace's shoulder.

"Look, girls. This is a good thing, the sooner I can start treatment, the sooner I can get back to normal."

"Can we visit you?" Lucy asks.

"Hopefully, yes. When I'm settled, maybe they'll send me home for a few days if things are going well." I look deep into Lucy's eyes, wiping her tears away with my thumbs.

"Now, you two girls have got to be strong for mummy. While I'm away, I want you to help mummy as much as possible, okay?" I look at them. They stare back

"Okay?" I repeat.

"Yes," Lucy says. Sadie nods her head. Her face was red and flushed.

"Good," I hold Lucy close to me and look at Grace, she has tears flowing down her cheeks, and so do I.

Part Two

I sit, upright, holding on to the black plastic handle on the door of the taxi. My grip tightens as we rock from side to side over the pot-holed roads, like a ship through rough seas. I look through the rain-soaked window on to the wet, dark streets of London. The melancholy outside reflects my mood. I'm thinking about last night. Grace and I put the kids to bed. They were both upset. They wanted to come with us this morning. I couldn't do that. It would be too hard. It's hard enough as it is. Grace phoned her sister, Elaine, she's there now, babysitting 'til she gets back. As I stare out onto the streets, a realisation of what's happening begins to hit home. I remember wondering, was I doing the right thing? What in fact, was I doing? I didn't know? I didn't want to go, but what choice did I have? I had to go.

"I hope the weather's a bit better in Romania," I say smiling at Grace, she knows I'm nervous.

"I don't think it'll be warm there?" She replies, trying hard to help me relax.

"It can't be any worse than this," I say, Grace doesn't answer.

The cab pulls up outside St Pancreas station. I check my watch, five past seven. We're a bit early. Grace gets out first, I follow her, struggling to rise from the sagging leather seats of the black cab.

"Are you alright?" She asks.

"Yes," I reply hesitantly.

The driver opens the boot, takes out my case, and brings it round to me. Grace pays the man, and we walk into the station. She tries to take my suitcase from me.

"I've got it. It's on wheels," I tell her sharply.

She looks at me, I see in her face that's she's unsure of how to be. I kiss her,

"Sorry, here," I hand her my case, then take hold of her other hand, and we walk into the grand entrance.

"This is a beautiful station," I say gazing up at the Victorian Gothic architecture, "I think this bit used to be a hotel."

Grace follows my gaze and looks up, "It's beautiful," she replies. I'm not sure she cares.

"What do they call it? Gothic?" I ask, persevering with idle conversation.

"I'm not sure, yeah, maybe?" We both admire the red brick arches.

"Amazing," I say, then we continue through the imposing entrance to the new, modern, wing of the station.

Open plan coffee shops, restaurants and newsagents line the station promenade. Crowds of people quickly manoeuvre past us, phones and coffee cups in their hands. The station is busy, people going about their daily routines, unaware of my imminent departure.

"Where is everybody going?" I ask.

"I know, it's madness," she replies.

"I liked the outside better," I say.

Grace nods her head in agreement. I point at the station notice board.

"Come on, let's see what platform I need."

We walk over to the electronic board hanging high above the walkway then look up in unison, at the train timetable. I see my train displayed.

"It's on time," I say.

"We're early," Grace checks her watch, "should we get a coffee somewhere?"

I don't want a coffee. I just need to get through passport control and get on my way.

"I think I'm just going to go through," I reply, turning to look at her.

"What? Why?" Grace replies, surprised, her eyes can't hide her sadness.

"I just need to get on my way."

"Oh, okay," she replies. I hold her close to me, her head buried in my chest. I fight hard to hold back my tears. I kiss her, then wipe away a tear from her cheek

"What we need to remember, is that this is a good thing," I say, trying my hardest to convince myself, as well as Grace.

"I know, I know," she replies.

I put my arms around her, hug her and kiss her forehead.

"It's just too hard. I need to just get on with it." I tell her.

Then take her hand and walk towards the Eurostar departure gate. The walk takes only a few minutes, the tension building between us.

"Well, we're here" I turn and look at her, she has tears streaming down her face.

"Hey, come on," I say, holding her again.

"It'll be alright. I'll be back in a couple of weeks, sooner if Jacks little plan goes wrong."

She kisses me on the lips. I taste her salty tears.

"I love you," she says.

"I love you too," I reply.

"Come on, Grace, I'll be fine. I'll be back soon."

"I know, I'm Ok," she says, insincerely.

"I'm gonna go through; it's no good stringing this out anymore," I kiss again, "I'll see you soon."

"Ring me."

"I will,"

I turn and wheel my suitcase towards the entrance barriers. A man greets me.

"May I check your ticket, please sir?" he enquires.

I hand him my ticket.

"That's fine sir, you can go straight through," he says, then hands me my ticket back.

"Thank you," I reply.

I turn to look at Grace, then wave. She smiles, kisses her hand and waves at me.

"Love you," I say, then take a deep breath and walk through security, leaving behind the life I once knew.

Hundreds of people sit in the waiting area of the station. I look around for Jack, unsure what I'm supposed to do if I see him, he's not there. I make my way towards a young lady standing checking tickets, the sign above her head displays, business lounge, I wait inline

"Hi, I think my ticket gets me in?" I say smiling, making light of my question. She checks my ticket.

"It does, lucky you," she replies, with a smile and hands me back my ticket. I proceed through the frosted glass doors. The ambience in the lounge is much calmer. I spot a vacant seat and make my way towards it, almost collapsing into the chair as I arrive. I take a deep breath, relieved I've made it this far.

"Excuse me, sir," I look up, "May I get you a drink?"

In front of me stands another young girl dressed neatly in a modern-day maid type outfit.

"Yes, thank you, tea would be lovely and some water please."

"No problem, milk and sugar?"

"Just milk thanks," I reply.

I look around again, no, Jack. A newspaper lays on the coffee table in front of me. I pick it up and begin scanning the front page. The waitress returns with my tea, placing it where the paper once laid.

"We have fresh croissants, fruit and juice if you would like something to eat," she gestures to a counter filled with breakfast delights.

"You can just help yourself," she continues.

"I'm fine, but thank you," I reply, she walks off. Her kindness has settled me. I take a drink of my tea, then continue to read the newspaper. A few moments later, I feel someone standing close to me. I look down at two shiny black patent leather high heels.

"Excuse me, is anybody sitting here?" a voice says.

I look up from the shoes. An eastern European woman stands beside me.

"No, please sit down," I reply.

"Thank you," she says, then pulls her small trolley case to the side of the chair and sits down.

"There's free tea and croissants over there if you're hungry?" I say she looks at me and smiles.

"I'm fine," she replies, making me feel slightly foolish, I don't know why I said that? I quickly lift the newspaper to cover my embarrassment. I then feel my heart miss a beat. I wonder if she is Cristina. I glance across at her. She's looking at her phone. She notices me and smiles. I smile back, "Shit! It can't be, this can't go wrong already before I've even left England."

Jack checks his watch, 8:30 AM.

"It's ok, we'll make it," Anna says, then indicates and turns the car sharply around a tight left-hand corner.

"We're cutting it close though," he replies, as the car slowly approaches a red light. Phil Collins, 'You Can't Hurry love,' is playing on the car Hi-Fi system.

"Don't worry. We're nearly there. Anyway, you weren't complaining an hour ago!" she answers, then smirks at Jack. That early morning act of lust might just make him miss his train. The lights turn green, and they set off. Moments later, Anna parks up outside the train station. Jack rechecks his watch, 8:40 AM.

"Shit! I hope check-in hasn't closed," he says, then quickly opens the car door and steps out of the car. He walks round to the boot, opens it and takes out his suitcase, slamming the boot shut. Anna joins him.

"What time is your train?" she asks.

"Nine twenty-four," he replies, "I better dash."

"Give me a cuddle first," she replies, then throws her arms around him, "I'll miss you," she says, he hesitantly returns her affection.

"I'll have to go," he states.

"I know, good luck, I hope it all works out."

"I do too," he replies, kisses her, picks up his case and begins to walk away.

"Don't get bitten by any vampires," Anna calls out, "I'll be checking your neck when you get back!"

Jack turns around. Smiles then continues his journey. Anna watches him disappear into the station.

Jack knows St Pancreas well, he makes his way directly to passport control and hands his passport to the security woman.

"Has the nine twenty-four started boarding yet?" he asks her, she checks her watch.

"Yes, go straight on through to the platform, your train will be leaving soon," she replies.

"Can passengers wishing to board the nine twenty-four Eurostar train to Paris, please make their way to platform one, the train is getting ready to depart."

I hear the announcement, take a last sip of cold tea, then reach for my walking stick. I force all my weight on to the cane and stand up.

"Can I help you?" I look across at the woman opposite, before I can answer, her arm links through mine, and I feel her grip me and carefully help me to stand. I turn to look at her. Her face is no more than a few inches away from mine. I notice her carefully painted lips, hazel eyes and perfect skin, she has a mole above her mouth. Her perfume immerses my senses,

"Thank you," I reply

"It's no problem, are you ok?" she asks

"Yes, yes. I'm fine. Thank you."

"Okay, have a nice journey."

"And you," I reply.

She then walks away from me, trailing her small navy overnight case behind her.

 I watch her leave.

Then collect my case, follow her out of the lounge, on to the escalator and up to the platform. Passengers manoeuvre around me as I stand motionless, unsure of which direction to go. I notice a train guard,

"Excuse me, can you direct me to my carriage please?" I ask, the man checks my ticket.

"Coach B seat 15, it's the next carriage along, enter by the first door and your seat is on the right," he replies, handing my ticket back to me.

"Thank you," I reply, then follow his instructions. I notice the woman from earlier, in the lounge, ahead of me. I'm sure she is getting on to my carriage, I walk up behind her, she turns and notices me

"Oh, hello again," she says, smiling.

"Hello," I reply, "don't worry, I'm not stalking you," she looks at me confused, I feel my cheeks go red with embarrassment. "I think this is my carriage."

"Can I help you with your case?" she asks.

"No, I'm fine, thank you."

"Okay," she replies, then boards the train. I notice her slim waist and tight-fitting skirt as he climbs the steps. I then manoeuvre my case on to the first step, quickly realising that I may need some help after all. I wonder which hand to steady myself with, juggling my suitcase and walking stick,

"Let me help," I look up, a man stands before me, he's dressed smartly in a navy overcoat, a spotted black scarf and a navy flat cap. He looks eastern European.

"Thank you," I say to him.

He moves in front of me, lifts my case on to the train, then turns to look at me.

"Where are you sitting?" he asks.

"I think I'm in this carriage," I gesture to my left.

"Okay, I'll put your case here." I watch him place my case on to the luggage rack.

"Thank you again."

"It's not a problem," he answers, then walks away down the carriage.

I let him take a few steps, before following him down the aisle, stopping at my seat. I place my rucksack onto the shelf above, then sit down.

"Are you sure you're not stalking me?" the woman asks.

Once on the platform, Jack checks his ticket, Coach A seat twenty-four. He glances up and down the platform, searching face after face, but he can't see me.

"I hope he's made it?" He thinks to himself, worried that maybe, just maybe, I'd changed my mind.

He joins the queue, boards the train, places his case onto the luggage rack and looks down the carriage aisle. His attention is soon diverted to the man glaring at him. He walks confidently towards him.

"Good morning Ivan," he says, then holds out his hand. Ivan takes a moment to respond, then stands, shakes his hand, then sits down, saying nothing.

"Hello," Jack says, looking across at Cristina, she is sitting in the window seat, next to Ivan.

"Hello," she replies, "We wondered where you were?"

"Let's just say, something cropped up," he replies with a sly smile on his face. He then takes his seat, opposite Cristina, placing his Ted Baker messenger bag on the empty seat next to him. An announcement is made over the carriage speaker system. The train is about to leave.

"Good timing," Jack says, Cristina's face remains expressionless. A waitress appears, carrying a stainless-steel jug, "Would you like tea?" she asks, in a French accent.

"No thank you, is there any coffee?" Jack enquires.

"Yes, it will be coming around soon."

"Okay, thanks."

She looks across at Cristina and asks the same question, she declines her offer. Ivan just shakes his head. The train jerks forward, they all look out of the window, watching the platform disappear before their eyes.

"And so, our journey begins," Jack says.

"It does," she replies.

"I'm looking forward to it."

"Good, I'm glad you are," she replies.

"Madame, would you like some coffee?" A waiter now stands before them.

"Yes, please, thank you," she replies. The waiter fills her cup, then Jack's; Ivan refuses his offer with a silent stare.

Jack takes a sip of his coffee, "Ivan, are you going to be this much fun for the whole journey?" he asks, smiling at him. Ivan turns his head, looks at him, his face severe and stern. Then turns his attention to the carriage aisle.

"Ivan," Jack repeats, Ivan turns to look at him again.

"We are going on a very long journey. Surely you can forget whatever it is I have done to upset you and make this a pleasant situation for us all."

"He is not upset with you," Cristina replies.

"Then what is it? His silence makes me very uncomfortable."

Cristina half turns her head towards Ivan. Jack observes their gaze. Without saying a word, they seem to understand each other. Ivan then stands and walks away down the aisle.

"Was it something I said?" Jack asks.

"No, he's fine," Cristina replies.

"I've never heard him speak, not a word, what's up with him?" he asks. Cristina looks straight at Jack, then pauses.

"What? What is it?" he asks.

"He cannot talk," she replies.

"He can't talk. Why not?"

"He has," she hesitates.

"What?" Jack repeats.

"He had a problem with his mouth, his tongue. He cannot talk."

Jack stares hard at Cristina. He remembers his conversation with Daniella immediately.

"What happened?" he asks.

"He had an infection. He had to have part of his tongue removed."

"Cancer," Jack tries to make sense of the situation.

"Yes," she replies.

Jack inspects her features as she explains, not believing a word of it.

"Bloody hell, how long ago was that?" he engages in the façade.

"When he was a child." she replies.

"Have you known him for a long time?"

"Yes, all his life."

"Did you go to school together?" Jack asks, she pauses before answering.

"Yes."

"It must have been hard for him, is that why he's so serious all the time?"

"He is, how he is. I cannot change that." she replies, "He is a good man. I trust him with my life."

"With your life?"

"You do not need to fear him."

"Fear him? I don't fear him. I'm interested to know why he's here."

"I have told you he is here to look after me."

"Do you need looked after?"

"That is not of your concern." She replies, bluntly.

Jack sits back in his seat and laughs, "I'm going on a journey, with a man who I know nothing about. Who never, sorry, who can't speak and it's not my concern?" Jack can't hide the irritation already flowing through him. "Don't make me out to be a fool, Cristina."

Cristina looks at him anxiously, "I'm sorry, I did not mean to offend you. All will be explained to you on our arrival at Heaven's Gate."

Ivan returns to his seat.

"Cristina has been telling me about what happened," Jack says, Ivan's eyes move slowly to look at him, "Your cancer, I'm sorry to hear about that."

Ivan holds his gaze; something in his eyes reveals the lies that have just been exposed. Jack relaxes back into his seat, look out of the window and reflects on the situation he, and I, are in.

"**Well this** is a strange coincidence," I say, sitting down.

"It is," she replies.

"My name is John, nice to meet you," I hold out my hand.

"Nice to meet you, John," she answers and shakes my hand, "My name is Maria." Her hand is small and soft in my grasp. I notice her perfectly manicured red painted nails.

"Well, it's nice to meet you, Maria. Who would have thought, we would be sitting opposite each other again?"

We are interrupted by a member of the train staff offering tea; we both accept her offer.

"Where are you going? Paris?" I ask, taking a drink of my tea. She looks at me slightly confused.

"Of course, you are," I say, feeling slightly embarrassed, "We're on the bloody Eurostar." I chuckle to myself and watch her smile at me. I'm feeling nervous. I look out of the window. St Pancreas station drifts off into the distance. A feeling of loneliness engulfs me. I'm unsure of what I'm doing. I already miss my kids.

"Are you okay?" she asks.

I immediately return to reality, "Yes, yes, I've just got a lot on my mind."

"You look like you have." She says, "Are you going on holiday?"

"No...Well, kind of."

"You don't know?" she looks baffled by my answer.

"Let's just say, it's business and pleasure, and you?"

"The same."

"Your mixing business and pleasure! They say you should never do that."

"I guess rules are meant to be broken."

"They are. So, what is your business?" I ask,

"Do you live in London?" I ask.

"I work as an interpreter,"

"An interpreter? Ou est la Bibliotheque!" I say in my worst French accent.

"Where is the library?" she replies, unsure of my meaning.

"Sorry, that's the only French I know," I laugh, "I guess your job takes you all over the world?"

"Yes, and you, what do you do?"

"Nothing much now, but I used to be a policeman."

"A policeman?" she repeats.

"Does that surprise you?"

"You do not look like a policeman."

"And what does a policeman look like?" I ask she laughs, then takes a sip of her tea.

"Have you been working in London? Do you live there?"

"I have been working, but I've been visiting a family friend in Brighton."

"Brighton is lovely, cold this time of year though."

"Not compared to Budapest."

"Budapest?" I reply.

"That is my home."

"Do you think it'll be cold there now?"

"Not so much, why do you ask?"

"I'm on my way to Romania. I'm guessing they're a similar climate."

"Romania?" she answers, surprised.

"Yeah, that's where I'm heading."

"Now that is a coincidence."

"What is?"

"I am travelling to Romania too."

"You are?" now I'm surprised.

"Yes, I have family there. Why are you going? Do you have friends there?"

I pause, unsure of how honest to be.

"I'm going for treatment."

"Treatment?"

"Yes, you've noticed my leg?"

"Yes," she replies.

"Well, it's not only my leg I have a problem with. I have a disease called Motor Neurons." I notice her expression change, "Don't worry, you can't catch it," I say, trying to make light of the situation.

"I have heard about this disease. I'm sorry."

"It's okay. I'm used to people's reactions."

"And there is a treatment for you in Romania?"

"I hope so."

"I didn't know Romania had such facilities."

"I didn't either."

"Are you flying there from Paris, we might be on the same flight."

"I wish….I'm travelling by train."

"By train! Why? Do you not like to fly?"

"Let's just say. I felt like I needed an adventure. It could be my last one."

"I hope you enjoy your adventure, John," she replies.

The waitress returns, offering us a menu. I take it and place it on to the table in front of me. Maria examines hers. I realise I haven't texted Jack. I get out my phone and begin to type.

I'm on the train, a beautiful woman sat opposite me, feeling good! Where are you?

I press send.

The countryside is replaced by darkness, as the train begins its descent into the channel tunnel. Jack checks his phone for any more messages from me, then places his phone back on to the tabletop.

"Next stop Paris," Jack announces, Cristina looks up from her book, then touches Ivan's arm. He immediately stands. Jack watches their interaction. She controls him.

"Please, excuse me," she says, then rises from her seat. "I won't be long," she states to Ivan, then walks away from the table, down the aisle. Ivan watches her intently, standing proud, arms crossed over his broad chest. Only when she disappears into the lavatory does he sit down.

"I'm surprised you're not in there with her," Jack says calmly. Ivan rolls his head toward Jack.

"Why are you here?" he asks, Ivan's face is expressionless.

"Are you protecting her?" Jack pauses, "Why does she need protecting?" he searches for a reaction.

"Do you love her?"

"Are you lovers?" he tries to provoke a response.

"I know you can't talk, but why you can't talk… well, a friend of mine told me this tale, a story, about men, who were born to protect, protect a special race." Jack examines Ivan's features. He doesn't react.

"These men… they are so committed to their task that they would give their lives and not only their lives, but also their voice, their tongues." Jack awaits a response.

"Are you that man?" he asks quietly, calmly. Then sits back in his chair.

"A gruesome but interesting tale, don't you think Ivan?" he says.

I wipe my mouth, lay the serviette on to my plate and take a deep breath.

"You were hungry," Maria says, looking across at my empty plate.

"Yes, I was," I laugh," I have to keep my strength up," I say, then tap my paunch. A smile appears across her face.

I feel a cramp-like pain in my thigh, and it takes me by surprise. Quickly I straighten my leg, holding it high in the aisle, stretching out my quadriceps and calf muscle. The pain is excruciating.

"Are you alright?" Maria asks, sounding concerned. I begin to rotate my foot, trying desperately to get the blood flowing around my leg.

"It's just my leg, cramp, it happens sometimes," I answer.

I feel the pain ease as the blood begins to circulate freely around my leg. I continue with my exercise until I'm sure the pain has gone. Maria is looking worried.

"I'm alright, honest," I say, putting her at ease. I then stand, bend my knees, squatting slightly and take my rucksack from the overhead compartment. Placing it on my seat, I remove a silver and black coloured wash bag. From it, I take out a circular plastic container, imprinted on the top of each section are the days of the week, my pillbox. Grace bought it for me so that I wouldn't miss my medications.

Written, across the front of it, in black sharpie is AFTERNOON. I place it on the table, search through my bag again and pull out another pillbox with MORNING written across the top of it. I take out the three pills I require, placing them onto the table and put my bag back on to the shelf above me. I sit back down and swallow down the tablets with a mouthful of water.

"The number of pills I take, I should rattle," I say trying to make light of my situation. She smiles, unconvincingly, back at me.

"Are you in pain?" she asks.

"No, not really. It's a strange kind of pain. Hard to describe."

"Can I get you anything? Would you like a hot drink?" she asks

"No, I fine honest." I lie.

Jack searches through his messenger bag, pulls out a clear plastic folder and places onto the table. From it, he takes out the printed map of his journey. The train has now completed its underground journey and is speeding through the French countryside. Jack admires the gold and red trees; the autumn sun illuminates the view.

"Beautiful countryside," he says, Cristina looks up from her book and turns to look at the view.

"It is," she replies.

"Is there a similar view in Romania?"

"Yes, it will be much colder, though. The trees will have lost all their leaves by now."

Jack studies the map.

"Have you been to Munich?" he asks.

"Yes, I visited Munich last year with Dr Schneider."

"With Dr Schneider?" he asks

"Yes, we had business there."

"Dr Schneider is allowed to leave Heaven's Gate?" Jack asks, Cristina looks confused.

"Of course, he is. He is not a prisoner. I don't understand?"

"I'm just wondering why the doctor didn't come himself,"

"Come?"

"To England, to meet with me."

"He is a very busy man."

"Or maybe, it is your decision and not his," he replies, looking at Cristina.

"I'm right, aren't I? You have the final decision, not him."

"Final decision on what?"

"On whether I should be allowed to visit."

"It is not my decision. Dr Schneider holds you in high regard. It was he who chose you."

"He chose me. Out of how many?"

"I do not know?"

"But it's you who will confirm his decision?"

"You are here now?" she answers bluntly.

"I passed the test then."

"What test?" she answers, looking mystified.

"Dr Schneider called me last night."

"I know, I spoke to him also."

"And what did you talk about? Me?"

"Yes, and some other business."

"What did he say to you?"

"He…We… want you to be impressed with our facility. There must be no mistakes."

"Mistakes, I think there's been a few of them already," he smiles.

"Then, there can be no more."

"I hope you're right," Jack replies

Maria's phone vibrates on the table top, I look up from my book. I'm reading something Grace gave me. She said I'd enjoy it. I'm not sure so far. I watch Maria pick up her phone, read the text, then fix her gaze on something behind me. She then turns her concentration back on her phone, starts to type, then looks beyond my shoulder again. She notices my attention, smiles, picks up her magazine and begins to reread it. I give it a second or two before picking my book up, placing it in front of my face, then turning around to see what's behind me? I feel like I'm in a scene from Death on the Orient Express, but once a policeman, always a policeman, I sensed something. To my surprise, the man who helped me earlier, with my case, is sitting behind me. He is reading a message on his phone.

I turn back around and look at Maria. My mind is racing with foolish situations; Did she just text him? Is he her boyfriend? Her lover? Am I thinking about this too much? I know my instincts if you feel something is wrong? It usually is. There's something. I know there is. I hear the man stand behind me, then watch him pass me. I wonder where he is going? The toilet? Probably. I wait for Maria to stand, make her way after him, then maybe they embrace, kiss, but she doesn't move, and I continue to try and enjoy my book.

Ivan sits upright in his chair. He has not moved since Cristina returned to her seat. Jack notices his frown; his eyes fixated on something coming towards him. Jack rotates in his chair, looking over his shoulder, trying to see what Ivan is looking at. All he can see is a man walking towards them, Jack looks beyond him, wondering what has taken Ivan's attention. Jack turns his head back to look at Ivan. He glares at the man as he approaches, turning his head as the man passes. Jack is unsure of what is going on? Both Jack and Ivan watch the man disappear into the train toilet. Jack looks at Ivan. Ivan turns his eyes towards Jack, moves slightly in his seat, then continues to scrutinise the carriage.

A few minutes later, Jack notices the man coming out of the toilet. The automatic door slides open. Jack sees Ivan twitch in his seat. Then, without warning, he quickly stands blocking the aisle, the man walks into the back of Ivan. Ivan spins and takes hold of the man, grabbing his shoulders. The man loses his balance slightly and takes a step back. Ivan holds him firmly. The two men, for a moment, are eye to eye.

"Excuse me," the man says. Ivan examines the man's features; he looks Eastern European too, then let's go of him and sits back down. The man seems confused, straightens his blue navy blazer then walks away down the aisle. Ivan watches him walk away. Jack turns to Cristina, calmly she asks Ivan if everything is alright? Without looking back at her, he nods his head slowly.

I notice Maria's mystery friend walking back towards me. I look at him as he passes, he is a handsome man, they would make a lovely couple. I return to my book. I'm bored with my book.

"How did you like Brighton?" I ask Maria looks up, slightly surprised, from her magazine. "Me and Grace used to take the kids down there every summer."

"Grace?" she asks, "Is that your wife?"

"Yes."

"And you have children?"

"Yes, two girls, Lucy and Sadie."

"Lovely names," she replies, "I had a nice time. My friend showed me around."

"Does your friend work in Brighton? Did you say he is family?"

"He is a she. She's an art teacher. My family is large and scattered all over the world."

"Cheap holidays then," I joke.

"Sorry?" Maria replies, not understanding me.

"Having family all over the world means you have somewhere to stay when you go to see them. Makes holidays cheaper."

She smiles but doesn't respond. I look out of the window, feeling embarrassed. I hear her phone vibrate again. She begins to read the message.

"Shit!" I hear her mutter to herself.

"What's wrong?" I ask.

"My plane, from Paris, has been cancelled."

"Oh, no, why? What are you going to do?"

"I don't know? My company are going to try and organise something."

"I think my journey goes through Budapest," I tell her.

"Budapest, by train," she smiles, "How long does that take?"

"I'd need to check my tickets, but I think I get the train to Munich this afternoon and travel on to Budapest tomorrow."

"Tomorrow?" she asks.

"Yeah, I'm having a night in Munich tonight, break up the journey. Then I get the train tomorrow."

"A night in Munich doesn't sound so bad. I'll let my company know."

I wonder for a moment what I am doing, am I organising a date with this woman? I didn't mean too. Grace is going to kill me.

Maria then begins to type into her phone, placing it back onto the tabletop. I look at her as her attention, again, is directed to the man sitting behind me. Her facial expression changes, she seems concerned. I hear the man behind me say something, then quickly he rushes past me down the aisle. Maria twists her body to watch him pass.

I knew there was something between them.

Ivan takes the phone from his pocket and looks at the screen. The phone vibrates in his hand. Jack watches him read the message. Calmly he shows the message to Cristina. She looks at him with a confused look.

"What does that mean?" she asks Ivan, sounding concerned. "Whose phone is that?"

Ivan scrutinises the message again before his attention is drawn to someone walking towards them. Jack follows his gaze and turns around to find out what he is looking at. The man who Ivan bumped into earlier, is striding purposefully towards them. The man looks annoyed as he approaches them. Jack turns to say something to Ivan, but before he can say anything, he has risen from his seat, blocking the man's route. Slowly Ivan raises his arm, unclenches his fist and reveals what lays in the palm of his hand, the phone.

"Bastard hoata!" the man shouts at Ivan, as he walks up to him, snatching the phone from his hand. The two men stand face to face. Ivan places his hands on the man's chest and pushes him away. He falls back, landing on the arm of a seat behind him.

"Ivan!" Jack shouts, getting to his feet. Ivan stands motionless, watching the man steady himself and stand upright. He takes a step towards Ivan. Jack turns to face him.

"I'm sorry about…." he begins to say, but the man interrupts him, shouting at Ivan. Jack cannot understand the dialect.

"Please, calm down," Jack tells the man, "There has been some kind of misunderstanding."

The man looks at Jack.

"Ivan found your phone and was going to return it," Jack says.

"I don't believe that for a second," the man snarls, "You should choose your friends more carefully."

"I'm sorry," Jack says apologetically.

The man looks across at Ivan, then Cristina, then back to Jack.

"Be careful," the man says, then turns and walks away from them. Jack turns to Ivan, who is watching the man's every move.

"Fucking sit down," Jack whispers to Ivan, who casually turns his head to look at Jack.

"Sit down, before we get thrown off this train," Jack continues.

Ivan notices the people around them, gazing up at the two men.

He then leisurely sits back down and looks across at Cristina. Jack sits down, leans across the table, and quietly asks Cristina,

"What was all that about?" anger present in his voice. She doesn't reply.

"I'm getting off this train at the next station and going back to London if you don't tell me right now what's going on?"

"We don't know what's going on?" Cristina replies, then glances at Ivan.

"Who was that man? Why did Ivan have his phone?"

"I do not know."

"You don't know? Then I think you should ask your friend there, what's going on?" They both look at Ivan.

"I do not need to ask," Cristina says.

"What?" Jack replies, confused.

"I trust his judgement,"

"What does that mean? Why did he have his phone?" Jack asks, then looks across at Ivan. "Did you steal it? Earlier.... when you knocked into him, did you take it then?"

Ivan doesn't reply.

"What if that man gets the police?"

"If he does, then we have nothing to fear," she answers.

"What?" Jack replies.

"If we were to get arrested, then we have nothing to worry about, but he will not." She says confidently.

"How do you know?"

"Ivan would not put me in danger."

"Stealing a phone doesn't put you in danger; it gets you arrested."

"As I have said, I trust his judgement."

"He doesn't know that man, why did he do that?"

"He has his reasons."

"What reasons?"

Cristina pauses, looking directly at Jack.

"He is here to protect me."

"What? Protect you, from who?"

"I don't know.... it's complicated."

"I don't understand, why would someone want to hurt you?"

"There are reasons."

"Tell me."

"That man, the message on his phone was in Romanian."

"And what did it say?" Jack asks, Cristina looks across at Ivan.

It said, "The information is correct; they are staying in Munich tonight."

"De Madame et Monsieur, ce train arrivera sous peu dans Paris Buttes-Chaumont, nous vous remercions d'avoir voyager avec Eurostar, et nous vous souhaitons un agréable séjour à Paris"

The train manager announces our arrival in Paris, the message is repeated

"Ladies and gentlemen, this train will shortly be arriving at Gare du nord, thank you for travelling with Eurostar, and we hope you have a pleasant stay in Paris"

"Well we're here!" I announce.

Maria appears worried, she ignores me and turns her head to look up the train aisle. The man is walking back towards us. He appears annoyed. She stands up to meet him, placing her hand on his arm, he glares at her then at me but doesn't speak. He ignores Maria's interest and returns to his seat. Maria sits down.

"Is everything ok?" I ask again.

"Yes," she replies, unconvincingly.

"Have you heard from your company? Do you know what your plans are yet?"

Her phone vibrates on the table, she picks up her phone quickly and reads the message.

"I do now," she replies.

"What does that mean? What does that have to do with you? Us?"

"Maybe nothing."

"Maybe?" Jack asks.

Ivan stands up and gets Cristina's bag from the overhead compartment. He ignores Jacks concerns.

"This is crazy. I need to know what's going on before I go any further." Jack says again.

Cristina follows Ivan, getting up from her seat. Jack grabs Cristina's arm,

"Wait!" Jack commands.

Ivan's hand appears on his. He feels the force of Ivan's grip.

"Let go!" Cristina says, scowling at Jack.

His eyes flick quickly between them, assessing the situation. Reluctantly, he releases his hold on her arm, Ivan holds on to him slightly longer than needed, before letting go.

"I will not be intimidated by you, or…" he looks at Ivan, "Him."

They both stand above him, considering their next move.

"I'm not going any further, tell me what's happening here!" he demands.

Passengers begin to queue behind them, Cristina sits down next to Jack.

"I am sorry about this. I did not anticipate any complications with me being here. Ivan is only with me as a precaution."

"But why? Why would somebody be following us? Why do you need Ivan?"

"I will tell you, but not now, later. We must leave the train," She replies.

The train comes to a standstill at Paris Gare du Nord. Passengers begin to shuffle past Ivan, who is blocking the carriageway. Jack glances up at the other passengers, takes a deep breath and regains his composure.

"You better had," he says sternly.

I step down from the train, on to the platform. My case thuds on the steps as I drag it behind me.

"Well, I hope your journey goes as planned, it's been nice to meet you," Maria says. She is standing on the platform in front of me.

"Yeah, it's been nice," I reply. "I hope you get your flight sorted," I shake her hand, it feels soft and small in my grasp.

"Thank you," she replies, "Are you sure you're okay from here?"

"Yes, I'm fine. I just need to get a taxi from outside to Gare du l'est. it shouldn't be a problem."

"Okay, if you're sure."

"I am, thank you."

I watch her as she walks away, I look around for her companion, but he's nowhere to be seen. I then wonder where Jack is? I think I can see him ahead of me, but the platform is so crowded, I can't be sure. I start to walk, slowly, letting Maria and Jack get away from me. I only get a few steps when I hear the sound of a horn beside me. I look up. An electric golf cart vehicle is parked to my right. It has Gare du L'est written on a laminated piece of paper attached to the door. I walk over to it. A young twenty-something man is in the driving seat.

"Bonjour, are you going to Gare du L'est?" I ask

"I can take you to the station exit, where you can get a taxi. Have you booked?" his English is excellent.

"I'm not sure?" I reply

"Let me check, may I have your name?"

"John Thompson"

He checks a list he has on a clipboard beside him.

"I see your name. Please get on. I will get your bag."

I'm surprised my name is there, I know Jack has planned this. I board the vehicle, as the young man throws my bag into the rear of the compartment. He then climbs into the driver's seat, switches the buggy on and presses the horn.

"Hold on," he says, looking over his shoulder.

"Oh, okay," I reply. The cart jolts into life, the young driver beeps the horn again, people look at us. I feel slightly embarrassed. As we drive down the platform, I wonder if I will pass Jack, I feel nervous. I can't see him. I look for Maria. I can't see her either. As the cart turns to exit the Gare du Nord station, I take one last look around me, to my surprise I see Maria's friend, the man who was sitting behind me. He is stood with two men, both tall and broad-shouldered, wearing in tracksuits, one is blue, Adidas. The other, white, I can't make out the brand. They both wear baseball caps. Together they look a strange combination, a suited man and two well I'm unsure who they are? They look like two thugs, but he is talking to them like he knows them. They listen intently to what he is saying. I wonder what their relationship is? Then the cart turns and takes me away from the three men and out into the Paris air. I'm greeted with a cacophony of noise, people shouting and cars beeping their horns. There's a line of, what looks like, a thousand people waiting for a taxi.

"Bloody hell, how long will a taxi take?" I ask the driver.

"Wait here," he replies, stopping the cart and stepping out onto the Parisian walkway. I watch him walk over to a man dressed in a black suit, white shirt and black tie. He asks him something, then waves over to me. I step from the cart, grab my case and walk over to him.

"This man will drive you to Gare du l'est," the driver says. I shake the suited man's hand.

"Thank you," I reply.

Jack walks in silence behind Cristina and Ivan.

"We should have a taken a taxi," Cristina says, glancing over her shoulder, anger present in her voice.

"I need some fresh air," he replies. His tone taught and sharp. He was giving me time to get to the station before them. They pass by a small grocery store, Jack stops.

"Wait! I need a drink," he says.

Cristina and Ivan stop, turn and stare at him.

"I won't be a moment," he says, then steps into the shop. He takes a breath and walks over to the open fridge. He stares at the drinks lined up in front of him. He wonders about his next move and the predicament he's got himself, and me, in to. He considers ending the journey now but can't. There's too much hanging on this. He takes out his phone and begins to write.

Hey John, hope you had a pleasant journey?

Have you made it to Gare du L'est yet?"

He presses send, places his phone back in his pocket and takes a bottle of Perrier from the fridge. He pays for his drink, steps out into the Paris streets and takes a sip of water.

"Okay, come on, we don't want to miss the train," he says sarcastically, walking past Cristina and Ivan.

My phone vibrates in my pocket.

I look out on to the Paris walkways. Its busy, people jostle for position on the streets. Paris has changed since I was last here, or maybe I'm the one who's changed. A wave of melancholy flows over me.

I think about Grace and the kids back home. I wish she were with me now. The sadness seizes me. I feel my eyes fill with tears. The cab rocks violently to one side, I slide across the red leather seat, desperately trying to find something to hold on to. The cab quickly adjusts, throwing me back across the seat. I reach out, grab hold of the door handle and hold on.

"Hey, take it easy!" I shout at the driver. Then turn my attention back to the streets of Paris. I feel my heart begin to race, out on the street, I see Jack, not more than a few feet away from me. He's taking a drink of water. The cab passes him, I turn my head and look back through the rear window, I notice a woman and a man accompany him. I sit back in my seat, releasing my grasp on the door handle. Immediately I'm thrown back across the seat, as the cab lurches around another corner.

"Fucking hell fella, take it easy!" I shout.

We come to an abrupt stop. The driver looks over his shoulder.

"We are here," he says, a broad grin across his face.

"Thank fuck!" I reply and pay the man.

The train slowly moves away from the station platform.

The seating arrangement is similar to the Eurostar. Jack sits opposite Cristina and Ivan. Nobody has spoken since they boarded the train and took their seats. Jack stares out on to the streets of Paris, as the train makes its way through the city, out into the French countryside, heading for Munich. He checks his watch, 2 PM. The train is five minutes late leaving Paris, nothing to worry about, we should still be in Munich on time. A tense wait at Gare du L'est was endured by the three of them, each considering their next move.

The train begins to rock rhythmically, as it picks up speed. Ivan stands, looks at Cristina, then makes his way down the train carriage.

"Who's he looking for? Are you expecting that man to be following us?" Jack asks, breaking the awkward silence.

"I don't know?" she replies.

"What's going on Cristina? please tell me."

She just stares at Jack, across the table.

"You should not be here. You should have flown."

"Well, I'm here."

"You do not need to know this side of my life."

"I think I do," he answers.

She turns her attention to the landscape, passing by outside.

"Where I come from, where I live. It is a special place,' she says, turning to look at Jack. "We have lived there for many years. There, we are safe."

"Safe from what? Who?"

"My family, my people, have survived for many years. But, we know the dangers."

"What dangers?"

"I know it sounds strange, but there are people who would want us dead."

"Want you dead?" Jack is surprised.

"Yes."

"But why? Who?"

"I have told you. My people have fled persecution many times, over many years. We are safe behind the walls of the citadel. Armies would arrive, wars continued. But, as long as we stayed within the walls, we were safe."

"That was then. This is now. You're talking about history, wars that ended years ago."

"Maybe for some, but not for all. There are people out there who would like us all killed. My people will never be safe outside the walls."

"What people? I don't understand, what is it that they hate about you? Your people?"

Cristina pauses, unsure of how to continue.

"I cannot tell you everything now. My superiors will do that when we arrive."

"Cristina, if you don't tell me, I will be leaving this train at the next station, and you can explain that to your superiors."

Cristina turns away, concentrating again on the rolling countryside. Jack doesn't avert his gaze. He glares at Cristina.

"We, my race, are not like you, not like other humans," she says calmly, still looking out of the window.

"What?" Jack says, Cristina slowly turns to face him.

"We are different. I am different. I might look the same on the outside, but inside, I am different. My body does not function like yours."

"You're not making any sense, what is wrong with you?"

"There is nothing wrong with me. I am different."

"Then tell me how?" Jack takes her statement seriously.

"You will not understand."

"Try me."

"Our blood, our immune system, is very different from yours." She pauses.

"How different?" Jack replies, confused.

"For us to exists, to live, we need more than food."

"More than food? I don't understand."

"Please, wait till we arrive at Heaven's Gate, all will be explained then."

"Cristina, please continue, tell me what's going on? What do you mean?"

"What I am about to tell you, you will find hard to believe," she pauses, "I am real, I am not what you might read about in stories."

"What I might read about? What stories?"

"Stories of vampires."

"What?" Jack laughs, "Vampires, what are you talking about?"

"You are not ready," she replies sternly.

"I'm not ready for what? To find out you're a vampire."

"I am not a vampire, they do not exist, but I, my race does."

Jack realises she's serious.

"So, why mention vampires? What have they got to do with it?"

"There are similarities, but we are real."

"What similarities could you possibly have with vampires."

Cristina stops and breathes deeply.

"Our blood, we need blood to survive."

Jack doesn't know how to respond, realising she's serious about her declaration.

"You need blood? Cristina, that's madness, what do you mean, you need blood."

"My heart, my lungs, every part of me, needs blood. But my blood is different. It needs to be replenished. It needs feeding; only more blood can do this."

"More blood?"

"I know what you're thinking, that I'm crazy,"

"I don't think you're crazy. I just don't understand what you're saying If it is true,"

"It is true," she interrupts

"Then what is this condition called?"

"It has no name. We are who we are. You will see when we arrive at Heaven's Gate."

"What does Heaven's Gate have to do with this?"

"Heaven's Gate is helping us, helping us to survive."

"In what way?"

"We are beginning to live without the need for blood. Heaven's Gate has developed medicines that can reduce our need for blood. But there is much work still to be done."

"How is this possible?"

"We, Heaven's Gate, is still trying to discover the reasons. But we know our metabolism is much slower than yours, our hearts beat slower. The protein in our blood is high. We do not need to pump blood around the body as fast. Our bodies live on the blood beneath our skin, not on the beat of our hearts."

"And that is why they want to see me? To help?"

"I do not know their plans, but yes, we hope you can help."

"Help how? I know nothing of this condition."

"Nobody does," she replies.

The carriage I'm sitting in is quiet. There are maybe only a handful of passengers dotted around me. I take a moment to look at my surroundings. I'm sat at a table for four in first-class again. I feel privileged to be here. The seats are large, soft and very comfortable. I inspect the empty place in front of me, lime green and grey, how does that colour combination work? I don't know. But, they look trendy, modern.

I pick up the menu, and a leaflet drops onto the table top, I open it.

TGVs (Train a Grande Vitesse) are the pride of the French fleet, running at up to 300Km/h, linking many towns and cities across France and Europe. Most are double-decker, with a combination of first and second-class seats. Promising a smooth and quiet journey.

"An upper deck?" I ask myself. I thought the train looked huge. I place the leaflet back in its holder and look out of the window. Paris begins to drift off into the distance, as we head out into the French hills. I wonder if I will remember any of this, my memory is not what it was. It could be the drugs I'm on or my depression. The doctor assumed when I enquired about my short-term memory is terrible. I should keep a diary, or write a blog, as my kids would say. But I know I won't.

"Bonjour Monsieur, would you like some café?" A waitress stands before me, holding a jug of coffee. A little cap sits, perched, on her head.

"Merci. Thank you," I reply. She fills my cup, then places a lunch menu in front of me.

"I will be back shortly to take your order," she says.

"Okay, thank you," I reply.

I read the menu. I wish Grace were with me. She would love this. I place the menu card on the table, turning my gaze to the trees passing by outside. I feel a tear roll down my cheek. It feels cold on my cheek. I can't help it. I've never cried for years, now it's a daily occurrence, even hourly. I begin to think about my kids. It hurts more. I quickly pick up the napkin, dry my face, take a sip of my coffee and breathe.

I'm tired of this.

Jack relaxes into his seat while the waiter fills his glass.

"Thank you," he says, then takes a sip of his red wine. Cristina and Ivan both have water in front of them. The waitress leaves the three of them together. Jack swirls his wine in his glass, examining the tears streaming down the glass.

"Are you okay?" Cristina asks.

"Yes," he replies abruptly.

"I am sure you have many more questions,"

"Oh, I do, I do," he replies, interrupting her.

"I, my superiors, will answer everything, but this is not the time or place," she continues.

Jack looks up from his glass, takes another drink of wine then stands.

"Where are you going?" Cristina asks, sounding concerned. Ivan begins to stand, Cristina, places her hand on his arm.

"Keep him in check, I'm going for a walk," Jack says, then walks off down the train aisle.

"Jack! Hi!" I say as I see him approaching me. He could not have appeared at a better time, interrupting my thoughts of melancholy. He smiles back and raises his wine glass,

"Hi, cheers!" He replies I lift my glass to his.

"Is anybody sitting here?" he asks, looking at the seat opposite me.

"No, sit down."

"How are you then? How's your journey been?"

"I'm good and the journey, well, look at all this," I say glancing around the carriage.

"Yeah, it's nice, isn't it?"

"Nice, fucking hell, how the other half live! It's gorgeous."

"I'm glad you're enjoying it. I was a bit worried you'd be having second thoughts."

"I have wondered what I'm doing," I reply, honestly, "But I'm excited, have you told them I'm here yet?"

"Who?"

"Who?" I look at him, confused, "Your friends."

"No, not yet, it's still a bit too soon. They'd throw us both on the next train home if they knew."

"What are you doing here then? Aren't you worried they might see us together?"

"No, they're having their lunch, it'll be fine."

"How's your journey been? Have they told you what they want you for?" I ask.

I notice his apprehension.

"What have they said?" I ask.

"It's strange, they're still not giving much away, but I'm fairly sure they're going to offer me a job."

"It's a strange interview they're putting you through."

"I know," he says then looks at me, "Don't worry John, it'll be fine," a broad grin appears on his face as he takes another drink of wine.

"Pardon me monsieur, would you like anything from the lunch menu?" The waitress has returned, interrupting our conversation. I quickly pick up the menu.

"Yes, may I have the Lasagne with salad please," I reply, she writes my request on her note pad then turns her attention to Jack.

"And for you, monsieur?"

"non, je vais bien, Merci" Jack replies in fluent French.

"Okay, si vous désirez quelque chose plus tard, faites le moi savoir," she replies smiling.

"Je vais, je vous remercie," he says. I watch her laugh, then walk away.

"Smooth bastard," I say to him, smiling, "What did you say?"

"Just that I didn't want anything."

"Sounds like you wanted something to me?" I say laughing.

"How did the transfer go at Gare du Nord?" Jack asks.

"It was fine, thanks. I felt a bit of an idiot sitting on that buggy thing."

"Why?"

"Being driven around in one of those electric buggies isn't the most stylish way to travel."

"No worse than that old Ford car you used to own."

"Piss off! I loved that car. It was a classic."

"It was a heap of shit. It kept breaking down."

"Only a couple of times, you have to expect that with old cars. I'd still have it if it weren't for Grace."

"Yeah, I remember that night, I had to come and pick you both up, she refused to get in it again."

"She made me sell it," we both laugh, then take a sip of our drinks.

"I'll tell you what was terrible," I say.

"What?"

"My taxi journey."

"What? Where? To St Pancreas?"

"No, in Paris, to Gare du L'est."

"That's only a five-minute journey," Jack says, surprised.

"I know, he drove like a bloody maniac. I reckon we got there in less than two."

"French taxi drivers," Jack answers, laughing.

"I think I saw you," I announce.

"Where?"

"In Paris, when I was in the crazy cab. Did you walk between stations?"

"Yeah."

"How come you didn't get a taxi? Not brave enough?" I smile.

"The taxi queue was too big. It's only a few minutes' walk. I needed to stretch out the legs."

I watch him. I don't believe a word he says.

"What's up?" I ask

"Nothing,"

"Come on, I know you, are you alright? You're not worried, are you?"

"No, no, I'm fine honest. I just wish I knew a bit more. But I reckon by the time we get there. I'll have got it out of them, her."

"Her," I ask.

"Yeah, Ivan doesn't say much."

"I saw him too, big fella."

"Yeah, that's him. He's a strange man."

I notice he looks worried again.

"You're sure you're alright?" I ask again.

"I should be asking you that I'm fine, honest."

"Don't worry about me. I'm enjoying the trip."

"Have you spoken to Grace yet?" he asks

"No, not yet. I've texted her," I pause, "I wish she were here with me."

"I bet you do," Jack puts his hand on my arm, "Fingers crossed we get you sorted, then we'll get her out here on holiday."

"She would love it."

"How was she this morning?"

"Okay, I think, you know how she is."

"Yeah, like a rock."

"She is, I tried hard not to make a big deal of it." I say, then pause, "My journey on the Eurostar was great though!" I try to lighten the mood.

"It's a nice train."

"Maybe, but not as nice as my travelling companion." A smirk covers my face.

"Ahh…So you said in your text. You're not missing Grace that much then," he laughs.

"No, no, it was nothing like that. We were just talking, but she was a good-looking woman. Something was going on, though."

"What do you mean?"

"My sixth sense was working overtime."

"You were making stuff up in your daft head then?"

"Maybe, but I was a good copper once you know. I can sense things."

"Like what?"

"I'm sure she was texting the fella behind me."

"The man behind you? What's strange about that?"

"I don't know, something. She kept looking at him."

"Maybe she knew him or fancied him. Women have needs too, you know."

"Funny you should say that that's what I thought."

"That she fancied him?"

"No, she was having an affair with him."

"Ha, ha. How did you work that out? Poirot!" he laughs.

"I'm sure they were texting each other."

"Bloody hell talk about making stuff up. Were you jealous, in your mad little mind," he laughs.

"Excuse moi."

We both look up. The waitress has returned with my lunch. She places it in front of me."

"Merci, thank you," I say to her.

"Would you like some more wine with your meal?" she asks.

I look across at Jack.

"It would be rude not to. Yes please," I answer.

"Okay, I'll leave you to it," Jack says, making his way out of his seat.

"That was short and sweet," I reply.

"Well, I don't want to push my luck. Enjoy your lunch and don't get too pissed. I'll see you tonight at the hotel."

"Okay, see you later." I raise my glass, "And thanks again!"

"No worries enjoy!" he replies and walks away back down the train aisle.

Cristina watches Jack, as he takes his seat, then picks up her glass of sparkling water and takes a drink. Jack smiles at her, then looks out of the window. The rolling countryside flashes by outside, farmhouses scattered across fields of varying colours. Trees are dressed in their autumn coats, a river slices through the view. The sun begins to set, its auburn glow throwing elongated shadows across the fields.

Jack questions his predicament, what to do next? Where to go from here? He searches through his bag, pulling out the plastic folder containing his itinerary. He takes a hand full of papers from the folder, places them on to the tabletop and flicks quickly through the documents. The black and white photo of the villagers catches his eye, he separates it from the other sheets and inspects its contents. Jack places the photograph onto the table, in front of Cristina.

"Who is that?" He points to the woman in the photo. Cristina looks at the picture then at him.

"Where did you get it?"

"It wasn't hard to find on the internet."

Cristina picks up the photo, contemplating her answer.

"There is so much more to reveal, please, I cannot answer your questions now."

"What questions? Who is that in the picture? Your mother?"

Cristina slides the photograph across the table towards Jack.

"That is me," she replies. Ivan turns to look at her. He then fixes his gaze on Jack.

"That's you?" he says, surprised.

"Yes."

"When was that picture taken?" he asks.

"That photograph was taken a long time ago."

"How long?"

"Many years."

"How can it be you then?" he asks calmly.

"As I have tried to explain, I am not like you. My body works differently. It's not easy to explain."

"Try," he interrupts.

"It is part of my condition. I do not grow old as you do," she replies

"You don't grow old?"

"I grow old slowly."

"Really, so, how old are you?"

"I do not know."

"You don't know?"

"We…my race… We don't celebrate birth. We celebrate being alive."

"This photograph," Jack picks it up and looks at it closely, "Must have been taken around the end of the war, nineteen forty-five, forty-six. That would make you seventy years old," he pauses. Cristina shows no emotion. "But you must be at least twenty when the photo was taken, that makes you…." he pauses again, "Let's say, about, one hundred years old." Jack waits for Cristina to answer.

"It is not how long a person lives, but what they do in that time that is important," she replies, Jack shakes his head.

"That may be true, but are you expecting me to believe that you are one hundred years old."

"Please," she pleads, "When we get to Heaven's Gate, my superiors will explain it all to you then."

"Your superiors… your superiors have a lot of explaining to do. Nothing you have told me makes any sense. I get the feeling I might be getting involved in something sinister."

"Sinister? What do you mean?"

"Your superiors…Dr Schneider…. Is he your leader?"

"What do you mean?"

"Are you part of some sort of cult?"

"What?" she answers, now she acts surprised.

"This looks to me like a band of brainwashed kids, believing anything they're told."

"This is real, I am real," Cristina protests. "I know what I have told you is hard to believe, but it is true, and I am here. You wanted to know, and I have told you."

"You have told me nothing. Right now, I'm ready to fly back and forget this ever happened."

"Dr Carlisle, please," Cristina appeals to Jack, "We are not some crazy cult, all will become clear when we arrive at Heaven's Gate. I understand your concerns, but please believe me."

Jack glares at her, then turns away.

Excuse me, could I have some water please?" I ask the waitress.

"Of course," she replies, notices my empty wine glass and says, "Would you like more wine?"

"Yes please, qui, thank you," I reply.

The waitress returns a few moments later with my water and wine. I check my watch, time for my afternoon pills. I forget what each tablet does now. I don't think about it anymore, I wash them down with the water and hope they work their magic. I follow the water with a large mouthful of wine, not to be taken with alcohol it says clearly on the label. My phone vibrates on the table in front of me. I pick it up. It's a message from Grace.

Have you taken your pills yet? Don't forget!! Love you x

I smile, "She's brilliant."

Yes, I have just taken them, thanks for reminding me!

How are you? How're the kids? Love you too xx

I place my phone on the table, as I do it vibrates again. I read the message.

Hi dad, I hope you're enjoying your holiday. I miss you loads and can't wait to see you. Love you x

It's from Sadie. I smile.

Love you too gorgeous girl, I'll speak to you tonight when I get to the hotel, love you loads xxx

I wonder where Lucy's text is?

I text Grace.

Is Lucy there? X

No, she's gone into town with her friends, she has her phone on her if you want to text her x

No, it's ok, I'll call later tonight x

Ok, love you x

Love you x

Jack checks his watch. It's nearly five o'clock. The mood is calmer now, Cristina is reading, Ivan just sits, waiting patiently, staring into space.

"I'm going to get something to eat," he announces, "Would anybody like anything?"

"No, I'm fine," Cristina replies.

"Ivan?" he looks across at him. Ivan shakes his head.

"Okay, I won't be long," Jack replies, stands and makes his way to the buffet carriage.

The train swings from left to right, Jack steadies himself holding on to a silver rail running around the carriage. He chooses a Croque monsieur sandwich and a bottle of Stella Artois beer, from the cold storage and hands it to the young man serving behind the buffet counter. The sandwich is placed into a microwave. "

"Eighteen Euros, please," the man says while opening the beer.

Jack pays him and waits for his sandwich, drinking the beer from the bottle. His phone vibrates in his pocket. He reads the message.

Hi, how's your journey going? Are you in Munich yet? I can't remember what time you get there. X

It's from Anna.

He replies,

Hi Anna, I'm still on the train. I should get there about half-past seven tonight. I'll call you when I get there. Have you had a lovely day? X

The man behind the counter calls out to Jack,

"Monsieur," he holds high a paper plate.

"Thank you," Jack says, taking his sandwich from the man and making his way to a spare table by the window. There are no seats in the carriage, only tall tables to perch against while you eat. His phone vibrates again.

I'm just out with Daniella. She's worrying me a bit about the hospital you're going to. She tells me it's evil?? I know, it sounds crazy, I don't believe her, but just be careful ok x

Jack begins to think that maybe Daniella is right,

Yeah, she said a similar thing to me when I asked her about it. I don't know what her problem is, don't listen to her.

I've been to worse places! X

Ok, just be careful, call me later x

Jack considers answering, decides against it, turns off his phone and puts it back in his pocket.

Munich station, we're here at last. I'm relaxed but tired. I need a snooze. I wait, let the other passengers leave the carriage. I check my paperwork, I'm booked into the Hotel Sofitel, and a taxi should be waiting for me to take me there. I step from the train, nervously, I look for Jack. He's nowhere to be seen, so casually, I begin to walk down the platform. As I approach the station exit, I'm greeted by several men, Asian in appearance, holding signs with people's names on. I can't see my name.

"Mr old man Thompson!" I hear a man call.

I look across and make eye contact with him. He's tall, thin, and wears a long camel coat that looks two sizes too big for his slender frame. He notices me, a broad smile appears on his face.

"Mr old man Thompson!" He asks again as he walks over to me.

I chuckle to myself,

"Yeah, I think that's me?" I tell him, "My friend has played a joke on me," we shake hands.

"You book a taxi to Sofitel hotel?" he asks, not understanding my explanation.

"Yes."

"Please come this way," he gestures with his hand, and I follow him out of the station. The situation outside Munich station is a mirror image of the scene outside Gare du Nord. Hundreds of people are waiting for a taxi. Cars shuffle around, blowing their horns, the noise is deafening. The man leads me to a quieter area of the concourse.

"Please, wait here. I will go and get my car."

"Okay," I reply.

I watch him walk off into the mass of people. I feel a cold breeze around my neck. It's a clear night. I pull my coat zip-up high and lift my collar, trying desperately to keep in the warmth. I look again for Jack, two men in tracksuits catch my eye. I look closely at them, they are same two men from earlier, at Paris Gare du Nord. One is dressed in a sky-blue tracksuit, the other a bright red one, they both have knitted beanie hats on their heads. I'm not sure why I'm surprised to see them, but something keeps my attention. I question, to myself, why are they here? They look like thugs. If I were still a policeman, I would be asking them questions. Men up to no good give off something, a vibe, a presence and they do that. I watch them smoke, one of them leans against the glass-fronted store, the other takes out a piece of paper and looks at it. I'm stood close enough to notice the rose tattoo on the back of his hand. My scrutiny of the two men is, surprisingly, interrupted by the appearance of Jack. He strides straight past the two men, as he leaves the station, followed by Cristina and the unmistakeable figure of Ivan.

They move away from me without looking over, for a moment I forget that they shouldn't see me, the two men so transfix me. My surveillance resumes, the man in the red tracksuit gestures to the blue tracksuit and they both turn and look at someone. I follow their eyes. I'm not sure what I'm looking at. I look back at them, then in the direction they both face. They're looking in Jack's direction, I'm unsure of my deduction. A car horn sounds behind me, the two men look up, then head in my direction. My heart begins to beat faster. I watch them approach, then pass me by, showing no interest in me. They throw their cigarettes to the ground, then open the back door of a black Audi car and get in.

"Mr Old man Thompson!" I hear a voice and look away from the two men.

My driver is beside me, "May I take your bag?" He asks.

"Yes, yes, thank you," I reply.

He takes my bag and places it into the boot of his car. I look back to see the Audi pull away from the kerb.

I get into my taxi, unsure of what to make of my surveillance. The cab nudges out from between cars. I hear a horn blow loudly from the car behind me, my driver ignores it and still pulls out into the organized chaos of the exit lanes. He weaves his machine through stationary traffic, ambling tourists and begins to add to the noise. Honking his horn at any obstruction, he steers my carriage out of the station and on to the highway.

We stop, abruptly, at a set of traffic lights. The driver looks at his phone and rings someone. I hear him shouting down the phone. The lights change, we move away. He steers the car with one hand. The other holds the phone tightly to his ear. He lets go of the wheel to change gear. The vehicle veers sharply right. I feel the car wheels hit the kerb. I'm thrown across the seat.

"Fucking hell fella, easy!" I shout.

He ignores me, sending the car into a vicious circle. We spin around, cross two lanes of oncoming traffic, then leave the main road entering the hotel foyer area. The taxi comes to an abrupt stop.

"Hotel Sofitel!" the driver announces.

I look out of the window.

"Bloody hell! That was quick, thank fuck," I say to him.

I get out of the car. The driver hands my bag back to me, then waits. I look at him. He looks at me. I realise what's happening. I have no money

"Have you been paid?" I ask, he looks at me.

"Yes," he replies but doesn't move.

"Okay, good," I reply, "I'm sorry, but I don't have any money for a tip."

The driver realises what I am saying, he looks at me disgusted, walks around the car, gets in and without acknowledging my existence, drives off. I take a moment to look at my surroundings; the outside of the hotel is brightly lit. A circular driveway runs around a central fountain display, water jets up from twisted steel flowers, glinting off the lights that surround the fountain. Lush green foliage, flank either side of the driveway, illuminated by neon lime green lamps. Tall, broad-leaved plants congregate together. It looks impressive. To my left is an outdoor eating area, to my right the same. Several people sit drinking and smoking.

"Excuse me, sir, are you checking in?" I turn, a man in a beige suit stands in front of me.

"Yes, I am," I reply.

"May I take your bag, sir?"

I hand him my case.

"Please, follow me."

He leads me into the hotel reception, I stand and admire the grand entrance, neon blue lights glisten above stainless-steel reception desks. Leather couches and giant plants, line either side of the large hall. The wooden floor beneath my feet seamlessly merges into a midnight blue carpet before me. It's beautiful. I follow the man to one of the desks. The concierge stands my bag beside me, wishes me a pleasant evening, then leaves.

The receptionist explains that my room and breakfast are paid for. That the hotel Wi-Fi is free to use for guests and asks me whether I would like a table booked in the restaurant for dinner. I decline his offer, I'm not hungry, but feeling very tired.

"You are in Room 4123, which is on the fourth floor. The elevators are just behind you on the left," he explains.

I take the key from him, turn and head for the lifts. A younger-looking man arrives at my side, pushing a gold trolley.

"May I take your bag?" he asks, I let him put my bag on to his carriage.

"Room 4123," I hear the receptionist call out to him.

"This way sir, follow me," he says.

We enter the elevator, exit on the fourth floor and finally make it to my room. I open my door and step inside. A broad smile appears on my face,

"Thank you, Jack," I say to myself.

My room is luxurious, decorated with silver grey and white walls. A super-sized bed engulfs the room, dressed in brilliant white sheets, with two gold cushions. Cushions on the bed? I don't get it. Grace would love it. The headboard, white leather, nearly reaches the ceiling. I walk over and feel it, soft, padded. I look around. A gilt coloured chair is placed in the corner of the room. Another stands in front of a large mirrored desk. Above the desk is an enormous gold framed mirror. The room is dimly lit, only the bedside lights are on. I need the toilet. I search for the light in the en-suite, bright spotlights beam down onto the brilliant white porcelain sink. The colour scheme has changed to browns and blacks. There is a bath, a separate large shower cubicle, as well as a toilet. I return to the main bedroom, walk over to the window, pull open the curtains, revealing a white leather window seat. I run my hand over the soft leather, then sit down. Outside Munich stretches out in front of me, bright lights, leading off into the distance. This is too much. It's beautiful. I wish Grace could see it. She'd love it. I need to bring her here. I need to live.

Jack takes the key from the man behind reception.

"Would you like a table booked for dinner tonight?" he asks.

Jack looks across at Cristina. She is checking in at the desk next to him.

"Cristina," he calls, "Should we book a table for dinner?"

"Yes," she answers, slightly surprised at his suggestion, "What time should we meet?"

"Nine o'clock."

Cristina checks her watch, "Okay, fine."

"A table for two at nine o'clock," the receptionist repeats.

Jack looks across his shoulder at Ivan, then back at the man.

"Yes, a table for two please," he confirms, "See you later," he says, then makes his way to the elevator.

Once in his room, he throws his bag to the ground, sits on the edge of his bed and runs his hands through his hair. Fear flows through him. Uncertainty engulfs him. His phone begins to vibrate in his pocket. He takes it out, looks at the number, the screen reads unknown, he answers.

"Hello."

"Hello, Dr Carlisle," Jack recognizes his voice immediately.

"Dr Schneider."

"Yes, good evening. I just thought I should give you a quick call."

"Yes, I think you should," he interrupts.

"Cristina has informed me about your concerns."

"Has she?" he interrupts again.

"It seems that you may be a bit confused about some of the things Cristina has told you."

"A bit confused is an understatement," Jack replies.

"Let me first assure you, that we are not some kind of…" he pauses, "Crazy cult."

"Then, what are you? I'm travelling with a young lady, who's telling me tales about vampires and thinks that she may be a hundred years old. How do you expect me to react to that?"

"Dr Carlisle, there are many things you understand, but much more that you do not."

"Then explain to me now, how any of what I've been told can be true?"

"There is too much to explain over the phone."

"Try me!"

"Dr Carlisle, you have unfortunately forced Cristina into revealing a number of facts about her, that are difficult to apprehend. She did not expect to be put in this position. She is finding it hard to answer your questions without confusing you."

"I'm sorry about that, but you have to understand my situation."

"We do," he interrupts, "But, I cannot tell you everything now. When you arrive at Heaven's Gate, I will answer all of your questions then. Only then will you will be able to appreciate what we are trying to achieve here."

"Tell me about Cristina," Jack asks, the line goes quiet.

"She is a special woman."

"She thinks she's over a hundred years old."

"What you need to understand Dr Carlisle, is that Cristina, her race, is the reason the hospital exists. We need to protect them, look after them. Not just for the good of their community, but also the good of mankind."

"Protect them. For the good of mankind. Is that why Ivan is here?"

"Yes," he answers quickly.

"He's a liability. He's going to get us arrested."

"Ivan is a good man. If he feels that something is wrong, he will act on his instincts. It is for him to decide."

"And what happened on the train today?"

"Yes,"

"You heard about it then?"

"I did."

"And you think that was alright, to act as he did?"

"I trust his judgement."

"I'm not sure that I do."

"Dr Carlisle, have you ever watched a situation escalate into something greater than it needed to be."

"I think I did today."

"He does not act recklessly. Ivan will not wait for a situation to develop; it is not in his training. He will act immediately, to stop any danger towards Cristina."

"His training. What does that mean?"

"All I ask is that you trust Ivan, trust me."

"You ask a lot."

"Maybe, but you will not regret your decision to visit us at Heaven's Gate. I can assure you of that."

Jack reflects for a moment, on the day's revelations. The realisation that I am here, with him, in this hotel somewhere.

"Okay," he replies, reluctantly.

"Thank you. Please, enjoy what is left of your evening and I look forward to meeting you tomorrow."

"How old is she?" Jack asks and waits a moment for the response.

"I do not know exactly, but she is older than you….and me." He replies calmly.

"Hi, Grace."

"John! How are you? Where are you?" she replies.

It's great to hear her voice.

"I've just arrived at the hotel in Munich."

"Is it nice?" she asks. I look around my room.

"It's okay," I reply.

"I had a look online today, you're at the Hotel Sofitel Munich, aren't you?"

"That's it."

"It's got five stars!" she proclaims, I chuckle.

"Yeah, it is, it's gorgeous."

"Lucky you."

"I wish you were here with me."

"I wish I were there too," she replies, there's a pause.

"How was your journey?"

"It was good, I've had some crazy taxi rides though, they drive like bloody maniacs over here!"

"That was how I used to feel with you."

"With me? What do you mean?"

"When we were young, you drove like a maniac."

"Ha, ha, you used to love it."

"I did not!" she protests.

"How are the kids?" I ask

"Good, they're here, do you want to speak to them?"

"Yes, please, put them on," I reply.

"Sadie, dads on the phone!" I hear Grace call out.

"Hi, Dad."

"Hi Gorgeous, how are you?"

"I'm good."

"What have you done today?"

"We went into town with mum. We went to McDonald's for a treat."

"Lucky you, did you buy anything in town?"

"I got a dress and Lucy got her ears pierced!"

"Lucy got her ears pierced, nobody asked me!" she goes quiet, "Do they look nice?" I ask.

"Yeah," she says.

"Did you get yours done?"

"No."

I feel the conversation begin to halt.

"Is your sister there?"

"Yeah,"

"Can you put her on?"

"Yeah."

"Love you loads, gorgeous girl," I say, "I'll see you soon."

"Love you too, Dad." she replies, "Lucy, dad wants you!" I hear her call.

"Hi, dad."

"Hi, gorgeous girl," I repeat, "How are you?"

"Good."

"How're your ears?" she goes quiet, "Do they look nice?"

"Yeah."

"Did it hurt?"

"No, not really."

"You didn't ask me."

"Mum said you wouldn't mind," she says cautiously.

"Did she? It's fine. You're a big girl now."

"Where are you?" she asks.

"In Germany, Munich."

"Is it nice?"

"Yeah, I wish you were here with me."

"Can we come?"

"Not yet, you know why I'm here, don't you?"

"I think so, to get better?"

"Hopefully," the line goes quiet, "You know I love you loads?"

"Yeah," she replies.

"Okay, well, you look after mum, and I'll see you very soon," my heart is breaking. "Is mum still there?"

"Yeah."

"Can you put her back on?"

"Okay?"

"Love you," I repeat.

"Love you too, dad."

I hear the phone being passed back to Grace.

"I told you she wanted her ears pierced," Grace says immediately.

"I know, I know, it's fine. I just wish I was there."

"And I wish I was with you too…" there's a pause, "What are you doing tonight?"

"Not sure? Jack said he would call me. Maybe go for a drink, but I'm a bit knackered."

"Go on, enjoy yourself."

"I'll try. Look I'm going to have to go, get a shower, sort myself out."

"Will you ring me tomorrow?"

"I will."

"Promise!"

"Yes, I promise."

"Are you ok?" she asks.

"Yeah, I'm good. I'll call you tomorrow."

"I love you," she says.

"I love you, too…. Bye."

"Bye."

I hang up and fall back on to the bed, my eyes streaming with tears.

Myles Davis, A Kind of Blue, plays out of a Bose Bluetooth speaker. Jack sprays himself with Tom Ford for men, then chooses a white Paul Smith shirt to wear with his black Hugo Boss trousers. His phone begins to ring. He checks the screen, Anna's number shows. She wants to Facetime. He hits the hang button, then places the phone back on to the bedside table. Moments later, the phone vibrates into life, Anna phoning. This time Jack answers,

"Hi!" he says.

"Hi, I just tried to Facetime with you,"

"It wouldn't connect, the hotels' Wi-Fi is rubbish. How are you?"

"I'm fine. How's your journey going?"

"I've just checked into the hotel, it's been a long day, but all's going well. I'm just about to go for dinner."

"With Cristina?" she asks, a sense of trepidation can be heard in her voice.

"Yes, with Cristina," the line goes silent, "So, how was your day?" Jack continues.

"That's what I'm ringing about."

"Your meeting with Daniella."

"Yes, she's got a real thing about that hospital you're going too."

"Heaven's Gate."

"Hell's gate, she called it."

"I've spoken to her about it, remember that time at the gallery."

"I thought something was going on."

"I'm not sure what her problem is, or how she knows about it?"

"She has family there."

"What? Where? At the hospital?"

"No, they wouldn't work there, somewhere in the area. I think she's grown up hearing folk tales about the people from that village, the only problem is, she doesn't think they're folk tales. She's sure they're true."

"What tales?"

"It sounds bizarre but, she says that the people who live in the village are cursed. They have a disease."

"What kind of disease?" Jack asks

"I'm not sure, she was describing them as…" she goes quiet

"As what?"

"I can't even say it. It's so ridiculous."

"Vampires," Jack answers.

"Yes, bloody vampires. How did you know she'd say that?"

"An educated guess."

"It's creepy. She hates the place. She was describing them as immortal; the only way that they could be killed is with a sacred knife."

"And why would they need to be killed?" Jack interrupts.

"She's convinced, they're cursed. The devil possesses their souls."

"Sounds plausible, carry on," Jack says sarcastically.

"Honestly Jack, she thinks they're vampires."

"Who would have known, that Bram Stoker's novel was not one of fiction but one of fact."

"I know, it's crazy, but I just thought I'd let you know."

"Why?"

"What do you mean?" she says, sounding confused.

"Why would you tell me that? I don't believe in vampires. You don't believe in vampires. So, why tell me this nonsense."

"She said you could be in danger."

"In danger? How?'

"She said, there are people out there, who if they knew she had left the village, would try and kill her."

"What? Anna, I seriously think you should choose your friends carefully. She sounds deranged, irrational. Please, I think you stay clear of her."

"She knew she had someone with her."

"Who?"

"You said she had a man with her."

"She has, Ivan?"

"Daniella thinks he's what's called, a follower, a protector. He would do anything to protect her."

"That's ridiculous," Jack answers,

"Can he talk?"

"What?"

"Have you heard Ivan speak?"

"Yeah, he never shuts up."

"I thought you said he never spoke."

"Maybe, he was just shy at first. What else did Daniella say?"

"Just be careful."

"I will be, I've been to worse places than this, I'm not scared of folk tales of vampires, I've been to war.

"I know, I know, I'm just worried about you.

"Well, don't be," he says, bluntly.

"Okay, okay….have you seen John yet?"

"Only briefly, I'm going to see him tonight, after dinner."

"How's he doing?"

"I think he's fine. Look, I'm going to have to go, it's getting late, and I'm starving."

"Oh, okay," she answers, sadness apparent in her voice.

"Don't listen to word Daniella says. It's madness. Honestly, listen to what you're saying."

"I know it is. She just seems so convinced."

"Well, please don't talk about me anymore. If she brings it up, say you don't know. In fact, don't see her for the next few days, at least till I'm back. This is supposed to be confidential." His voice now raised.

"I won't," she says quietly.

"I just don't want this going wrong, and if she's got family out here, who knows what they might say."

"Okay"

"Alright, I must go. I'll speak to you tomorrow. Bye."

"Bye…sorry," she says quietly.

"It's fine, just don't say another word."

"I won't."

"Bye," Jack says again and hangs up

"Shit!" He says out loud.

Cristina looks up and waves, Jack stands at the entrance to the restaurant. He notices her, raises his arm and makes his way over to the table.

"Good evening," Jack says, as he takes his seat, opposite Cristina.

"Hello."

Cristina is looking beautiful; she's dressed in a red scooped neck dress, a gold necklace looped around her neck.

"You're wearing make-up," Jack announces.

"Does that bother you?" She asks.

"No, not at all, you look stunning."

"Well, thank you," she replies, not able to hide her embarrassment.

A waitress appears at their table, hands them their menus and asks if they would like a drink.

"Yes, may I have a white wine please," Cristina asks.

"I might join you in a glass of wine; could we please have a look at your wine list?" he asks the waitress.

She hands him the wine menu. Jack quickly examines the wines on offer.

"Seeing as we're in Germany, I think a Riesling may be in order? Is that okay with you?"

"Yes, that would be lovely."

"May we have a bottle of the Sherborn Riesling please," he asks, handing the menu back to the waitress. She then leaves the two of them.

"Where's Ivan tonight? Have you given him the night off?" he asks.

"He had to go somewhere. I'm sure I'm safe enough with you tonight."

"Hopefully you are," Jack replies.

There is a short pause.

"I know we've only sat down, but I've got to asks again, what's going on?" Jack asks, then smiles.

"What's so funny?" she enquires.

"I don't know how many times I've asked that question, in the past twenty-four hours."

"Quite a lot."

"Will you answer?"

Cristina considers her answer.

"You spoke to Dr Schneider," Jack asks.

"I did."

"What did you say to him?"

"I told him about us."

"And what has happened, today?"

"Yes, he said he would call you."

"He did."

"Good," she replies.

"Do you want to know what he said?"

"No."

"No?" Jack asks, "Why not?"

"It is a private conversation between you and the doctor."

"But it involves you."

"I trust him. He would not betray me."

"Betray you," Jack shakes his head, "You sometimes have a strange choice of words."

The waitress returns with their wine, interrupting their conversation. Jack tastes the wine,

"That's gorgeous," he declares.

The waitress fills both their glasses, places the bottle into a stainless-steel wine cooler and leaves the table. Cristina picks up her menu and looks through it. Jack watches her, unsure whether to continue with the conversation.

"Cheers," he says, Cristina's eyes look up from the menu. She picks up her glass.

"Cheers," she repeats, "To the future," she adds.

"To the future," Jack replies, then picks up his menu.

"What would you like to eat?" Jack asks.

"I'm not sure everything sounds lovely."

"Do you have to be careful, with what you eat?" He asks.

"What do you mean?"

"If it is true, what you say, then surely you need to be careful what you eat?"

"I can eat most things, like anyone else, but protein is high on my list of priorities."

"Steak again then?" Jack suggests.

"Maybe," Cristina replies, placing her menu on to the table.

"Are you ready to order?" They both look up at the waiter standing by their table.

"Please, you go ahead, I'm still looking," Jack says.

"The steak please," she says.

"And how would you like it cooked?" the waiter asks

"Rare please."

"And for you, sir?"

"I think I'll try the Rouladen please."

"Good choice, sir," the waiter replies, then walks away.

"Rouladen?" Cristina questions his order.

"Have you ever had it?"

"No."

"It's a lovely traditional dish. They wrap thinly sliced beef around a filling of bacon, or pork belly, with onions, pickles and mustard."

"Sounds interesting."

"Why did you to order steak?"

"I like steak."

"I thought there might be another reason."

"What would that be?" she asks carefully.

"You mentioned needing protein, what's better than a steak? Rare."

"All the goodness is in the blood."

"You would say that," Jack replies.

Cristina is unsure how to respond.

"I'm sorry that was uncalled for."

"What were you suggesting?"

"Nothing, please, I'm sorry," Jack apologises.

Cristina takes a sip of her wine and looks at him.

Jack picks up his glass,

"Here's to a lovely evening," he says.

Cristina considers her response, raises her glass, and they both take a sip of wine.

"Did, Dr Schneider put your mind at rest?"

"Kind of."

"What does that mean?"

"He assured me that I was not entering a cult."

"I cannot believe you thought that?" she says.

"And yet, you want me to believe everything else you've told me."

"I would not lie to you."

"Good…" he pauses, "I asked him about you."

"I thought you might, what did you ask?"

"Your age."

Cristina glares at Jack.

"And what did he say?"

"I thought you didn't want to know?"

"Jack, please don't play games with me," she says sternly.

"I'm sorry, he didn't say much, but he did say that you are older than him…..and me."

Cristina calmly takes a sip of her drink.

"He also said that you were special, your race is special, and you need to be protected," Jack observes her.

"Protected from who? Or what? He would not say. Will you explain to me who, and why, someone might want to hurt you?"

"This is not the time."

"I think it is."

"Whatever I tell you, will only lead to more questions, you will not believe me."

"I'll try, please, I need to know. My life might be in danger, if what you say is true."

"They do not want you."

"They? Who are they? Why do they want you?"

Cristina closes her eyes and takes a deep breath.

"My race has always had enemies. People find it hard to understand. You realize that now."

Jack nods in acceptance.

"The way we lived…. in the past — the way we were forced to live, hiding within the walls, hunting for food by night. Our existence became the narrative of many myths. We were demonized."

"Did they think you were vampires?" Jack asks

"Vampires!" Clarissa smiles, "That word did not exist for many years. It is the most famous story to be born from my race."

"How is that possible?"

"Do you want me to tell you?"

"Of course, please carry on," he answers.

"Have you heard of the man Ármin Vámbéry?"

"No,"

"But you do know of Bram Stoker."

"Yes, he wrote Dracula."

"Ármin Vámbéry was a friend of Bram Stoker. He was a Hungarian man who was travelling through our lands."

"When was this?"

"Many, many, years ago. He was a writer. He hoped his adventures in Romania would make an interesting story. One that would make him his fortune. His journey eventually brought him to Transylvania, where he heard tales of a mysterious race of people, a race that lived within the walls of a citadel.

A citadel built high on the crest of a mountain. A race that could not be seen during daylight hours, only appearing at night."

"Why only at night?"

"We were like prisoners. We could not leave the walls during the day. It was too dangerous. Back then, life was hard. If we were found, discovered, away from the walls of the citadel, we would be arrested and tried for crimes we had not committed. There was no justice. We would be killed. Our heads displayed like trophies on wooden spikes. Only at night were we able to hunt, survive. They forced us to live that way, like animals."

"Why did they think that? Why did they keep you there?"

"We cannot hide the way we are,"

"I don't understand."

"We live longer, much longer. The surrounding villagers thought of us as demons."

"And, this Amrin, wrote about this?"

"Yes, He wrote about a village of demons…" she pauses, "Can you see how this story is unfolding?"

"And it was a success, his book?"

"Ármin Vámbéry took these tales back to England with him. But, he did not write a tale of fiction, he said his story was true. He was ridiculed; no one believed him. Why should they?"

"I wonder why?" Jack smiles.

"But that was not the end. One of his friends enjoyed his tales and began to write."

"Bram Stoker?" Jack asks.

"Yes, he wrote a story of fiction."

"Dracula."

"Yes, We think so?"

"Bloody hell!" Jack sits back in his chair and takes a drink of his wine.

"Excuse me," they both look up, a waitress stands, holding their meals.

Ivan stands motionless by the entrance of the hotel, dressed in a black roll neck jumper and jeans, hidden by the shadows. Taxi's come and go, delivering tourists. They hurry past him with excited faces, patiently he waits, observing their every move. A black Audi A6 drives past him without stopping. He watches the car come to a halt just before the exit barrier. The barrier slowly begins to elevate. The back doors swing open, and two men get out, both dressed in black suits. They quickly slam shut the car doors and begin to walk towards the hotel. The car exits and the barrier returns to its dormant state. Ivan takes a step backwards, as the duo pass by him and enter the hotel. He waits a moment, then confidently follows them into the hotel reception. The two men head directly for the hotel bar. Ivan breathes deeply, then follows them into the bar.

The two men are standing at the bar, one of them orders a drink, the other examines the room. Ivan places his glass onto the table next to him, sits down and begins to inspect their every move. The bartender returns with two drinks. One of the men hands over the money, his hand is illuminated by the halogen spotlights. The tattoo on the back of his hand, clearly visible to Ivan.

"Tell me about Ivan," Jack asks, placing his knife and fork onto his plate.

"What do you want to know?" Cristina replies.

"I've worked out he's here to protect you," Jack asks, "I'm right, aren't I?"

She takes a moment to consider her reply.

"Yes."

"One man is that enough?"

"Nobody knows I am here. Nobody knows I have left Romania. I should be safe. He is only here as a …."

"A precaution," Jack interjects.

"Yes, precisely," she answers.

"And what was that on the train? An innocent man accosted, robbed."

"We do not know his innocence. I trust Ivan…his judgement."

"Have you been speaking with Dr Schneider?" He asks.

"Why do you say that?"

"He told me the same thing."

"Then you should believe us."

"He could have got us arrested. We're lucky that man didn't press charges."

"Then what does that say about him?"

"Nothing, he probably thought it wasn't worth the hassle."

"Maybe."

"What? You think he was following you?"

"I do not know. I hope not."

"Cristina, we can't continue this journey with Ivan robbing and assaulting innocent passengers. We, he, are eventually going to get arrested."

"I don't think so," she answers.

"Tell me again, why he lost his tongue, was it cancer?"

"Is everything ok with your meal?" They both look up. The waitress has returned to their table.

"Yes, it was lovely, thank you" Jack replies.

"Would you like to see the dessert menu?" she asks while collecting their plates.

Jack looks at Cristina.

"Would you like anything else?" he asks.

"No, I am fine, thank you…maybe some water," Cristina replies.

"Certainly, I'll get that for you now."

"Well?" Jack asks.

"All will become clear when we arrive at Heaven's Gate."

"Heaven's Gate," he pauses, "This is very strange. I mean, ridiculously so."

"I understand your worries, concerns, but please believe me when I say that Heaven's Gate is a special place. All its secrets will be revealed to you when we arrive."

"Secrets, there better not be any bloody werewolves there, that would freak me out."

Ivan watches on, as the men take their drinks

to an empty table, set back into one of the corners of the bar.

"Excuse me."

Ivan slowly turns his head.

"We are sitting here; do you mind leaving?"

Ivan glares at the man, then at the woman, sitting beside him. Ignoring them, he returns his gaze to the two men.

"Excuse me!" The man says annoyed, "I said, will you leave us alone, we were sitting here."

Ivan ignores his protest. The couple mutter to themselves, then gather their things and leave the table. They are complaining as they move to an adjacent vacant table.

One of the men checks his watch, then takes a slug of his drink. They sit quietly, barely saying a word, casually looking around the bar. Moments later, a woman walks up to them and sits down. The men shuffle in their seats, sitting upright, as though their mother has entered the room. The woman bends down, places her bag on to her lap and takes from it an envelope. She slides this across the table top, towards the two men.

One of the men picks up the envelope and, without opening it, places into his inside pocket. Ivan slides slowly across to the chair next to him, the shadows covering his face.

The woman then stands and, without speaking, leaves the two men. Ivan watches her, walk into the lobby and head directly to the elevator. The doors open, she enters, then disappears. Ivan's eyes are directed back to the two men. One of them gulps down, what looks like vodka, says something to his partner, stands and walks out of the bar. Ivan's interest is again, taken into the hotel lobby. The man strides across the foyer and enters the toilets. Ivan slowly rises from his seat and leaves the bar.

"Please, excuse me," Jack announces, "I must use the toilet."

He then stands, places his chair back beneath the table and walks towards the hotel foyer. As he leaves the restaurant, he notices Ivan walking across the hotel reception area. He wonders where he has been.

"Hi, I wonder if you could point me in the direction of the toilet, please?" Jack asks at reception. The lady directs him to a door left of her.

"Thank you," he replies, then walks away.

Jack checks the signs on the toilet doors. Then pushes open the door, looks up and sees Ivan. He has his back against the toilet wall and his arm around the neck of a man.

"Ivan!" he calls out.

The man is grasping furiously at Ivan's arm, trying desperately to release himself. Ivan turns to look at Jack.

"Let him go!" Jack shouts.

Ivan momentarily relaxes his grip. The man pulls himself free from Ivan's grasp, turns to face him and strikes Ivan hard with his head. Ivan stands steady, a small wound appearing above his eye and a trickle of blood streams down his face.

Ivan retaliates stretching out his arm, grabbing the man around the throat and thrusting him towards the porcelain urinals. Jack watches as the two men collide against the wall, the force of Ivan crushing the man against the white porcelain bowl. A streak of red appears against one of the bowls. The man, concussed, slumps to the ground.

"Ivan!" Jack shouts again.

Ivan ignores him, bends down and begins searching the man's jacket and trouser pockets. He then stands, finding nothing, twists his head, a trickle of blood drips from his brow as he looks at Jack.

"What's going on?" Jack screams.

The toilet door opens behind him. Jack looks over his shoulder at the man entering the toilet. He looks at Jack, smiles, then turns and sees the man lying on the floor and Ivan's bleeding face.

"What has happened?" he asks.

Ivan moves quickly past Jack and the man, into the foyer.

"I don't know. I came in and found him like that," Jack says. He then approaches the man lying on the ground. He checks his pulse.

"Is he alive?" The man asks.

"Yes," Jack can see an open wound on the man's forehead, rivers of blood run over the man's face and puddle on to the toilet floor.

"I'm a doctor, but I think this man needs an ambulance," Jack says, "Could you pass me one of those towels?" pointing at the pile of fresh white hand towels folded neatly next to the basin. The man hands him a towel, and Jack holds the cloth to the man's head.

"Should I get an ambulance?" the man asks.

"Yes, please," Jack replies.

The man then shuffles quickly out of the toilet. Jack releases the towel and looks at the deep wound. The man lets out a groan, turns on his side and opens his eyes.

"Just stay still, you've banged your head, an ambulance is on its way," Jack tells him.

The man's eyes focus on Jack; he blinks quickly, then violently pushes Jack away from him. Jack falls onto the hard tiled floor.

"Hey!" Jack calls out, as he watches the man get to his feet.

The man looks at himself in the mirror, then across at the toilet door as it opens.

"The ambulance is on its way," the man announces as he re-enters the toilet. The bleeding man looks at him, then forces himself past him, barging him into the door. The startled man looks down at Jack.

"What's going on?" he asks.

"Fuck knows," Jack mutters.

Ivan marches straight across the hotel foyer and

into the bar. He looks over to where the men were sitting. The table is vacant. Spinning on his heels, he hurries out of the hotel entrance. His eyes focus on the scene before him. A taxi pulls up and its occupants, a man and a woman, climb out of the back doors. They embrace, kiss, then walk hand in hand past Ivan.

"Sir, may I help you?"

Ivan looks down at the concierge, who has asked the question, then back at the dimly lit landscape.

"Sir, I think you have a cut on your eye,"

Ivan pays no attention to his show of concern, takes one last look around, then re-enters the hotel. Straight ahead of him stands the man he has just attacked. Ivan watches the man enter the elevator. Quickly he sprints towards the closing doors. Striking the elevator buttons on his arrival, to no avail, the elevator begins its ascent.

"Ivan!" Jack calls out, striding over to him.

Ivan focuses his attention on the numbers incrementing slowly above him.

"What the fuck is going on?" he whispers, angrily, into his ear.

Ivan turns and frowns at Jack.

"Stay there, do not fucking move," Jack says, then storms off towards the restaurant.

He walks straight over to Cristina, who notices him approaching and also his furious expression.

"What's wrong?" she asks, on his arrival.

"Come with me," Jack commands.

Cristina does not question his order, gathering her bag and immediately vacating her seat. Jack waits for her to join him.

"Excuse me, is there a problem?"

They both turn to look at the waitress beside them.

"No, no, everything is fine, thank you. We're just running late for another appointment. Please put the bill on room 1732."

"Okay, I hope you have a lovely evening," she replies.

With that, Jack and Cristina leave the restaurant.

"What's wrong?" Cristina asks.

Jack looks at her then points at Ivan, who is sitting in a seat directly opposite them. Blood streaming down his face. They stride towards him.

"What's happened, Ivan?" She asks, then stretches out her hand. Holding his chin, she moves his head to the side, displaying the wound. His eyes gaze into hers. Jack watches their interaction.

"My room now!" Jack instructs them.

They both turn to look at him.

"Come on, before the police come," he continues.

"Excuse me."

Jack turns, to see the man from the toilet standing beside him.

"Is everything alright?" he asks

"Yes, fine, thank you," Jack replies.

"Your friend," the man points at Ivan, "Does he need an ambulance?"

"No, he will be fine" Jack replies.

Jack pushes open his door, turns on the light and enters his room.

"Sit down," he instructs them.

Cristina and Ivan follow him, then perch themselves on the end of the bed.

"What happened?" she asks Ivan.

"What happened?" Jack interrupts, "what happened was....this maniac attacked another man, in the toilets, downstairs."

"And where is this man now?" Cristina calmly responds.

"What?"

"Where is this man he attacked?"

"I don't know?" he shouts.

"Did he get the police? Is he standing at reception now, reporting this attack?" Cristina's voice gets increasingly louder.

"What are you suggesting?" He asks, Cristina glares at him.

"You can't be serious?" he announces, then shakes his head, a smile grows across his face.

Cristina launches herself towards him, slapping him hard across the face.

"Fuck you! After all, I have told you. This is not a game. This is my life, Ivan's life."

Jack recoils, shocked by her actions. Slowly he raises his hand to his face then takes a moment to look at her then Ivan. Cristina scowls back at him.

"I need a drink," he says.

Jack then stoops to open the mini bar, taking from it two miniature bottles of Johnny Walker. He unscrews one cap, gulps down the contents and breathes deeply.

"I could be in danger; do you not understand?" Cristina asks.

"No, I don't understand!" Jack replies.

"We must leave…. tonight," she says with some urgency.

"I'm going nowhere," Jack replies casually.

"My life is in danger!" she protests, "I'm risking my life, being here for you and you do nothing."

Jack twists open the second bottle of whisky and takes a sip.

"Your life is in danger, from who?" he asks.

"I don't know, but somebody knows I am here. We must leave tonight, please," she appeals.

"Who was that man?" He says, his eyes shifting sideways to looks across at Ivan.

"I cannot be sure. Probably from the old town, or at least, paid by them." She says.

"Paid by them? What? To kill you?"

She turns to look at Ivan. He looks up at her solemnly.

"Yes, we think so. It is not safe."

He knows he can't leave. He can't leave me.

"It makes no sense, none of this makes any sense. Ivan attacking suspected hitmen, you can't expect me to believe this."

Cristina picks up her bag from the bed, opens it and gets out her phone. She starts to dial.

"Who are you phoning?" Jack asks.

She holds the phone to her ear, ignoring his question.

"Who are you phoning?" Jack repeats.

Cristina waits patiently for someone to answer. Jack steps towards her seizing the phone from her hand. Ivan immediately retaliates, grabbing Jack's arm, twisting it aggressively behind his back. Jack drops the phone and the Johnny Walker bottle in his other hand. He screams out in pain, falling to his knees.

"Get him off me!" Jack calls out.

Cristina calmly picks up her phone, looking at Jack as she does so.

"Ivan, let go of Jack," she says quietly but firmly.

Ivan releases his hold on Jack, stands and sits back down on the bed. Jack regains his composure and gets to his feet.

"You've got to stop doing that?" Jack says, rubbing his arm.

"Who were you phoning? Dr Schneider?"

"Yes."

"Why?'

"When I explain to him what has happened. He will organise transport tonight to get us away from here."

Jack thinks quickly. He has to delay her request.

"Stay here tonight," he looks at them both, "Get your things and stay here in my room. We'll all stay here tonight."

Cristina shakes her head.

"That man? Whoever he is? He's gone?" He looks across at Ivan. "You said yourself if he was still here, he would have told the police. He hasn't, so he's gone. We are safer here tonight."

Cristina looks at Ivan.

"Ivan, you know we are safe here. It's late. There is nothing we can do tonight. There is more chance of something else happening if we leave this room."

Ivan momentarily holds his gaze, turns his eyes towards Cristina and nods in acceptance. Jack observes Ivan's response.

"Good, who knows? Maybe after tonight, they will give up. Whoever they are?" Jack says.

"They won't. I won't be safe until I'm back at Heaven's Gate." Cristina replies.

I'm woken by my phone, pulsating next to me, my eyes open. I blink rapidly, finding it hard to adjust to the light. I take a moment to realise where I am, remembering my phone call with Grace. The phone stops vibrating. I sit up, my backaches. I pick up my phone. It's a missed call from Jack. I check my watch, ten fifty-six. I text him back.

Hi Jack, I fell asleep, is everything ok?

I look intently at the screen, waiting for his reply; the phone begins to vibrate in my hand.

"Hi, Jack," I answer.

"John, how are you doing?" He asks

"I'm fine, just had a little nap."

"Sorry, did I wake you?"

"No, yes, but I'm glad you did. Are you alright?"

"Yeah, yeah," he answers.

I hear the apprehension in his reply

"What is it? Have you told them about me?" I ask

"No, no."

"Then what? Somethings up, I can tell."

"I just need a drink, are you up for a nightcap?" he asks

"Are you buying?" I ask

"Yeah, tight arse," he laughs, "Meet you in the bar downstairs, in ten minutes."

"I'll just freshen up, and I'll be down. Are you sure everything's alright?" I ask again.

"Everything's fine, stop worrying."

"Okay, see you in ten," I reply and hang up.

I know something's wrong.

"*Come in,*" Jack says, standing to one side allowing Cristina and Ivan to enter his room. "Make yourself at home."

They walk briskly past him, dropping their bags in the corner of the room. Jack walks over to Ivan.

"May I?" He asks, pointing at the open wound above Ivan's' eye.

Ivan stands perfectly still, as Jack touches the wound.

"That needs stitches," he says, to Cristina.

"He will be fine," she replies.

Jack walks over to his case, searches through his clothes and pulls out a small red bag.

"Here," he throws it onto the bed, "look in there and clean him up," he says.

Cristina looks at the case.

"It's a first aid kit," Jack says.

"I know what it is," she replies.

"Then use it!" Jack replies abruptly.

She takes a step towards the bed and picks up the small case.

"Ivan, come with me," then, directs him to the bathroom.

"While you're doing that, I'll go down to reception and order some extra bedding."

Jack walks towards the door.

"There is no need, we can call them from here," Cristina says, turning her gaze to the telephone sitting on the bedside table.

"I could do with some fresh air," Jack says.

"It is not safe," Cristina says, angrily.

"I am going for a drink," Jack replies, "I'll be fine."

He then opens the door and without looking behind him, strides out into the corridor. The door slams shut behind him.

Jack steps from the elevator and walks towards the bar. Cautiously he looks around him, unsure of what he is looking for.

"John!" He calls out, as he enters.

I hear the voice behind me and spin around.

"Hi, Jack,"

He gives me a big hug. I can smell the whiskey on his breath.

He looks around the bar then points at a small round table that's unoccupied.

"Grab that table, and I'll get the drinks. What do you want?" He asks.

"A lager," I look at what's on offer, "A Stella, please."

I casually walk over to an empty table and sit down. I check my watch, 11:17. I take a moment to look around the bar. It's quiet. A young couple are sitting in a shadowy alcove, he whispers in her ear, she laughs then kisses him. From my seat, I can see the hotel foyer and the reception desk. I notice a woman standing talking to the receptionist, there's something familiar about her. I continue to examine her, she twists, points to the exit doors and then continues her conversation with the receptionist.

"Is that Maria?" I wonder.

I continue my surveillance as she ends her conversation, turns, then walks towards the hotel entrance.

"It is her."

I wonder whether to call out, but I don't. I watch her leave the hotel.

"Who are you looking at?"

I look up at Jack. He places the two drinks down on the table and sits down.

"I think I just saw the lady from the train this morning."

"Who? Where?" Jack asks, then takes a drink of his double whiskey.

"Just over there, by the reception."

"Have you been chatting up women?" He asks, smirking.

"No, no, nothing like that, it's just unusual to see her here."

"There's a lot of unusual things going on here," Jack replies.

"What do you mean?" I ask, then lift my drink, "Cheers," I say.

"Cheers," he replies, "It's nothing, I'm just a bit confused about what's going on?"

"She still hasn't told you then?"

"No, not exactly, I have to wait until I get to Heaven's Gate, to get the full picture," he replies.

"It's bizarre, are you having second thoughts?"

"No, no, I'm fine. We're halfway there, there's no turning back now," he laughs.

"Has she said anything?" I ask.

"Nothing that makes any sense. The boss rang me earlier."

"Who?"

"The head surgeon, Dr Schneider, he runs the place."

"And what did he say?"

"Just that he was looking forward to meeting me, showing me around the facility and all would become clear on my arrival."

"He's going to offer you a job. He has to."

"Maybe?"

"And what will you do? Have you thought about that?"

"Not really, I'm only doing this because of you."

"Don't blame me!" I laugh, "You must be slightly intrigued."

"I am a secret hospital in the middle of nowhere. Yeah, I'm intrigued, alright."

"How come we're meeting here in the bar? What if they see us together?"

"They won't. They're wrapped up in bed. They won't be coming down."

"Have you any idea what you're going to tell them….about me?"

"No, not really. I need to see what they can offer first."

"You know where this place is, don't you?"

"Yeah, Romania."

"Yes and no, I looked it up. Brasov is in bloody Transylvania."

"So what? You're not scared, are you?"

"I just don't want to get bitten by some fucking vampire and spend all eternity walking the earth. That would be just my luck."

"You'll fit in if that happens, you look like the living dead now."

"Fuck off!" We both laugh, "Looks a lovely place though," I add.

"Yeah, I had a quick look too, it looks beautiful."

"And where's Heaven's Gate?"

"It's about twenty minutes away from there, near a place called Rasnov."

"What if there's nothing they can do for me?"

"Then you've had a little adventure. But, fingers crossed they can."

He notices my apprehension.

"Look, at least we're trying something. It's better than wallowing in self-pity back home."

"I know, I know," I say, then I take a drink, "I feel bad about how I've been. I've had time to think."

"To be fair, you've got a good reason."

"Maybe, but how I've been with Grace, the kids I've been horrible. This trip, it's making me think about things."

"What things?"

"I don't know. That I might have something to live for. I could make a trip like this with Grace, maybe even with the kids. Before I get too ill."

"You could."

"I might ask them when I get back."

"They'd love it. You'd love it."

"I don't mean to be an ill-tempered wanker. It's just this disease, the waiting, waking up every day wondering what part of me isn't going to work today. It pisses me off."

"I bet it does. I understand your frustration. It's a horrible disease. I'm glad you're feeling a bit more positive."

"Just a little bit," I smile.

"It's a start, let's just see what Heaven's Gate has in store for us, then we can think about our next step."

Jack takes a deep breath, touches his key against the electronic lock, turns the handle and enters the room. Cristina is perched on the edge of the bed. A syringe inserted deep into her forearm.

"Cristina!" he calls out.

She ignores him and continues to inject the contents into her vein. Jack rotates, looks across at Ivan, then returns his gaze to Cristina.

"What are you doing?" he asks, sounding concerned.

Cristina removes the needle from her arm, places the syringe into a plastic pouch, stands and deposits the pouch into her suitcase.

"What was in that?" he asks.

"My medication."

"For what?"

"It is something I need to do."

Jack grabs hold of her arm; Ivan immediately stands.

"Stay there!" Jack shouts at him.

Ivan looks menacingly at him but stays where he is. Jack inspects her forearm.

"What are you expecting to see?" she asks calmly, "Do you think I'm a drug addict?"

"There is no mark," he replies.

She pulls her arm from his grasp.

"I heal quickly," she replies.

She takes a step backwards, turns her back on him and begins searching through her bag, pulling out a tattered paperback.

"I'm tired, I think we should sleep, it will be a long day tomorrow," she says.

"I agree," Jack answers.

He notices Ivan still standing beside him, awaiting instruction. His face, cleaned, now displaying two plasters. Blood beginning to seep through the fresh bandages.

"His face looks better," Jack says to Cristina.

"I'll check it tomorrow before we leave."

"Good," he replies, "Anybody need in the bathroom?"

They both ignore his question. With that he enters the bathroom and closes the door behind him. He takes out his toothbrush and begins to clean his teeth. Moments later, there is a scraping, dragging noise coming from the bedroom. Jack opens the door and looks out, Ivan is pushing the couch in front of the door, barricading the entrance to the room. He looks across at Cristina, she is now in bed, engrossed in her book. Jack then finishes his night time routine and walks back into the bedroom.

"Where am I going to sleep?" He asks, looking around the room.

"Ivan will sleep on the couch, we will share the bed," she says, confidently.

Jack walks over to his side of the bed, sits down and takes off his shoes. Removing his jeans, he gets into bed.

"This is cosy," he says, turning to look at Cristina.

She gives him a glance before rolling over onto her side and snuggling under the covers. Jack watches Ivan, as he manoeuvres himself beneath his duvet, lying on his back, he fixes his gaze on the ceiling.

"Goodnight," he calls out, then turns off his bedside lamp.

The room descends into darkness and silence. He closes his eyes and reflects on the day's events. Unsure of what the future might bring.

My alarm echo's around the room. I open my eyes,

stretch out, pick up my phone and turn off the incessant noise. Pain shoots from my hand to my shoulder. I take a deep breath. The first minutes of the day are the worst. I can feel every throbbing ache, as my muscles begin to come alive. I drag myself from beneath the covers, resting on the edge of the bed. I raise my arms above my head, bring them slowly down by my side and repeat. I feel surprisingly good about myself. I'm not sure why? I'm still dying, I still hurt, but I sense something, that something is hope.

I raise to my feet, continue my stretching routine then shower, dress and make my way down to breakfast. I enter the restaurant, check to see if Jack is there. I can't see him. I'm escorted to a table by a teenage waitress.

"Help yourself to whatever you like from the buffet," she says, pointing to the large display of cuisine on offer.

"Thank you," I reply.

I place two slices of bread into the toaster, wait a few minutes for them to pop up, then take my seat at an empty table. I take out my phone and begin texting.

Good morning, what are you doing today? X

I send it to Grace. I don't wait long for a reply.

Hi

I have to go into town this morning, meeting Susan for lunch.

How was your evening? Did you meet Jack? Have you taken your pills? Are you at the station yet? Are you ok? How are you feeling? X

I smile to myself, so many questions. I want to hear her voice, so I ring her.

"Hi,"

"Hello John, this is a nice surprise. Are you alright?" She asks.

"I am, you asked so many questions. I thought it would be easier just to call you."

"You're feeling okay then?"

"Yes, I am. I met Jack last night for a nightcap. He seemed upbeat about the situation."

"Has he told them about you yet?"

"No, not yet."

"Has he found out any more about this Heaven's Gate?"

"All will be explained on his arrival, he was told."

The line goes silent. I can feel the tension from Grace. I know she isn't happy with the situation I'm in.

"Are the kids there?" I try to change the conversation.

"Yes, do you want to speak to them?" she asks.

"Go on then," I say.

I hear her call Sadie.

"Hi, Dad."

"Hi gorgeous, how are you?"

"Good, I got nine out of ten in my maths test yesterday."

"Did you? Brilliant!"

"When are you coming home?" she asks abruptly.

"Soon, I hope."

"Where are you?"

"I'm in Germany," I reply.

I hear Lucy in the background, telling her to get off the phone.

"Is that Lucy shouting at you?" I ask.

"Yeah, she says we're leaving for school, now."

"Put her on."

"Okay, bye, dad."

"Bye. Gorgeous."

I hear the phone being passed to Lucy.

"Hi, dad."

"Hi Lucy, are you okay?"

"Yeah."

"How are your ears?"

"A bit sore."

"Do you regret having them done?

"No, I like them….mum saying, we have to go to school."

"Okay, you go then. I'll speak to you again soon."

"Okay, bye, dad."

"Bye."

"Sorry about that, but the school bus is going to be here soon," Grace says, getting the phone from Lucy.

"You go and get them sorted. I'll speak to you later."

"Alright, are you ok?" She repeats.

"Yes, why?"

"You sound different."

"I am. Well, I hope I am."

"What's happened?"

"Nothing…" I pause, "I love you."

I hear the girls shout that the bus has arrived.

"Go on, get the kids to school."

"I love you," she says.

"I know, I love you too."

The train leisurely leaves the station, idling through the Munich suburbs. The railjet, a streamlined red bullet, is Austria's fastest locomotive. Jack looks on as the buildings drift off into the distance, and the journey accelerates through the pretty Bavarian countryside. The morning had been uneventful.

The three of them dressed, ordered breakfast to the room, then took a taxi to the station.

"Cristina," Jack says.

She looks up from her book.

"It's beautiful out there," he tells her.

She turns to admire the scenery — the train sprints past tiny villages, nestled in green valleys. Picturesque chalets and Bavarian churches, with their tall, slender spires, complement the scene.

Jack is sat in one of the four leather seats in his compartment, a complimentary orange juice resting on the table in front of him. Cristina and Ivan sit opposite him. They occupy the end compartment in the carriage. Jack studies Ivan's face and posture. He seems relaxed.

"How come he hasn't checked the train?" Jack asks.

"He knows there is danger…. he does not need to go looking for it," she replies.

Queen, 'Don't stop me now,' plays through my headphones as I finish my second breakfast of the morning. A croissant containing ham and cheese. Freddie's lyrics thunder around my head, stimulating me, I feel great. The seat opposite me is unoccupied, allowing me to stretch out my aching limbs. I wonder where we are. A waitress passes me,

"Excuse me, could you tell me where we are?" I ask.

She checks her watch then stoops to look outside.

"I think we will soon be in Salzburg," she replies.

"Salzburg, thank you," I reply.

"You can see the Alps," she says, pointing out of the window.

I turn and look at their snow-capped magnificence, standing tall in the distance.

"They're fantastic," I say, as the waitress walks away.

The train begins its approach into Salzburg, crossing the tree lined, Salzach river. Jack admires the emerging architecture. Salzburg's citadel appears in the distance, standing proud, high above the city.

"Cristina," Jack says.

"Yes," she replies.

"Salzburg Citadel," he points through the window, "does it remind you of home?"

She turns her gaze to the impressive structure.

"It has similarities," she replies.

"But no hidden secrets?" he smiles.

"None that I know of."

After pausing for a few minutes, to let passengers on and off, the train continues its journey. Leaving Salzburg and its citadel behind. Quickly gathering speed, it snakes through the undulating Austrian panorama.

Jack stands up.

"Would anybody like anything from the buffet?" he asks.

Both of them look up at him.

"No," Cristina replies.

"Okay, I won't be long," he says, then strides off down the carriage.

"Jack!" I shout when I see him approaching.

Then pull my headphones from my ears.

"Alright, alright," he laughs, "no need to shout."

"Where are you sitting?"

"I'm just in the carriage next door," he says, pointing up the train aisle.

"This is a nice train," I tell him, stroking the arm of my chair, "I could get used to this."

"I bet you could. How's your day been?"

"Good, no problems."

"Did you sleep, alright?"

"I did, I was knackered, but I feel surprisingly well today."

"It's all the fresh air."

"You know what?"

"What?" he answers, looking concerned.

"It just might be. This trip, getting away from home. It's making me feel different."

"How different?"

"About my disease, my life."

"You've only been gone a day, what could have changed in a day?" he asks.

"I don't know. It seems to have cleared my head. I've been so caught up in everything, well…." I pause.

"Well, what?"

"I don't know. I just feel different."

"Good, keep that up then. Should I get us a coffee?"

"Yeah, go on then."

I watch him stand and walk away. Moments later, he returns, placing a bottle of beer in front of me.

"Funny looking coffee," I say, smiling.

"We're on holiday….kind of, might as well enjoy it," he replies, raising his bottle. I raise mine.

"Here's to holidays," I say, then turn my attention to the view outside. "What about this scenery?"

"I know, I've been engrossed in it myself. Did you see the citadel, on the hilltop, at Salzburg?" he asks

"I did, it would have been nice to have had a couple of hours there, to look around. It looked a bit like the one in Brasov."

"It did. Have you been doing some research then?"

"A little bit. I checked out the fortress, citadel, whatever you want to call it? It's a fantastic building, how did they build that, on that mountain?"

"I've no idea," he says, then takes a drink.

"There's no mention of any hospital though. Not called Heaven's Gate anyway."

"I know, talk about top secret."

"Why's it so secret? Have they said?"

"No."

"What are you going to do then? If they offer you a job?"

"I don't know…depends on you."

"Depends on me?" I laugh, "Don't blame me!"

"Then who am I going to blame?" He laughs.

"Seriously, what are you going to do?"

"Seriously," he repeats, "I don't know. I'm just going to have to wait 'till I get there. Hopefully, it'll all make sense then."

"It's all very strange. Are you worried?"

"No, no, I'm sure everything will be fine."

"You seem a bit worried."

"Do I?" He asks, seriously.

"Somethings up, I can tell."

I wait a moment for him to answer.

"It's just that I've never heard of this Heaven's Gate before. Makes me a bit nervous."

"Makes you nervous, what about me? I'm the one who should be nervous."

"Don't be, honestly. It'll be fine if it's not, then we just go back home. You've just said that you're feeling a bit better about things."

"I know I am."

Wind turbines dominate the scenery, rows and rows of them. Standing tall, amongst the green fields.

"I always think they look kind of sinister," Jack says.

"What do?" Cristina asks.

"The wind turbines, don't you think they look kind of Sci-fi?"

"I don't know. Maybe?" she answers, without conviction.

"Well they do to me," he mumbles to himself, then checks his watch.

"Not long now. I think we're on time. We should get to Budapest for about four-thirty. What time was the night train?"

"Nineteen ten," she replies, without hesitation.

"What are we going to do for three hours? Do you want to get some food somewhere?"

"I think we should, the food onboard the sleeper is…" she pauses

"Rubbish," he interrupts.

"Yeah."

"Let's get some food then, have you been on the train before?"

"Yes, a few times," she replies, then stands, "Please, excuse me. I just need to use the facilities."

Ivan stands up to let her pass then follows her. Jack watches the two of them make their way down the train carriage. While Cristina enters the lavatory, Ivan positions himself on guard, outside. After a few minutes, the pair return to their seats.

Jack leans forward, "Can we talk?" he whispers.

Cristina leans over the table, "Yes."

"Please, sit beside me."

Jack moves his bag from the empty seat beside him. Cristina accepts his request.

"How are you feeling?" he asks.

"I'm fine. Why do you ask?"

"I'm concerned….after everything that's happened."

"Don't be."

"Do you think whoever that was… has gone?"

"I don't know?"

"I'm sorry, but I just don't understand why they would be following you?"

"They have their reasons."

"But surely it would be easier to get to you in Romania."

"What do you mean?"

"The citadel… it's open to tourists. People walk freely within the walls. Anyone who wanted to hurt you, well, they could do it there?"

"We are protected within the walls. Nobody would attack us there."

"Really?"

"Yes, we are safe there."

"Is that why you have Ivan with you. To protect you, outside of the citadel?"

"Yes."

"But he is only one man."

"He has served me well so far."

"Maybe, but if someone had a gun, God forbid. Then what chance has he of saving you?"

"They will not kill me that way."

"They won't? Why do you say that?"

"Whoever it is? They believe the stories, about me, my race."

"What stories?"

Cristina momentarily pauses, glancing across at Ivan.

"That I'm evil…that my soul is evil. They believe that the only way I can be killed is by using a Boline knife."

"A Boline knife?" Jack asks.

"It has a crescent blade and has been used to kill animals, during rituals, for hundreds of years."

"That sounds ridiculous."

"It is, but the tradition works for us. We helped create it."

"Why?"

"We are not evil; a bullet would easily kill me. Their beliefs, this knife, it makes it difficult for them. They need to get close to us, to me. That, we can guard against."

"With Ivan."

"Yes," she replies, Jack looks across at him.

"Why didn't you fly? Wouldn't that have been much safer than this."

"I don't fly."

"Are you scared?"

"We were not born with wings. It is not natural to fly."

"It would have saved a lot of trouble. They wouldn't have been able to get a…. Boline knife on a plane."

"It was not an option for me, and we did not expect to be followed."

"Then why is Ivan here? If you thought, you were safe."

She, slowly, looks across at Ivan.

"He will never leave me."

I wait for the other passengers to leave the carriage, before standing. The train has arrived at Budapest station. I'm excited about being here. I check my watch, four-thirty, three hours to kill before I board the night train. My phone vibrates into life. I have a text from Jack.

We're going to find a restaurant near the station to get some food. Cristina thinks the menu on the train won't be that good, so get yourself something to eat, and I'll see you later.

I grasp my suitcase, descend from the train and look around me. Budapest's Keleti station is an impressive building. I admire the ironwork above my head, blackened through years of service. As I look around, I notice Jack and his travelling partners, standing about twenty meters away from me. They are standing together, talking. I stand, frozen, unsure of how to proceed. My heart begins to race. I have nowhere to hide. The woman gestures to the exit. Jack nods at her. Then they begin to walk away from me. I stay where I am, static, watching them. Eventually, they are engulfed by the other passengers, and I lose sight of them. I breathe deeply and take a stride forward. I was slowing my pace to allow them to get ahead of me. As I enter the station foyer, I stop again and look for them. I can't see them anywhere. I wonder where they are? I get out my phone and text Jack.

Where are you?

I saw you on the platform, which restaurant are you in?

I wait a moment before getting a reply.

We're in the first-class lounge. You can slum it at McDonald's.

See you later.

I look up from my phone, notice a McDonalds ahead of me and head for the entrance.

"Hi."

"This is a nice surprise," Anna replies, "Is everything ok? Where are you?" she asks

"I'm at Budapest station, just waiting to get the night train." Jack answers.

"It's nice to get a phone call from you," she says.

"Look, I just need to ask you something."

"Yes, I'm fine, thanks for asking." She replies, a sense of sarcasm present in her voice.

"It's about Daniella,"

"What about her?"

"What have you told her? Have you told her where I'm going?"

"Why? What's happened?"

"Have you? Does she know I'm travelling to Heaven's Gate?'

"Well yeah, that's when she told me those stories."

"Did you tell her who I was with?"

"I'm not sure, yeah maybe Why are you asking?"

"Does she know how I'm getting there?"

"What do you mean?"

"Did you tell her I was travelling by train?"

"I don't know, probably, why? It's not a secret, is it?"

"What did you tell her?"

"Why? What's going on?"

"Does she know which trains I'm getting?"

"What? I don't know?" Her voice sounding concerned, "What's this all about?"

"So, she does?"

"She does what?"

"She knows everything?"

"Not everything, I don't know everything. You don't bloody know everything. What's going on? You're worrying me now. Are her stories true?"

"Of course, her stories aren't true, don't be stupid. Just don't say anything else."

"Why? What's she got to do with your trip?"

"I don't know, maybe nothing. Nobody's supposed to know I'm making this journey. The hospital takes it's confidentiality very seriously."

"So, what's happened?"

"Nothing."

"Then, why call me? Something's wrong?"

"Just don't tell her anything more."

"Jack, you're making me worried now. What's going on?"

"Look, I'm going to have to go. I'll call you tomorrow when I get there. Just don't talk to Daniella, okay."

"Jack, what's going on?" she shouts.

"Nothing, I'll call you tomorrow,"

"Jack!" she shouts.

He hangs up and turns to face Cristina.

"So, they know you're here?" she asks.

"They?" he asks.

"Whoever they are, they know you're here with me."

"I don't know? Maybe?"

Cristina looks to the sky then walks away, back into the lounge.

"Fuck!" Jack mumbles to himself.

I make my way back down the station platform. The time is nearing six-thirty. I'm a little early, but I'm keen to board the train before Jack. A leaflet, left on my table in the restaurant, described the train as a modern air-conditioned Romanian sleeping car. With carpeted, one, two or three berth compartments, each containing a comfortable bed and a washbasin. The train, called the Ister, also has Deluxe compartments, each with a private shower and toilet. I hope I'm in one of them.

I climb aboard, unsure of where my berth is. A cleaning lady exits the compartment ahead of me.

"Excuse me, do you know where my room is please?" I ask, showing her my ticket.

She grabs her chest, in shock, surprised to see me and mumbles something in her language.

"Sorry, do you know where my room is?" I repeat.

She pulls her glasses down from her brow, studies the ticket, then points to the front of the train.

"Thank you," I say, then walk past her as she enters another booth.

The train has a corridor running along the left of the carriage. The sleeping compartments are on my right. Each door has a number screwed to its surface. I, slowly, manoeuvre my way along until I find my cubicle and enter the room. I'm greeted with a single bed, positioned against the wall, a small basin, toilet and a shower cubicle. Though the room is compact, I'm happy with my surroundings. I place my case on to the bed, take off my coat and sit on the bed. I feel my phone pulsating in my pocket. I read the message.

Don't forget your pills!

Love you x

The message is from Grace. I search through my bag, take out the pill case and place five pills onto the laminate shelf in front of me. I look for my bottle of water.

"Shit!" I say, out loud, I've left it in McDonald's.

I wonder, for a moment, whether the tap water is okay to drink. My better judgement suggests not.

"Maybe the cleaning woman has some?" I think to myself, then leave the room.

I can see her ahead of me, leaving my carriage, crossing into the next. Quickly I follow after her, not noticing a passenger boarding the train. I walk straight into him.

"Sorry!" I say as I collide.

"It's okay," I hear him reply. I recognise his voice.

"Jack!" I announce.

He glares back at me. For a moment, I'm unsure of his response. I then notice, behind him, his two travelling partners. I look directly into Cristina's eyes, then shoot a glance sideways, at Ivan. She seems confused, Ivan scowls at me.

Without saying another word, I put my head down and step away from the situation. Heading into the adjacent carriage.

"Shit, shit, shit," I think to myself.

More passengers are now boarding the train. I'm unsure of how to proceed. My mind is racing. I notice a train guard, in front of me, holding a suitcase as he helps someone onto the train. I tap him on the shoulder,

"Excuse me, is there a restaurant car I could use?" I ask.

The guard looks over his shoulder at me, shakes his head, then responds in a language I don't understand.

"Sorry I don't understand. Is there anywhere I could get some water?" I ask.

He mutters something again, then shrugs his shoulders.

"He doesn't speak any English."

It's from another voice I recognise.

"Maria!" I say, surprised.

"Hi, John," she replies.

"What are you doing here? I wasn't expecting to see you."

"I wasn't expecting to see you again either," she answers, with a sly smile on her face.

"What happened?" I ask.

"It's complicated."

The train guard says something to me. I don't understand him.

"Do you know what he's saying?" I ask Maria.

"He says, the restaurant car is that way," she points to my right, "But, it won't be open until the train departs from the station."

"Oh, okay," I say, sounding slightly worried.

"What's wrong?" she asks.

"It's nothing. I just forgot to get some water before boarding the train. I can't take my pills without water. It's ok. I'll wait."

"I have a bottle in my bag, you can have it," she replies.

I notice the guard looking at us, there is a queue of people behind Maria, waiting to board the train. She speaks to the guard again; he places her bag down and makes his way down on to the platform.

"Please follow me," she says, picking up her bag.

"Let me," I say and take the bag from her.

"Thank you."

She then manoeuvres around me. I follow her to her room. I hold the door open as she enters her berth. She places her bag on to her bed, unzips the case, searches inside and pulls out a bottle of water.

"Here you go," she says, handing me the bottle.

"Thank you, are you sure you don't need it?" I ask

"I can get something later."

"Let me get it for you."

"There's no need, honestly."

"No, please, I'd like to. If not water, then, maybe something stronger?" I ask, she smiles.

"It's going to be a long night. I might need a drink to get through it."

"Great, I'll meet you later then. What time? About eight?"

"Yes, eight is fine."

"I'll see you later then. Thanks for this," I say, holding the bottle of water aloft.

Her door closes behind me. I stand in the train corridor. People are waiting for me to move so they can pass with their cases. I walk the opposite way to my booth and stand at the end of the carriage, allowing the passengers to pass by me. I open the bottle of water, take a drink, then remember my encounter with Jack.

"Shit!" I say out loud.

Jack enters his room, then turns to look at Cristina.

Ivan closes the door behind them.

"Who was that?" Cristina asks, sternly.

Jack says nothing.

"Who was that?" She repeats, her voice raised.

"John," he replies, calmly.

"John, your friend who is dying?"

"Yes."

"Why is he here?"

Jack turns away from her, pulls the zip on his suitcase and takes out his washbag. Cristina grabs his arm and turns him around.

"Why is he here?" She shouts.

"I'm taking him to Heaven's Gate."

"What?"

"I said. I'm taking him to Heaven's Gate."

"He cannot come. He must go home now!"

"I need to help him. He needs help."

"We cannot help him."

"I need to find that out for myself."

"He must leave now," she demands.

"He's going nowhere."

"How did he know we were here? Have you told him about our plans?"

"What?"

"Did you tell him our plans?"

"Yes, I told him our plans," Jack answers.

Cristina twists her head to look at Ivan. Jack notices her look.

"You don't think John has anything to do with you… us being followed, do you?"

Cristina glares at him.

"That's ridiculous," he says.

"Who else knows we are here? Who has he told?"

"You're paranoid. He has nothing to do with this. He used to be a policeman, for God's sake."

"You have put us all in danger."

"What? He knows nothing."

"What have you told him?"

"That there's a hospital, that I've been invited to and it just might, might be able to help him."

"But they can't."

"I will ask Dr Schneider when we arrive at Heaven's Gate. Until then, he travels with me."

"You will not. He leaves tonight." She screams at him.

Calmly, Jack places his toothbrush into the glass by the basin and whispers

"He stays."

Behind him, he hears the door open and the sound of them leaving the room. He glances, over his shoulder and watches the door close.

The train jolts forwards, I steady myself against the carriage wall. The platform, outside, slowly disappears into the darkness. I take a moment to consider my situation. The door window is slightly open. A cool breeze caresses my face. I turn my head slightly, to look down the train corridor. There's nobody there. Slowly, I make my way back to my booth, praying I don't see Jack. I push open my door, enter my compartment and sit on the bed. The pills are still there, waiting for me. I gulp them down, unsure of the trouble they have caused me. I lean back against my compartment wall and stare, vacantly, out of the window. I feel my phone vibrate. I take it from my pocket and look at the screen. Jack is calling me. Nervously, I answer.

"Hi, Jack."

"Hi, John."

"Have I messed everything up?" I ask.

"No, No, they had to find out sometime."

"What did they say?"

"They said they have a room for you ready, and they knew you were travelling with us."

"Piss off, don't joke about it. What's going on?"

"It's fine. It'll get sorted."

"Do you want me to meet with them?"

"No, not yet. I need to talk with them first."

"Is it over?"

"No, it's not over. I said I would get you to Heaven's Gate and I will. Just leave it with me."

"Were they annoyed?"

"No, they were fine."

I know he's lying.

"Jack, I need to know what's going on?"

"Look, it's all good. They were always going to find out. They've just found out slightly earlier than I would have liked. But the trains on its way, you're here, I'm here, so what can they do? They want me, so they get you, end of story. I'll come and see you later. Relax, it'll be fine. Don't worry."

"Relax, I feel like shit."

"Go and have a beer. I'll call you later. Stop worrying."

All I hear are lies. I don't answer.

"John, are you ok?" He asks.

"Yeah, I'm fine," I answer, reluctantly.

"What if I bump into them again? What should I say?"

"You won't. They'll stay in their room, now we've set off."

"But, how do you know?"

"I just know. Go and have a drink, relax. I'll sort it."

The time is seven fifty-five P.M. I need a drink, a beer, something to relax me. I leave my room and head to the restaurant. Entering the carriage, I am pleasantly surprised by my surroundings. The walls are covered in an oak wood cladding. Teal tablecloths cover small tables, lining both sides of the carriage. Each table has its table light and Romanian flag. The seats are covered in blue velour, I'm impressed.

The carriage is almost empty, apart from the bartender. He stands at the far end of the coach. He notices me as I enter, I smile at him, and a broad grin appears on his face. Maria holds up her hand and waves. She's sat at a small table for two. I make my way towards her.

"Hi," I say.

"Hello again," she replies.

I sit down opposite her. She's wearing a white blouse, the top three buttons unfastened. A cross hangs around her neck, beautifully displayed. I notice she has no drink in front of her.

"Would you like a drink?" I ask.

She twists her body to look at the bartender. He makes his way from behind the bar; in his hands, there is a tray.

"Andrei is just getting me a beer."

He walks over to us and hands out the beers — one to Maria, then one to me.

"I took the liberty of ordering one for you, is that ok?" she enquires.

"That's more than ok, thank you."

Andrei fills both our glasses, halfway, with the beer. Then he walks away.

"Thank you, Andrei," I say, as he leaves, "And thank you. I need this."

I hold up my glass to Maria. She picks up hers, and we clink glasses.

"Cheers," I say.

"Noroc," she replies.

"Noroc?" I repeat, not sure of the meaning.

"The Romanian word for cheers," she answers.

I gulp down the contents, emptying my glass.

"I think I need another one of these?" I say, pouring the last of the bottle into my glass.

"Is everything alright?" she asks.

"Yeah… I'm fine," I reply, unconvincingly.

I look across at Andrei, he notices me, I hold up my empty bottle, and he acknowledges my order,

"You don't look very happy," Maria looks at me forlornly.

"I'm ok, just a bit tired. What about you? What's happened? You can't be pleased, if you've ended up taking the train?"

"It's complicated; let's just say…." she pauses, "It was easier to just get on a train."

"Your plane was cancelled then?"

"Yes, and I had some other matters to deal with."

"Work matters?"

"Yes, something needed to be sorted quickly."

"I'm glad we bumped into each other then."

She looks at me, puzzled.

"So, I could tell you about my journey. You might never have known there was another way?"

"I guess you're right…thank you."

Andrei arrives with my bottle of beer.

"Thank you, do I pay you now?" I ask.

"Later," he says, with a smile on his face.

I gulp down the rest of my glass, then quickly refill the empty glass. I notice Maria inspecting me.

"Sorry, did you want another drink?"

"No, I'm fine," she replies.

I take another drink.

"What's your plans then?" I ask

"Plans?"

"Where are you heading tomorrow?"

"Bucharest."

"That was for work, wasn't it?"

"Yes, but hopefully I will meet some friends there."

I pause, for a moment.

"I thought I saw you last night."

"You did, where?"

"At my hotel…in the reception. Was it you?"

"No, that wasn't me," she says sternly.

"Must have been your doppelganger then."

"Excuse me?"

"You must have a twin. I could have sworn it was you."

"Maybe?" she says.

I'm unconvinced. It was her. Why would she lie?

"Have you been on this train before?"

"No."

"This is very nice," I say gazing around the carriage, "But the rooms, well… they're not what I'm accustomed to."

She laughs.

"They're okay, I've had worse," she says, "What's your plans? Didn't you say you were going to visit a hospital in Romania?"

"I am."

"You must be excited about that, what treatments can you get there, that you can't get in London."

"I wouldn't say I'm excited, more nervous. I'm not sure what to expect."

"Have they not explained what's going to happen?"

"Not exactly."

"How can that be? I don't understand, why would you travel all that way, not knowing what treatments you are getting?" she replies.

I laugh, "I know I must be mad."

She looks at me, confused.

"I shouldn't tell anyone."

"Tell anyone what?"

"That it's not planned…my arrival."

"The hospital doesn't know you're arriving… tomorrow?"

"No," I laugh, "Sounds crazy, doesn't it?"

"It does. What if they can't help you?"

"Then, I go home."

"Sorry, but none of this makes any sense. Why would you do that?"

"Travel all that way for nothing."

"Yes."

"Hope."

"Hope." she repeats.

"Yes, I need something, there's nothing at home."

"But, how do you know they can help you?"

"I have a friend. He's a doctor. He thinks they can help me."

"Then why hasn't he organised your arrival?"

"It's not as simple as that,"

"Why?"

"It's not what you'd call a conventional hospital."

"Then what is it?"

"More confidential, than conventional."

"Confidential?" she repeats, looking confused.

"Yeah, the hospital, it's what you might call… top secret."

"Top secret. It all sounds very strange. You must trust your friend."

"I do…with my life."

"Why isn't he travelling with you? Is he there already?"

"He is travelling with me. He's on this train."

"Now?"

"Yes, he's travelling separately to me?"

"Why?" she asks.

I look at her, unsure of how to proceed. She notices my apprehension.

"Sorry, am I asking too many questions?" she asks

"No, no, it's okay."

"It's just. Your story is so interesting. I didn't know Heaven's Gate was so secret."

I'm surprised by her words.

"How did you know I was going to Heaven's Gate?"

She looks back at me apprehensively.

"You must have mentioned it earlier."

"I don't think I did. I'm sworn to secrecy."

I try to put her at ease, but I know I hadn't mentioned it.

"Well then, I must have put two and two together and come up with Heaven's Gate. It's the only hospital in that area," she laughs as she answers.

Jack stares at the number thirteen, screwed to the brown laminate door. He notices hundreds of tiny scratches all over the surface. He waits a moment, then lightly knocks. There's no response. He knocks again.

"Cristina, it's me," he calls out.

The door opens slightly, Ivan appears, he looks at Jack with his familiar glare, then allows him to enter. Cristina is sitting on one of the two single beds. On the other bed lies two suitcases, unopened. Ivan closes the door behind him. She looks up at him.

"So, what happens now?" he asks, "Have you spoken with Dr Schneider?"

"Yes," she answers, calmly.

"And what did he say?"

Cristina doesn't answer immediately but turns and looks out of the window.

"You can continue your journey," she replies, without turning around to look at him.

"Good," Jack replies, "I'm happy about that."

Cristina turns to look at him.

"You're happy," she repeats.

"Yes, we have come this far, it would be stupid to cancel everything now."

"I think you are the one who has been stupid."

"I did what I had to do… for John."

"You have done nothing for him."

"What did Dr Schneider say about him?"

"He agreed with me. John must go home. He cannot come to Heaven's Gate." she says, sternly.

Jack smiles.

"He agreed with you?"

"Yes, arrangements have been made."

"What arrangements?"

"When we leave the train at Brasov. John will continue to Bucharest, where he will be picked up by car and taken to Bucharest airport. An airline ticket will be waiting for him there, to fly him back home."

"Will he?" Jack answers sarcastically.

"It will be done. You have put us in danger."

"I have not put you in danger." Jack interrupts.

"Inviting someone to Heaven's Gate, without our knowledge, puts us in danger. I have explained this to you."

"I will speak with Dr Schneider."

"There is nothing to discuss."

Jack sits down next to Cristina.

"Look…my friend has no future. He was…is suicidal. I had to try something."

"And giving your friend false hope is helping him?" she asks.

"I don't know that."

"I have told you."

"I need to find that out for myself."

"That is not possible. There is nothing we can do for him."

"Then I will fly home with John."

Cristina's eyes fixed on Jack's.

"But what about Heaven's Gate?"

"The only reason I am here is because of John."

"Because of John?" Cristina answers, sounding confused.

"Yes, do you think I would still be here? After all you have told me. After all that has happened,"

Jack turns and looks up at Ivan.

"This whole….thing…journey… Heaven's Gate. It's too much. Too much to believe, understand. I don't need this in my life, but maybe John does. That's why I am here. If he goes back, then so do I."

The room descends into silence. Jack looks intently at Cristina.

"Then you can leave," Cristina replies, calmly.

"What? But Dr Schneider has agreed for me to continue my journey."

"Your journey, only you."

"Call him now. Let me speak to him."

"There is nothing more to say."

"Look, John is no threat to you or Heaven's Gate He's just a very ill man, who needs help."

"We cannot help him. Why do you not believe me?"

"There must be something. What makes Heaven's Gate so special? If they can't help a dying man? Then what kind of hospital is that? I know you take in patients for research purposes, clinical trials. Why can't he be involved in something like that?"

"Now, you are ridiculous."

"Why? Call Dr Schneider now, let me talk to him." Jacks voice begins to rise.

"No! There is nothing we can do."

"I will leave. I will not continue this journey without him."

"Then I will inform Dr Schneider of your decision. You can leave," she says abruptly.

Jack hears the door unlock. Ivan has hold of the handle and is staring at Jack. He gets to his feet.

"Get him to call me!" Jack pleads.

"There is nothing to discuss."

"There is everything to discuss!" he shouts. "I will wait for his call. Now let me out!" he glares at Ivan.

Ivan opens the door.

"Get him to call me now!" Jack demands, then leaves the room.

He hears the door shut behind him, and the lock clicks into place.

"So, you've heard of it?" I ask, intrigued to hear her answer.

"Yes, I have," She answers, then shuffles in her seat.

I feel her uneasiness.

"You're the only person in the world who has then."

"That is because…" she considers her words.

"What?" I interrupt.

"They do not want you to know."

"Know what?" I ask.

She studies my reaction.

"You should not go," she says calmly.

"What? Why?"

"It is not safe."

"Maria, you're talking in riddles. It's a hospital."

"You must take my advice, leave this train and go home to your family. Tell your friend, that what you desire cannot be found at Heaven's Gate."

"What I desire? That's a strange way of saying it. I need help, that's all. There's nothing for me back home."

"There is nothing for you there."

"How do you know? Have you been there?"

"No, I will not go there."

"Then you don't know what facilities they have, what treatments they can do."

I watch her as she becomes more animated.

"That place is evil. It will do you no good."

"Evil…" I laugh, "Maria, That's ridiculous. It's a bloody hospital."

"It is much more than that," she snarls.

I start to feel uncomfortable, as she glares at me. I notice her eyes flick left, over my shoulder. Something has caught her attention. I twist my torso to look behind me. Two guards have entered the carriage, dressed in full army uniform. They look over at us. Maria begins to stand.

"Where are you going? Sorry, have I upset you?" I ask.

"Sorry, but I must leave."

"Oh, okay, was it something I said?"

"No, but please, take my advice. Do not go to Heaven's Gate. Leave this train and return to your family."

"I can't do that," I reply.

"Then I have nothing more to say to you." She answers abruptly. Then holds out her hand. I take her hand and lightly shake.

"Goodbye and good luck," she says.

"Goodbye," I reply.

She lets go of my hand and walks towards the two guards. I watch her as she approaches them, nervously they both hold their gaze on me. I don't react and continue to observe the meeting. She says something to the first man, who then nods his head. Maria then walks past them, leaving the carriage. The two men follow her. The guard at the rear adjusts his beret.

I notice a flower tattoo on the back of his hand.

Jack steps from the shower in his room; he hears his

phone ringing. Quickly he picks it up, number unknown.

"Dr Schneider, hello," he answers.

"Hello," a voice replies.

"How are you?" Jack asks.

"I am very good. Thank you for asking. And, how are you?"

"I'm good too, looking forward to meeting with you tomorrow,"

The line goes quiet.

"Cristina has spoken with you?" he asks

"Yes."

"And…"

"Dr Carlisle, the invitation was for you and you only. I thought you understood that."

"I don't understand anything. I don't understand why Heaven's Gate is so secret. I don't understand why I have been escorted across Europe, by a two-hundred-year-old woman and her bodyguard. And as I have just explained to Cristina, if it weren't for John, I would not be here right now."

"I am very sorry to hear that. I thought you were beginning to understand why Heaven's Gate is so…" he pauses, "Well… we need to protect what we have here."

"And what is it that needs protecting? John is no threat to you, Cristina or Heaven's Gate."

"We cannot help your friend. I am sorry."

"Really? there's nothing you can do?"

"Your friend has Motor Neurone Disease?" he asks.

"Yes."

"And you expected us to take him in as a patient. Develop a cure."

Jack can hear a tone of surprise in his voice.

"I just thought there might be something. I know you take patients on clinical trials. I was hoping there would be something there."

"You brought your friend all this way, without knowing. You should have spoken to me."

"I knew you would say no."

"Then why put your friend through this?"

"He needed something. Heaven's Gate was a chance. It came at the perfect time. John's mental health is not good. I was scared that he would do something stupid. I know you receive terminally ill patients at Heaven's Gate."

"That is a different situation."

"Is it? You must be experimenting on them, testing new drugs."

"Experimenting…. Dr Carlisle, we do not experiment on anyone at Heaven's Gate."

"Then why take patients you cannot cure? You must be using them for something?"

"Those patients are treated with respect in their final hours. We do not use them."

"Then take John."

"And do what with him?"

"I don't know. Whatever you do with the other dying patients."

"That is not how we operate. It is not how any hospital operates. You should know that, and now you have wasted your friends time and our time." Irritation present in his words.

"I had to try something."

"Dr Carlisle, I understand your willingness to help your friend. I respect your decision, but please, don't waste this chance to come to Heaven's Gate. You have only started to discover the secrets we hold."

"I'm sorry, but if I can't even get you to look at John, then I will be flying home with him tomorrow."

There is silence on the line. Jack is calm, awaiting the answer.

"I am sorry to hear that. What can I say to change your mind?"

"Just say you'll see him."

"I cannot say that. Dr Carlisle, you are throwing away a great opportunity."

"I am...maybe? But so are you? Goodbye, Dr Schneider."

Silence again. Jack hopes for a last-minute reprise.

"Goodbye," the doctor eventually replies, then the line goes dead.

I'm woken by a severe, deafening, knock on my door.

My mouth is dry. I open my eyes. The single light bulb shines brightly above my head. I blink rapidly and rub my eyes. There's another knock on my door.

"Hello!" I shout.

I sit up. My book falls on to the floor. I must have fallen asleep while reading—another knock, this time harder, with more urgency. I ache as I manoeuvre off the bed, stand up and open the door. Two guards greet me, both dressed in full army uniform, guns holstered to their hips.

"Hello, is there a problem?" I ask.

"Passport," one of the men says, bluntly.

I take a moment to look at his uniform. I recognise the badge on his chest, Hungarian army.

"Oh, okay, just a minute," I reply.

I step back into my room and the door slams shut. I find my passport and open the door.

"Sorry about that," I say, handing the guard my passport.

The two men look sternly back at me. One of them flicks through the pages. Eventually stopping at my photograph. He holds it up to my face, his eyes flick back and forth, from the photo to me. Then, casually, he hands it back to me and walks off. I watch them knock on my neighbour's door, and the routine begins again. I take a moment to look at their faces, then their hands. They are not the same men who met Maria earlier. One of the guards turns his head. He notices me looking at him. I smile, close my door and sit back down on my bed.

The train is at a standstill. I look out of my window on to the station platform. I read the sign.

CURTICI

I open my case and take out the folder containing my itinerary. I spread the pages on the bed, find what I am looking for and begin to read.

At Curtici station, Hungarian Guards will usually join the train to check passports. This is the last post before the train continues to Romania, the Carpathian Mountains and finally crossing through Transylvania.

A realisation of where I am hits me, and another wave of melancholy flows over me.

Jack throws cold water over his face, then stares at himself in the mirror. He notices the tiredness in his eyes. His beard needs trimmed. He rests against the basin and closes his eyes, letting the cold water stream down his face. There's a knock on his door. He picks up the hand towel, rubs his face, checks his watch. Eleven P.M. then opens the door.

"May I come in?" Cristina stands before him. Ivan behind her.

"Yes," he replies. Then twists his body to allow them to enter his room.

Jack closes the door. Ivan leans across him and locks it.

"Have you spoken to Dr Schneider?" he asks.

"Yes," she replies, solemnly. Then sits down on the single bed. Jack sits beside her.

"I am sorry it has ended this way," she says.

"I am too."

"You can change your mind."

"And, so could you."

Cristina turns her head to look at him but says nothing. She doesn't have to.

"Have you come to convince me?" He asks.

"I'm not sure? Would I be wasting my time?"

"Probably, I can't leave John."

"Why don't you come with me. Meet with Dr Schneider. Maybe, in the future, you may be able to help him."

"In the future? He has no future. This is his last chance. If I don't help him now, then he'll either kill himself, or his disease will kill him. It's now or never."

"Did you think this would work?"

"What?"

"Your plan, to smuggle John into Heaven's Gate?"

"I don't know, maybe?"

"It would never have worked. Heaven's Gate is no ordinary hospital."

"That's why I wanted to take him. I thought you could have enrolled him on a clinical trial."

"And that is how it works in England? You smuggle patients on to clinical trials."

John looks at her.

"Then why would we be any different? I thought a man of your intelligence would understand. You cannot just smuggle a man into a hospital. Does your friend even know that this was your idea? Is that fair on him?" she asks

"I had to try something."

"And you have, but it has failed. Sometimes in medicine, you fail. Maybe it's been a long time since you've felt like that?"

"Shit!" Jack says.

He feels a hand rest on his shoulder.

"Please Jack, take your friend home, then come back and spend some time with us… at Heaven's Gate. You will not be sorry."

"Maybe?" he replies, turning to look at her.

She smiles at him, then stands up.

"I will see you before we leave in the morning," she says.

Jack looks up at her.

"Before you leave?" He repeats.

"Our journey ends at Brasov. You and John will continue to Bucharest, where you both will be collected from the station and taken to the airport. Your tickets have been taken care of."

Jack forces a grin, resigned to the fact, the journey is over.

"Okay, thank you."

"We will speak again," she says, then turns to Ivan.

Ivan opens the door, leans out into the corridor and surveys the unknown. Then steps from Jacks room.

"Goodnight," She says.

Jack stands, takes a step forward and puts his arms around her.

"Be safe," he says.

I brush my teeth, rinse my mouth out with bottled water,

place my toothbrush back into my wash bag and begin to unbutton my shirt. I'm exhausted, and my small bed looks inviting. I turn, quickly, surprised to hear another knock on my door,

"Hello!" I shout.

"John, it's me."

I open the door.

"Jack!"

"Hi John, can I come in?" he asks.

He looks miserable, forlorn.

"Yeah, of course," I say.

He walks past me.

"What's up?" I say, closing the door.

He doesn't need to say anything, I can read him like a book.

"I'm not going, am I?" I ask

"No," he replies, "I'm sorry."

I slowly sit myself down on the bed.

"I'm sorry John," he says, then sits down next to me, putting his arm around me.

"Well, it was a long shot anyway, wasn't it?" I say with a laugh.

"I guess it was," he replies.

"What did they say?"

"Just that they couldn't help you. I was wrong to think they could."

"And were you wrong?"

"I don't know? Maybe? I just wanted to help, give you some hope."

"False hope?"

He turns away from me and looks out through the window into the darkness.

"Sorry, I shouldn't have said that. I know you were only trying to help."

"I've dragged you halfway across Europe for what....? Nothing. I must be mad, I'm so sorry.," he says, continuing to look away from me.

"Hey!" I say, patting him on his back. "I'm as much to blame. I went along with your mad plan. I should have listened to Grace."

He looks at me over his shoulder.

"Yeah, you should have. She's going to kill me."

"She won't. I've had a blast. Travelled across Europe, for one last time, in first class. It's been great, honestly. These last few days, I've felt better than ever, better than I have done in a long time. Thank you."

I can see, he doesn't believe me.

"Honestly, Jack, I feel different. Being away from home has given me a new perspective on life. Maybe I do have something to live for. Being here, seeing all this. I want to do something with Grace…and the kids."

"Really," he says, looking confused.

"Really. I've been a right miserable bastard. I needed a kick up the arse, and you gave it to me. I've changed, somethings changed in me. On this journey, I feel different."

"In what way?"

"I'm not sure. I think just getting out of London, away from everything. It's made me appreciate what I have. I know I'm going to die, but just maybe, I can enjoy these last few weeks I have left."

"Well, I'm pleased. I'll try and sort something for you when we get back."

"Piss off! I'm not going on another fucking wild goose chase!" I say, smiling.

He turns to face me, then throws his arms around me. We hug.

"What's the plan now then?" I ask, "Am I flying home tomorrow?"

"Yeah."

"So, I'll see you when you get back from Heaven's Gate then. You can tell me all about it."

"I'm not going." He says.

"What? What do you mean, you're not going."

"I'm coming home with you."

"You're fucking not!" I say, annoyed.

"The decision is out of my hands."

"What? After all they've done to get you here. Are they going to just let you go? I don't believe you."

"I made a mistake, lied to them."

"So what! We all make mistakes. What number cabin is she in? I'll go and speak to her."

"No, no, honestly, it's okay. I'm ready to go home."

I stand up. I don't believe a word he's saying.

"I'll go and see her now. I know you're lying."

He gets up quickly and stands in front of me.

"It's my decision, John. I'm going home with you."

"Why?"

"I need to get you home."

"I know where I bloody live, I don't need you to hold my hand," I say, my voice raised.

"I'm not going, John. Heaven's Gate isn't for me. I was only doing this to get you in there."

"Are you not intrigued? Do you not want to find out what they do there that's so secret?"

"Not really, it's too much—too much secrecy. I get the impression they would ask too much from me. I don't need it right now."

"Are you sure?"

"Yes." He replies.

I shuffle the papers between my fingers. The photocopied sheets that held so much hope. Now it's gone, finished, over. I place them back into the clear plastic folder and click the little, round, plastic fastener, shut. Jack had been gone maybe an hour? Maybe two? I'm not sure. I just lay on my bed, staring at the ceiling and contemplating my future, Jacks future. He had explained what was going to happen. We would fly home together tomorrow, from Bucharest. I feel okay. Maybe I always knew that this would come to nothing. I miss Grace, my kids. I wonder whether to call them, let them know what's happening and that I'd be coming home. Maybe I will, later. But now, I needed to sort Jack out. I couldn't let him throw away his chance to visit Heaven's Gate. He said he wasn't bothered, but I knew he was. It was my time to try something. I had to find Cristina, talk to her, try and change her mind. Get her to take Jack with her, to Heaven's Gate.

I stride, purposefully, out into the corridor. Standing there, I realise I have no idea about which cabin she is in. I consider knocking on every door on the train. I will, if needed, but I have a thought.

"Maybe Andrei, the bartender, could he find out for me?"

I hurry down the aisle to the restaurant car. I stagger as the train sways, nearly falling. I take a moment to steady myself. Looking ahead of me, I can see the two train guards, standing together, talking. I'm unsteady on my feet. The train is travelling at what feels like top speed, rocking furiously from side to side. I approach the two guards. They make little effort to move out of my way as I walk towards them. My eyes meet there's, they stop talking and scowl at me.

"Sorry, excuse me," I say and squeeze by them.

I lose my balance and fall into one of the men. I feel his hands grab my shoulders to steady me. I notice the hands holding me and the tattoo. I look him directly in the face. I recognise him. They are not the soldiers who checked my passport. They are the guards who met Maria. But now I see him close up. I see more. I never forget a face. They are the men I saw in Paris and Vienna.

I'm confused?

"What the fuck?" I think to myself, "Why are they here?"

"Sorry," I say to them.

They don't reply. The man, holding me, let's go. I straighten my shirt, take another look at them, then continue my journey to the restaurant car. As I enter the carriage, Andrei looks up from his seat. He is sat on his own, at one of the tables, reading. He is the only person in the carriage. He looks up at me and smiles, then places the book down onto the table and stands. I walk up to him.

"Hello," I say.

"Beer?" He asks.

"Yeah, why not? thanks, Andrei," I reply.

I watch him walk behind the bar, take a bottle from the refrigerator and open it. He reaches below the counter and brings out a glass.

"I don't need a glass, Andrei. I'll just have the bottle, thanks." I say, picking up the bottle and taking a drink.

He watches me. I realise he wants money.

"Shit!" I say out loud.

Placing the bottle back on the counter, I check my pockets. I have no money.

"Andrei, I have no money. I've left my wallet in my room. Can I pay you later?" I say.

A big grin grows across his face.

"Okay, okay, on the house," he replies.

"Thank you," I raise my bottle, "Cheers, or should I say Noroc?"

With that, he bends down and picks out another bottle of beer. He opens it then holds it aloft.

"Noroc!" he shouts, then drinks down a mouthful of beer.

I smile, then mirror his actions.

"Andrie, I wonder if you can help me?" I ask.

He looks at me, confused.

"I have a friend travelling on the train. I'm supposed to meet with her, but I've forgotten which room she's in. Could you find out for me?"

I can see, he still doesn't understand. I repeat slowly.

"I…have.. a friend.. on the train.."

"That woman," he says, interrupting me.

He surprises me.

"Yeah, that woman," I reply, "I can't remember which room she told me to go to? Could you find out which room she's in?"

He looks up to the ceiling, thinks for a moment, then turns and takes a creased set of papers from the bar behind him. He places them in front of me, on the bar. It's a list of names. I scrutinize the list.

"What's her name?" he asks.

It's at that point. I realise I don't know Cristina's surname.

"You know what Andrei?" I look up at him, "I don't know?"

He continues to smile at me.

I look through the names. I find J. Carlisle, but I don't recognise any other surnames. I look back at Jack's name. It has a booking reference next to it. I look again down the list of names.

"There it is."

Next to the same booking number is a name, two names, in booth thirteen.

"Thank you, Andrei," I say.

He is, greedily, drinking down the remains of his bottle. I hand him the papers back. He throws them behind him, without looking where they land. I pick up my beer and take a long drink.

"You're a star Andrie," I say.

"Noroc!" he says, again.

"Noroc!" I repeat.

I then take my beer and leave Andrei behind me.

I walk through the doors and into the adjacent carriage. As I enter, I see the two guards, from earlier, ahead of me. They disappear as they leave the carriage.

Ivan stands outside of room thirteen. He breathes deeply. There's a noise from inside. He takes hold of the handle, opens the door and enters the room. Cristina is kneeling on the floor, looking for something. She looks up at him,

"I've dropped my phone," she says.

Ivan bends down and picks up the phone that lays by his feet. He hands it to Cristina.

"Thank you," she says, getting up from her knees.

The door of the cabin, flies open, crashing into Ivan's back. He grabs hold of the door and spins round. Two guards charge into the room. Ivan pushes the guard, nearest to him, away. Grabbing him around the throat, forcing him up against the cabin wall. Ivan feels something connect to his torso. He cries out, falling to his knees as the electrodes take hold, sending electricity through his body.

The guard throws the Taser to the floor, lunges at Ivan and thrusts a blade deep into his side. Cristina screams, the second guard strikes her hard across the face. She falls, dazed, onto the bed. She feels herself being dragged up the bed and turned onto her back. The guard climbs on top of her, straddling her waist.

"Do it now!" shouts the guard, standing over Ivan.

Cristina's eyes open, the guard grabs her chin and spits in her face, then leans in close to her ear.

"Time to die, evil bitch," he says.

He then sits up straight and pulls, from a holster under his arm, a crescent blade. Cristina's eyes widen. She reaches up, grabs the man's arm, then loses consciousness as a second blow lands on her chin. The guard looks across at his accomplice and nods his head. With that, he positions the blade above Cristina's heart and raises his arm.

I push open the carriage door, just in time, to see the two guards barge their way into a cabin. I'm not sure what's going on? Then I hear a scream. Quickly, I rush towards the cabin. As I approach, I notice the door is slightly ajar. I look at the number, thirteen. I can hear the commotion from inside the room.

"Shit!" I say, then push open the door.

I walk in. My eyes flick around the room. A guard stands in front of me, a man lays on the floor at my feet, and another guard is kneeling across a woman on the bed. He holds a crescent blade in his hand.

"What the fucks going on here?" I shout.

The guard standing in front of me lunges at me. Instinctively, I defend myself, striking his head, with my beer bottle. It shatters as it hit the bone. The broken bottle slices through the skin on his cheek. He drops to his knees. I turn to the man on the bed, the crescent blade, still held aloft in his hand.

"Put the knife down!" I roar at him.

Without warning, as if in slow motion, he swings his arm towards me and plunges the blade deep into my chest. I feel the burn as the steel enters my body. My eyes widen, I take a deep breath of air then thrust my broken bottle into his neck — blood squirts from the fresh wound, covering me. I watch as he holds his neck and falls on top of the woman.

The room goes black, and I collapse.

Cristina feels the weight of the dead man lying on her. Unsure of her situation, she lays stationary, eyes closed. She grimaces as she opens her mouth to take a breath. The pain in her jaw, intense. She focuses on the sounds around her. The only noise she hears is the train's wheels on the tracks. She waits, breathes again, blood trickles into her open mouth. She clamps her lips together, halting the flow. A noise, movement, beside her, stops her breathing. A man groans beside her. She hears him rise from the floor, then a moment of silence, before the door is opened and the man leaves the room. She waits, then feels safe enough to breathe out, opening her eyes in unison. She can smell him, the fragrance, repulsive, intrusive. The dead man's head lays, lifeless, next to hers. She moves her head slowly. From where she rests, she sees a man, bent over, seated on the floor. Beside him, lays Ivan.

"Ivan!" She calls out.

Then pushes, with all her strength, the dead man. Forcing him away from her, squeezing herself from below him. She falls to the floor, landing on the legs of a stranger. She stumbles towards Ivan, cradling his head in her hands. Slowly she raises his jawbone. Ivan's eyes stay closed. His skin was cold.

"Ivan," she whispers.

He sits, lifeless. She looks down at his clothing. Ruby-red blood seeps through the material. Carefully, she lifts his jumper. An open wound in his side pulsates, oozing blood down his torso. She holds his head close to her shoulder, stroking his hair. Over her shoulder, she notices a streak of blood, running up the wall beside her. Her attention is drawn to violence in the room.

Blood splattered walls. Blood soaked sheets, a dead man on her bed, a dead man on her floor and Ivan.

"No, No, No," she wails, cradling him in her arms.

Unexpectedly his head spasms, moving slightly.

"Ivan!" she calls out.

Then holds his face in front of her. His mouth opens, gasping for air. His eyes flicker beneath his lids, then open quickly. He stares at her.

"Ivan!" she calls again, "Can you hear me?"

Slowly he blinks in acknowledgement. Quickly she stands, turns on the basin water tap, grabs a towel and soaks it in the flowing water. She places it against Ivan's face and begins to wipe away the spots of blood. Ivan grimaces with pain, growling. Cristina lifts Ivan's jumper again. Blood still pumps from the wound. She looks around her. Glass fragments lay everywhere. She picks up a diamond-shaped shard, rolls up her sleeve and jabs the point deep into her wrist — blood surges from the wound.

"Ivan," she calls.

He doesn't respond.

"Ivan, open your mouth."

He sits motionless. Cristina pushes his head back then forces her fingers into his mouth; it feels dry to her touch. Ivan groans again, his eyes open, he looks at her with a blank expression.

"Drink!" She instructs him.

She then holds her open wound to his mouth and squeezes her arm. A river of blood pours from her wrist, filling his mouth — streams of red liquid, trail from his lips.

"Drink!" She orders, closing his mouth with her hand.

He swallows, then coughs, splattering blood over Cristina's face. She ignores his refusal. Forcing his mouth open and squeezing more blood from her wrist into his mouth.

"Drink!" she says, with more urgency.

Ivan swallows hard, holding down the liquid, then breathes out deeply.

"Good," She says, relieved.

From behind her, she hears a noise. I cry out as I momentarily regain consciousness then drift back into blackness.

"Jack! Jack!" Cristina shouts, then bangs hard on the door.

Quickly, he jumps up from his bed, fumbles with the handle then opens the door. Cristina stands in front of him.

"Come with me," she demands.

Jack inspects her blood-soaked clothing.

"Cristina, what's happened? Is that blood?"

"Please, come with me," she pleads, then hurriedly walks away.

Jack slams the door and follows her.

"What's happened?" He asks again, "Where's Ivan?"

She ignores him and rushes off down the train corridor. Jack follows, staring at the blood, covering Cristina's clothing. She stops abruptly when she reaches room thirteen, slowly turning to face Jack. He looks at her, then at the blood, smeared, on the door. Slowly he pushes it open and walks inside. He sees Ivan, sat upright, on the floor. His eyes wide open, glaring at him. Confused, Jack looks around him, at the blood-stained walls, the man on the bed and then, at the man lying face down at his feet.

"John!" He calls out and drops to his knees.

He turns my body over, then realises my situation. The crescent blade, standing proud from my chest.

"Fuck!" He says, then searches for a pulse. I'm still alive.

"Cristina!" he calls out.

She appears at the door, shaking, frightened.

"What happened?"

"We were attacked," she replies.

Jack scans the room, then reaches out and picks up Ivan's wrist. He looks directly into Ivan's vacant stare.

"Ivan! Can you hear me?" he shouts at him. Ivan blinks slowly.

"They're both still alive," he announces.

An arm hangs over the side of the bed. Jack lifts the tattooed hand.

"This man's dead," he calmly says, looking up at Cristina.

"He attacked us."

Jack feels for my pulse again. I breathe out, desperate for air.

"Come on John, stay with me….. Cristina, go to my room, get some clean towels and get the sheets from my bed."

Cristina stands fixed.

"Quickly!" he shouts.

Cristina responds, hurriedly, leaving the room.

Jack carefully examines the knife. Bloodstained and buried deep into my chest.

"What are you doing here?" Jack whispers to himself.

He feels my neck again.

"You're doing fine John. Just lay still, I've got you."

Jack looks directly at Ivan.

"I'm just going to see what's going on under here, Ivan."

Jack, nervously, lifts Ivan's sodden jumper. A steady stream of blood leaks from the side of the wound. Jack is surprised to see a scab forming. Jack's eyes flick quickly back at Ivan's.

"Just stay still Ivan."

Ivan blinks slowly.

The door swings open. Cristina returns. Jack stands, takes the sheets from her and lays one on me and one around Ivan. He stands and faces Cristina.

"What happened?" he asks.

"They came for me."

"Who did?"

"I do not know," she pauses and looks across at the dead man. "There were two of them."

"Where's the other one gone?"

"I don't know?"

"What's John doing here?"

"I don't know. He came in when they were attacking us," she pauses, "He saved my life."

Jack looks down at me, lifeless, on the floor. He rechecks my pulse. Slowly it throbs between his fingers.

"He's dying. We need to get to a hospital quick."

Cristina looks at Jack, then pulls her sleeve up to her elbow, displaying the scar on her arm. Sealed with dried blood.

"Are you hurt too?" Jack asks.

She looks around the crimson floor, picks up a slither of glass and tears a fresh wound in her arm.

"Cristina!" Jack calls out, shocked, "Stop! What are you doing?"

Blood pours from the wound. She offers her arm to Jack.

"Make him drink it." She says with urgency.

"What?" he replies.

Cristina kneels by my side. Blood drips from her arm onto the white sheet covering me.

"Open his mouth. I will feed him my blood."

"What?" Jack repeats, confused.

He doesn't move. Cristina forces her fingers into my mouth, pulls my jaw down and offers up the gaping wound to my mouth. Slowly she squeezes her arm. Jack watches as the blood runs around my lips and down my cheek.

"Hold his mouth open!" she demands.

Jack kneels and carefully clasps my chin. Blood flows out of my mouth and over Jack's hand.

"He needs to swallow it."

"He's unconscious. He can't."

"We need to get my blood in him,"

"But why? What will it do?"

"It will help."

Jack stares at Cristina.

"I have a syringe in my room."

"Go and get it quick."

"Will it work?" he asks.

"We have to try or… your friend will die."

Jack looks at me.

"Wait on me John, don't you dare fucking die on me," he says, then stands and leaves the room.

Jack grasps his bag, empties the contents onto his bed, finds his first aid kit and pulls open the lid. There's one syringe. He picks it out, searches for anything else useful then rushes out of the room and back to Cristina.

"Here," he says, showing the syringe to Cristina.

"Take my blood," she replies, offering up her forearm.

"Are you sure?"

"If you want a chance of saving your friend, use my blood," she answers.

Jack removes the syringe from its packaging, takes hold of Cristina's arm and forces the needle into her vein. The vessel quickly fills with blood.

"Now, give it to your friend," she instructs him.

Jack removes the needle from her arm and looks up at her.

"It might kill him."

"We have no choice."

Jack kneels beside me and takes holds of my arm. Slowly he injects the contents into my bloodstream.

"How much?" he asks

"All of it," she responds.

Jack empties the vessel and pulls out the needle.

"What will it do?" he asks

"I hope it will stop the bleeding."

"You hope?" he says, looking at her.

"Yes."

Jack feels for my pulse again. I'm still alive. Ivan twitches beside me and groans, as he tries to manoeuvre himself into a more comfortable position. Cristina crouches beside him.

"Are you ok?" she asks him.

He nods, then moves again, forcing himself into a seated position.

"What are we going to do? Where are we?" Jack asks.

"I'm not sure?"

"We should call the police. Stop the train, get these two to a hospital."

"No police."

"This isn't time for games Cristina, we need to get these two to a hospital fast."

"I will take them to Heaven's Gate."

"Heaven's Gate!" Jack repeats, "we're miles away from there."

"Somebody is coming to get us," she admits.

"Who is? When?" he asks.

"Ivan and I were planning to leave the train at Sighisora."

"Where is that? I thought you were travelling to Brasov?"

"There was no need for us to travel with you any further; you were going home."

"You were going to leave me?"

"We were in danger. We had to leave."

I moan, distracting Jack.

"John!" He says, dropping to his knees.

My eyes stay closed as he feels my brow.

"He is dying. We must get off this train and get him to a hospital."

Cristina checks her watch.

"I think we are near Medias."

"And where is that?"

"Maybe twenty minutes away from Sighisora?" she replies, "I will call Dr Schneider now."

Cristina looks around for her phone, then forces her arm under the dead man lying on the bed, pulling out her phone. The screen wet with blood, she wipes it against her jeans, then dials.

"We have been attacked," she says calmly. "No, I am fine, but Ivan…." she pauses, "And John are hurt."

Jack observes her reaction.

"Jack is okay. He is here with me. I think we are approaching Medias."

Cristina goes quiet while she listens to Dr Schneider.

"Okay," she replies, then hangs up.

"What did he say?" Jack asks.

"He will ring me back."

"What's happening?"

"Dr Schneider will organise our journey to Heaven's Gate. He will call me back soon."

Jack feels for my pulse, happy that I'm still alive, he checks my wound. The knife stands proud from my chest. He eases the cloth of my jumper, away from the blade. Carefully he tears the material, allowing him to view the area around the cut. A dark red crust is forming, solidifying around the edge.

"Look," he says to Cristina.

She stoops and inspects the wound.

"What's happening?" Jack asks her.

"My blood is helping the wound heal. I think you should remove the knife."

"What? He'll bleed to death."

"He won't. You cannot leave it in there. You must remove the knife."

Jack examines the knife entry again. Pressing his finger against the newly formed scab.

"I've seen nothing like this." He says.

"Remove the knife," Cristina instructs him.

He looks up at Cristina, then takes hold of the knife handle.

"Stay with me, John," he says.

Then, with a firm pull, he draws the knife from my chest. A single bead of blood drips from the open lesion. I feel something inside me contract. I gasp for air, jerk forward, coughing blood onto Jack's shirt, then collapse.

"John!" Jack calls out.

He checks my pulse. I'm still alive. Cristina's phone begins to ring.

"Hello," she says, as she answers.

Then falls silent, as she listens to the voice on the line.

"Thank you," she replies, then hangs up.

"What did he say?" Jack asks.

"Somebody is coming to collect us now."

"Where? The next station? Medias?" Jack asks.

"Yes, we will leave the train there."

"And is there a hospital near Medias?"

"I do not know; we will take them both to Heaven's Gate."

"That's fucking miles away. They need to be taken to a hospital now!" Jack's voice is raised in annoyance.

"Please, trust me. We will be at Heaven's Gate very soon."

"He won't make it."

"Then it makes no difference where we take him."

"What? I don't believe this. You go back to Heaven's Gate with Ivan; I'll take John to a hospital."

"He needs to come with us. He has my blood flowing inside him. Heaven's Gate will look after him."

"If he survives?" Jack answers, inspecting the wound.

"Yes, if he survives," Cristina repeats, "Get your things from your room now, we must act quickly."

Jack rechecks my pulse, then stands.

"I won't be long," Jack says, leaving the room.

Quickly he heads back to his booth. He pauses, before entering, to examine the blood-smeared onto the laminate door surface. With the sleeve of his jumper, he wipes away the blood and enters. He finds a pair of clean jeans and a jumper. Washes his face and hands. Then, hurriedly, throws his remaining possessions into his suitcase and rushes back to room thirteen.

As he approaches Cristina's room, anxiety grips him. Nervously, he pushes open the door and enters. Ivan stands before him.

"Are you ok?" Jack asks, surprised to see him upright.

Ivan slowly moves his head.

"He will be fine, for now," Cristina answers. Jack crouches down, places his fingers on my wrist and checks my pulse.

"He's still alive," Cristina says.

"He is. Now what?" Jack asks.

"When the train stops at the next station, we wait."

"For what? Who is coming?"

"I do not know."

"What if the train leaves before they arrive?"

"It won't," she replies, sternly.

"And what about all this?" Jack looks around the room, "It's like a fucking war zone in here."

"It will be taken care of," she replies.

Maria reads the message on her phone.

There has been a problem. We need to leave the train, call me now

Calmly she opens her bag and places her phone inside. She then removes a small, cylindrical container. Twists open the top and pours the contents into a bottle of water, that stands on the table in front of her. She places the empty vessel and the bottle of water, into her bag, then leaves her room. Hurriedly she walks down the train aisle. She stops, turns and inspects the blood-stained handle on the door. She takes a deep breath, then knocks. The door slowly opens. Maria enters.

"What happened?" she asks, staring at the mans' bloodied face.

"We must leave now!" he shouts at her.

"What happened?" she repeats, then reaches out and pulls the man's hand away from his head. The bloody towel sticks to his hair as it lifts from the gaping wound. Blood drips into the man's eyes.

"We have to get off this train!" the man shouts, placing the towel back against his brow.

Maria, calmly, looks around the room. Blood smeared sheets lay on the bed. Blood soaked towels lay on the floor. She opens her bag and takes out the bottle of water.

"Calm down, drink this," she says, handing the man the bottle.

The man takes it from her and quickly gulps down the water.

"Stay here. I will organise for us to be collected at the next station," she says, then spins on her heels and opens the door.

"Where are you going?" the man asks.

"I need to get my things. I'll meet you back here soon. Clean yourself up."

The man begins, again, to chatter at her. She ignores him, pulls open the door and leaves the room.

The train, slowly, trundles into Medias station. Jack and Cristina squeeze together, observing the platform through the carriage window. Both of them searching, hoping, for some sign of life.

"There's no one here," Jack announces.

Cristina ignores his observation, continuing to look out on to the deserted, dimly lit, platform. The train slows and jolts to a final stop.

"Now what?" Jack asks.

"We wait," she replies, calmly.

They notice a train guard walking onto the platform and a solitary passenger, a woman, leaving the train, making her way to the exit.

"Ivan!" Cristina shouts.

Ivan immediately gets up from the bed. Jack notices his face contort. Ivan places a hand to his torso, then leans between them, to gain a view onto the platform.

"Have you seen that woman before?" she asks. Pointing to the lady leaving the train.

Ivan has only a split second to see her as she disappears out of sight. He turns to look at Cristina and shakes his head. The room descends into silence. Ivan steps back and sits back down. Jack, again, notices the grimace on his face. The pain he is feeling, he cannot hide.

"Are you feeling okay?" Jack asks him.

He twists his neck to look up at him, sweat, glistening, on his brow. Jack places his hand on his forehead.

"He's burning up. He needs to get to a hospital." Jack declares.

"They are here." Cristina says.

Jack looks out of the window. A soldier has appeared on the platform. Moments later, another one follows him. They watch, as the two soldiers make their way towards the front of the train. Jack places his face against the cold pane of glass, trying hard to follow them.

"It is time. We must go now." Cristina says.

A group of, maybe, five or six policemen, now are gathered on the platform.

"The police are here!" Jack says, sounding concerned. "What's happening? Are we going to be arrested?"

"No," she answers, "Both of you, get hold of John, we have to leave quickly."

Jack stands motionless.

"Quickly!" she repeats.

Ivan crouches down and threads his arm under my armpit and around my back. He looks up at Jack. Immediately he drops to his knees and replicates Ivan's hold.

"Are you okay to do this?" Jack asks him.

Ivan nods.

"After three," Jack says, "One, two, three!"

The two men stand. Ivan cannot hold in his pain, crying out as he lifts me to my feet.

"Ivan are you ok?" he asks again.

Ivan ignores him, turning his attention to Cristina.

"Alright, John, stay with me, we're nearly there," Jack whispers to me.

Cristina pushes open the booth door, holding it open. Jack and Ivan drag my lifeless body out of the room and into the corridor.

Cristina hurriedly walks ahead of them. She stops, turns, just to make sure the two men are following. She reaches the carriage door, pulls on the handle and steps from the train. I'm dragged, feet beating onto the steps, as I'm hauled onto the platform. Jack watches Cristina walk over to the police. One of them notices her approaching and leaves the pack, greeting her as she arrives. They talk, the policeman then points to the exit of the station. Cristina nods. He then turns to the other police officers standing behind him, directing them to walk towards us. Jack nervously waits for their arrival.

"Jack!" Cristina shouts.

Jack looks past the police towards Cristina. She raises her arm and beckons them to her. Jack and Ivan drag my lifeless body past the oncoming police. They ignore the strange sight that greets them. Jack smiles nervously at the policeman standing beside Cristina. He doesn't respond, says something to her then walks away from them. Jack looks over his shoulder. He can see the police boarding the train.

"Follow me," Cristina says, then walks away from them.

Jack hears a moan from Ivan and looks across at him. Sweat pours from his brow. He glances at Jack then takes a step forward. The two men haul me across the station platform, out of the station. Jack stops and looks around. An ambulance is parked at the entrance. Two men, dressed in bright red overalls, stand centurion like either side of the open back doors. Between them, a wheeled stretcher awaits my arrival.

"Nearly there, John, hold on," he whispers to me.

Cristina walks up to the two medics and begins to speak with them. Jack and Ivan wait for her instructions.

"Put him on the stretcher," she says.

"Grab his legs," Jack says to Ivan.

Carefully they lift me on to the stretcher. Jack feels my pulse; a steady throb is still present. He feels a hand on his shoulder and turns to see one of the medics behind him. Jack steps away from the stretcher and watches as the two medics lift me into the ambulance. They quickly work on me, inserting a tube into my arm.

The three spectators wait in silence, by the open ambulance doors, watching the procedure taking place. Moments later the two medics step from the ambulance and speak to Cristina. They speak in Romanian. Jack doesn't understand what is being said.

"Come on," she says to them. Then boards the ambulance.

Jack and Ivan follow her. As soon as the three of them are seated, the back doors slam shut. Jack hears the ambulance starting up. Then grabs hold of his seat, to steady himself, as the ambulance moves away.

"What's going on?" Jack asks.

"We are being taken to Heaven's Gate."

Jack looks at me, lying on the stretcher. An oxygen mask covers my face. He stands and checks the label on the saline bag fixed to my arm.

"Is that it? A saline drip?"

"There is nothing more we can do."

"He will die if we don't get him to a hospital."

"We are going to a hospital," she replies.

"How long will that take?"

"Maybe three hours."

"Three hours! He needs to be taken to a hospital now!" Jack shouts.

"Your friend would be dead already if it was not for me. Only Heaven's Gate will know how to proceed. He cannot be taken anywhere else."

At that moment, Ivan slips from his seat and falls to the floor.

"Ivan!" Cristina screams.

Jack immediately crouches beside him, searching for a pulse.

"He's dying," he announces, then pulls Ivan's shirt up, revealing the damage. Blood flows, freely, from the open wound.

"Shit!" He turns to look at Cristina, "Check the cupboards; see what we can use."

Cristina stands and frantically searches through the cabinets. Ivan stares, vacantly, at Jack. His eyes are wide.

"Quickly!" Jack shouts as he feels Ivan's body go limp in his arms.

"Is there a defibrillator somewhere?" He asks.

Then tears at Ivan's clothing.

Cristina finds the machine and hands it to him. Quickly, he opens the box and sets the controls.

Cristina places a hand on Ivan's face.

"Stand back," He says, placing the electrodes on Ivan's chest.

The machine exerts its power. Ivan's torso jerks violently as the electricity passes through him.

"Check his pulse," he instructs Cristina.

She feels his wrist. Turns slowly towards Jack, then, with tears in her eyes, shakes her head.

"Stand back!"

Jack places the electrodes back on his chest. Ivan's body rises and falls with the resulting shock.

Cristina repeats the check.

"There's no pulse," she says.

"Can we use your blood?" he asks.

Cristina ignores him. Slowly she places her hand under his head and rests it on her knees. She strokes his hair.

"Cristina, can we use your blood? There must be a syringe here somewhere?"

Cristina looks up at Jack, her eyes glistening red with tears.

"No," she replies.

Jack surveys the architecture appearing outside, as the countryside, slowly, vanishes behind them.

Ivan lays, motionless, on the ambulance floor. His body covered in a sky-blue sheet is stained with blood. Cristina sits beside him, his head on her lap. She hasn't moved for the whole journey. Jacks looks down at her. She holds Ivan's limp hand. Jack reaches out and picks up my wrist, checking my pulse. I'm still alive. He checks his watch.

"Are we in Rasnov?" he asks.

Cristina, gently, looks up at him, then past him, to the view outside.

"Yes."

The ambulance comes to a stop. Jack stands and looks outside.

"Why have we stopped, are we here?" he asks.

"No, not yet," Cristina replies.

"Shit!" Jack replies as the ambulance continues its journey.

"How long?" he asks.

Cristina looks up at him and points out of the window.

"We're here."

Jack turns to look. On the mountain above him, written in large white letters, is the word, RASNOV. It reminds Jack of the Hollywood sign, in the hills, above LA. The letters dwarf the trees surrounding it. Then, beyond the sign, the citadel comes into view. Standing proud, on the crest of the mountain. The bright sunshine lights up the yellow, cream, walls of the buildings and red slate roofs. Within minutes Jack feels the ambulance begin its ascent to the top of the mountain. Turning sharply, the ambulance rocks from side to side. He grasps my hand.

"Nearly there, John!" he says.

Slowly they manoeuvre the twisting climb to the summit.

The ambulance comes to a stop. Immediately the back doors fly open. A portly man stands at the exit. He's dressed in a white coat, sky-blue shirt and navy tie. He has a grey goatee beard and long grey hair, pulled, tightly, back across his head. Small, round, tortoiseshell glasses are perched on his nose.

He focuses his gaze on Jack, then slowly turns to Cristina. She stands and quickly leaves the ambulance, throwing her arms around the man. He wraps his arms around her.

"Ivan is dead," Cristina declares. Tears, streaming down her face.

"And the other man?" he asks her.

"He is alive," she answers.

They both turn towards Jack. He sits upright, waiting for instruction.

"Dr Carlisle," he says.

"Are you Dr Schneider?" Jack asks, climbing from the ambulance.

"Yes," he says, shaking Jacks hand.

"How is….John?"

"He's alive, but his pulse is weak. He needs treatment now."

"Then we must act quickly," he says.

He then motions to two similarly dressed men, standing behind them. They climb aboard the ambulance. One examines me. The other concentrates on Ivan. Moments later, they inform the doctor of their findings. A wheeled stretcher appears, guided by two more doctors.

"Take Ivan to the crypt," the doctor instructs them.

The four men carefully lift Ivan's dead body on to the stretcher. Something falls from behind his back as he is moved. They all look down on the crescent blade that lays before them. Ivan must have had it hidden on him. Dr Schneider leaves Cristina's grasp and bends down to pick up the knife. My blood stains the silver blade. He looks at it, then at Cristina.

"Go with them," he says.

She walks over to Jack.

"I hope he survives," she says.

Then follows Ivan into Heaven's Gate.

"What is his, John's, injury?" he asks Jack.

"He had that," Jack points to the knife in Dr Schneider's hand, "forced through his rib cage. I do not know what damage it has done."

Dr Schneider looks again, at the blade.

"And he did not die?" he asks.

"I used a syringe and injected Cristina's blood into him."

"Cristina's blood?" he ponders, then walks towards the two men left with them.

He shows them the blade, then talks to them in Romanian. The men shout for assistance, and more medics appear. Carefully they lift me from the ambulance.

"Be careful!" Jack shouts.

The men ignore his concerns and begin to wheel me away, into the fortress.

"We will take him straight to surgery," the doctor explains.

"Good," Jack says, "I will go with him."

"No, you are in no state."

"He's my friend. I won't leave him."

"Dr Carlisle, we have him now, he is in good hands."

Jack turns on his heels and catches up to the men, stopping them.

"John, I'll see you soon mate," he says and kisses me on the forehead.

The men then swiftly push me away. Jack looks on.

"Come, you must be tired," the doctor says, placing a hand on Jack's arm. The doors of the ambulance slam shut, startling Jack, who turns and watches as the ambulance drive away.

"All we can do now is wait," the Doctor says.

Jack paces the floor in Dr Schneider's office.

Moroccan rugs lay on top of a grey stone floor. A mahogany desk stands proud by the large, rectangular, window that looks out onto the village square below. The outside is hidden from sight by a veil of cream textile, hanging from an ornate pole. Jack pulls the curtain to one side and watches the people outside.

"Please, sit down."

Jack turns and looks at Dr Schneider. Then makes his way to a large leather couch positioned at one end of the room.

"Would you like some tea?" he asks.

"Do you have some water?" Jack asks

"Yes."

Dr Schneider walks over to his desk, places the crescent blade on to the surface, then makes his way over to the corner of the room. He opens a wooden cabinet, revealing inside a fridge. He takes out a bottle of water, walks over to Jack and hands it to him.

"Thank you," Jack says.

Dr Schneider walks back to his desk, picks up the phone, says something in Romanian, then turns to look at Jack.

"Tea is on its way."

"I'm not here for afternoon tea," Jack replies.

"It may be a long afternoon," he replies, removing his white coat and placing it on a wooden coat stand.

Jack turns his attention to the four walls surrounding him. One is full of books, another, covered in photographs and paintings. Dr Schneider slowly walks to his desk and sits down.

"Your room will be ready soon. You can wash and rest," he says.

"Why am I here?" Jack asks.

Dr Schneider looks at him, then picks up the crescent blade.

"You have had quite a journey," he responds.

"Yeah, you could say that. Why am I here, Dr Schneider?"

"Do you know what this knife is?" he asks.

"Yes, It's a sacred knife. Cristina called it a Boline knife." he pauses. "It's used to kill demons… vampires."

Dr Schneider smiles.

"That is, of course, ridiculous, a ritual born from witchcraft and fables."

"Why am I here?" Jack repeats.

"Cristina is not a vampire Dr Carlisle."

"I never, for one moment, thought she was. But what is she?"

"She is special. Her race is special. They are not like anything or anyone you have ever encountered before. If your friend survives, you will have seen that for yourself."

"What is in her blood?"

"That is the million-dollar question."

"You don't know?"

"We have an understanding, but the answer to that question… is a secret we have not discovered yet. Her body does not operate like ours. It is complex."

"Why am I here?" Jack asks again.

"Dr Carlisle, we have monitored your career for many years. You have a very impressive Curriculum vitae."

"I'm here for a job? I've gone through all this for a job?" Jack replies, finding it hard to hide his frustration.

"I think you have gone through all of this… to save your friends' life."

"And now I may have killed him."

"Nobody could have predicted what has happened. Even we did not take the threat towards Cristina as seriously as we should. It's been a long time since anybody has tried to harm one from our village."

"What about Ivan, you sent him, didn't you? You must have known she would be in danger if you sent him."

"We did not send him. It is what he was made to be. His life was devoted to protecting her."

"And now he has given his life."

"I'm afraid so. It is a sad day."

"A sad day!" Jack raises his voice, "My friend is dying, and Ivan is dead!"

"I can assure you that we will use all of our resources to find out what has happened. How this nightmare was able to transpire."

"That isn't going to help John or Ivan."

"Of course not, but there is a bigger picture to think about. Heaven's Gate is more important than Ivan, your friend and even me. We are just here to continue the work being done here."

"Heaven's Gate… what goes on here? I'd never heard of it, and now it's all I hear. As far as the outside world is concerned, this place doesn't exist."

"Then we are doing our job well," he answers.

A knock on the door disturbs them.

Dr Schneider rises from his desk and strides to the door. A man enters, dressed neatly in a white shirt, red tie and black trousers. He carries a tray, on it a teapot and two cups. He makes his way over to the couch where Jack is sitting and places the tray on to the small oak table in front of him.

"Thank you, Michael," Dr Schneider says, as the man leaves the room.

Dr Schneider, sits down next to Jack, on the large couch and begins to pour the tea into the two cups.

"Milk." he asks, then hands Jack a cup.

He then hands Jack the freshly brewed tea.

Jack takes it from him, then waits, before taking a sip.

"I'll ask you again, what am I doing here?" he says.

"This is not how I imagined our first meeting to be," he answers, picking up his cup and taking a drink. "I wish it was under different circumstances. You should have flown, as we expected you to do. It surprised us when you said you wanted to travel with Cristina. I know now why you chose that way."

"I'm not the man you thought I was then?"

"You're all the man we thought you were. You have shown great composure and commitment to a cause. Ideals that we strive for here at Heaven's Gate."

There is another knock on the door. The doctor stands and makes his way to the door. Michael has returned, he says something in Romanian, and the doctor turns to face Jack.

"Your room is ready if you would like to shower, change your clothes. Maybe get some sleep?"

"You have not answered my question," Jack says sternly.

"Dr Carlisle, I will answer all your questions soon. Please, go to your room, relax…."

"Relax!" Jack interrupts, then stands. "I've had enough of this, where is John? I want to see him."

"Please," Dr Schneider says calmly, "Look at yourself. Go to the room we have prepared for you, wash, rest. I will keep you informed if there are any developments."

Jack looks down at his blood-stained hands holding the white china cup.

"We can continue our conversation later."

Jack scowls at the doctor.

"There is a phone in your room. Call me when you have washed and rested, we will talk then," he says, turning to look at Michael.

"Show Dr Carlisle to his room," he says, Michael nods.

"Please, this way," Michael says to Jack.

Jack takes a moment to think about his situation, then places his cup down onto the table and walks towards the two men.

"Call me if you hear anything," he says, then follows Michael out of Dr Schneider's office.

Michael leads Jack through whitewashed stone corridors. For the first time, since his arrival, he takes notice of where he is. Landscape paintings and portraits hang on the walls. A woman, in maids clothing, is cleaning a large mahogany sideboard ahead of them. She hears their footsteps and looks over her shoulder to see who's approaching.

"Hello," Jack says. Noticing her curiosity.

She looks at him, cautiously and nods.

Michael then stops abruptly in front of a large oak stained door. He turns the handle and pushes the door open.

"Your room," He announces.

Jack looks beyond the open door into the space.

"Thank you, come and get me, as soon as Dr Schneider hears anything," he replies and walks past him into the room.

The door slams shut. Jack stands and surveys his surroundings. A king-sized bed, with a large, carved, dark wood headboard is directly in front of him, dominating the room. Either side of the bed are two bedside tables, made from a similar wood, each with a gold stemmed lamp and wine-coloured shade. A cream and gold blanket covers the bed, decorated with autumn coloured cushions in red, brown and gold, scattered on the bed. At Jack's feet, there is a teal and gold, floral designed rug. Covering a grey slate floor. An arch-shaped bay window is to Jack's left. Dark, maroon coloured velvet curtains hang from a carved wooden rail. A two-pronged candelabra hangs from the ceiling. Jack begins to pace through the room. He opens a closed-door, on his right, to find a bathroom. Modern in design, with a gleaming white suit and gold taps. Jack closes the door behind him, makes his way to the bed, sits down and holds his head in his hands.

"Shit!" he says out loud.

He notices the dried blood on his hands, looks down at his clothes and stands. Quickly he removes his jumper, throwing it to the floor. He takes his phone from his jean pocket; checks the time, ten thirteen in the morning. He has one message.

Hi, have you arrived yet?

Call me xx

From Anna.

He casually throws his phone on to the bed, removes his trousers, underwear and walks into the bathroom. He turns on the shower, stands beneath the flowing water and runs his hands through his hair. The water, dark ruby red, streams down his legs and swirls around his feet. A single bar of soap sits on a gilded tray in front of him; he picks it up and washes.

He dries himself, examining his reflection in the bathroom mirror, every line on his face immersed in worry. He turns off the light, returns to the bedroom and walks over to the window. He gazes out onto the streets below. A central grassed area has a cobbled walkway around it. Villagers go about their daily routine. Some are dressed in traditional costume. Tourists swarm around small stalls selling, what looks like, carved miniatures of the fortress. He pulls the heavy curtain across the opening, blocking out the outside light, climbs into bed, stares at the ceiling, closes his eyes and immediately falls asleep.

A dull thumping sound echo's around the room. Jack turns onto his side, blinks quickly and opens his eyes. Confused, unsure of where he is, he sits up, resting on his arms. He hears the knock again, looks around the room, then to the door. Immediately, he jumps from the bed, throws a towel around him, rushes towards the door and pulls it open.

"Hello," Cristina greets him. Michael stands behind her.

"What's happened? Is it John? Is he ok?" Jack replies.

"John is still in surgery," she replies.

"What time is it?" he asks.

"Four o'clock."

"What? Shit, I've been asleep. He's been in theatre a long time, have you heard anything?" he asks

"John has a serious wound, it will take time to work on his injuries," she says seriously.

Jack looks at her, not sure how to continue.

"Your clothes have arrived," she says.

Michael walks past her, into the room and places two suitcases by the bed.

"Arrived?" Jack wonders.

"From the train, I have Johns as well."

"Oh, right, thank you," he replies, slightly bemused.

"Dr Schneider would like to see you if you are ready?"

Jack looks at himself.

"Give me a moment, come in," he says.

Cristina enters as Michael leaves the room and closes the door behind him. Jack walks over to his case, throws it onto the bed and unzips it. A bloody mess is squashed into the case. One by one, he picks out the clothes and throws them to the floor. He turns to look at Cristina

"Can you get rid of these for me please?" he asks.

She looks down at the pile of clothes.

"Yes, I will have them washed and returned to you."

"I don't want them, just get rid of them," he says sharply.

He removes a clean pair of jeans, underpants, socks, and a navy Hugo Boss jumper. He holds them under his arm.

"Can you get rid of everything please, including the case, I'll buy another one," he says.

Then makes his way to the bathroom.

"I won't be a moment," he says.

"*Come in,*" Dr Schneider says, as he welcomes Jack and Cristina into his office.

"How's John?" Jack asks immediately.

"Please take a seat," Dr Schneider answers.

Jack and Cristina make their way over to the couch. Dr Schneider steps behind his desk and sits down.

"How is John?" Jack asks again.

"He is still in theatre. I have told them to contact me as soon as there is any news."

Jack stares at him.

"Why am I here?" He asks again.

The doctor looks across at Cristina, then back at Jack.

"You are right in thinking that we want you."

"You want me to work for you?" Jack interrupts.

"Yes," he responds, "We would like you to join our facility."

"So, why didn't you just ask me? Phone me? Isn't that normal procedure?"

"We…. Heaven's Gate has to be very careful who we invite. There is no," he pauses, "Normal procedure. Individuals are selected, observed, then approached. It is a system we have used many times and, until now, with success."

"Until now," Jack repeats, "I think it might be time for a change."

"Maybe? But we have to protect what we have here. We have to know that the secrets held within these walls are kept in good hands."

"What secrets?" Jack asks.

Dr Schneider looks back at Cristina.

"Cristina is special. Her family, her race, are like nothing else on earth. Everything she has told you about herself is true."

"Everything? Even her age?" Jack asks.

"Yes," Cristina responds.

"How can that be true?" Jack asks.

"We have yet to discover the answer to that question. How can she live so long? Is still a mystery to us. The blood that flows through her veins, it operates very differently. It contains secrets that we have yet to uncover, secrets that could change medicine forever."

"Cristina told me she was over a hundred years old. It just can't be true, look at her."

"It is hard to believe, but it is true." Dr Schneider answers.

"You expect me to believe that? How do I know that you haven't just brainwashed this woman?"

"This woman!" Cristina interrupts sharply, annoyed. "Has lost a friend because of you. I nearly lost my life because of you. When will you realise that what we are telling you is the truth?"

"I have worked in medicine all my life. It's just not possible. This place, Heaven's Gate, I've never heard of it, nobody has. How can that be?"

"We have friends in, very, high places Doctor Carlisle."

"Who?" Jack asks, confused.

"Your government, for one."

"What? My government knows about this?" Jack answers, surprised.

"Yes, and many other governments around the world."

"And what do they know?"

"They know that we are protecting a very rare and precious race of people. And, that if we don't help them, they will disappear from this earth forever."

"Why? Because people want to kill them?"

"I wish it was that simple. If that was the only danger, we could manage that threat."

"Then what is it?"

"Do you remember, I told you I was interested in a paper you wrote on Rhesus disease?" Cristina asks.

"Yes, I remember."

"Cristina," Dr Schneider interrupts, "And her race has developed a fault in their genes, in their blood. In ten years, there have only been sixteen births. If that continues? Cristina's race will eventually die out. We cannot let that happen."

"And, you think it's because of Rhesus disease?"

"Maybe?"

"How can I help? I am not a fertility expert."

"The problem, we think, maybe similar to Rhesus Disease. Antibodies, in the pregnant mother's blood, could be destroying the baby's blood cells."

"I have no formal training in that area."

"Your knowledge of the human body, the way blood circulates inside us, is very impressive. Your paper had interesting theories. We were very excited about your results."

"There was nothing in that paper. I explained that to Cristina."

"There was, but you don't know that yet. We have people working here, who will help you."

"Help me. What people?"

"You would not be working on this alone. We have other specialists, fertility experts, working on this problem. They are struggling to understand the way the baby uses the mother's blood in the womb. The development of the foetus is different from a normal birth. Your knowledge will help them in their research."

"It will?" Jack says, not convinced.

"We need to understand what keeps them alive, which makes their blood different from ours. We cannot begin to help them until we have a greater understanding of how their bodies work. And you Dr Carlisle, know more than anyone."

"I think you're asking a lot. I wouldn't know where to start with this."

"Then, we will help you."

"You've planned all this."

"We have discussed this. Prepared for your arrival."

Jack sits back in his chair.

"And how does this work?"

"What do you mean?" The doctor asks.

"If I was to accept your invitation? What do I do? Fake retirement like you did?"

The doctor smiles.

"That is one way," he replies.

"I have to give up my life. My kids. For Heaven's Gate."

"We do not expect you to give up your life and children. Family is important. My family moved here with me. We have a good life."

"My kids won't move here. I can't just disappear from their lives."

"Then it is up to you when you see them, bring them here, go back to see them when you want. Heaven's Gate is not a prison. All we ask is your discretion and trust."

"Do you trust me?" Jack asks, "I could leave now, tell everyone back home about this mysterious hospital I have found. What would you do? Have me killed?"

"Mr Carlisle, we do not kill people, Heaven's Gate is about saving lives. You can go, say what you think is true, but who would believe you? And what would that gain? We do know you. You care about people, your profession, your friends. We trust you."

Jack turns to Cristina.

"And do you trust me?"

"Yes," she answers, calmly.

"What about yesterday? On the train, surely that will be in the newspapers today. The police will be looking for us. Are you not worried about that?"

"It has been dealt with. The authorities are working with us. There will be no reporting of the incident."

"How can you be sure?"

"The police protect us; we have an arrangement with the Government."

"The British Government?" Jack interrupts

"Yes, as well as our own, here in Romania."

"I don't understand. Does the British Government know about you? Let you work here in secret…. with no one to answer to?"

"We answer to Cristina, her family and the others in her race. The Romanian Government will do anything and everything to protect them. Your government too. We keep them all updated with any developments we make."

"What developments?"

"We are not only working here to save Cristina's race. We are developing new drugs. Treatments that could change the future of medicine. You have seen for yourself what Cristina's blood can do. John would be dead, right now, if it weren't for Cristina's blood."

"And how can that be? What is in Cristina's blood?"

"That is the million-dollar question. We do not know."

"And you think I can work that out?"

"Maybe, maybe not. But you can try. It is a great challenge."

"A challenge," Jack repeats, shaking his head.

"I know what I have told you, what Cristina has told you, is…."

"Bizarre?" Jack interrupts.

"Yes, bizarre. But, if John survives, you will have seen for yourself the miracles that can happen. That you can make happen."

"What will happen to John? If he survives?"

"Then, as I have said, he will be taken care of."

"You will take care of him. What if I want to take him home?" Jack asks.

"When he is well enough, you can."

"Do you trust him to say nothing?"

"Do you trust him?" Dr Schneider asks.

"Yes."

"Then our trust is with you."

"What about his disease."

"He has Motor Neurone Disease?" the doctor answers.

"Yes, is there anything you can do for him?"

"I think he has another fight on at this time."

"But, if he survives, he needs help."

"We have no treatments at this time. If we did? I would say."

"At this time?" Jack echoes, "But, you might in the future?"

"It is a condition we have not investigated."

"But you could?"

"And, so could you. As I have said, we do not know what breakthroughs we might make in the future. Does that prospect excite you?"

"Excite me? Maybe?"

Just then, there is a knock on the door.

"Excuse me," Dr Schneider says.

He stands, walks over to the door and opens it. A man wearing a white coat greets him. The doctor invites him into the room.

Jack watches him approach them. He's tall, thin, with a moustache.

"This is Dr Alexandru Bogdan. He is the surgeon who has been operating on your friend, John."

"John!" Jack says, standing, "How is he?"

"He is in a serious condition… but right now, he is stable."

"Is he going to live?" Jack asks.

"It is too soon to say; his injuries were severe."

"What injuries did he sustain?" Jack asks.

"The blade penetrated the chest, cutting through the cartilage of his fourth rib cage, fracturing two ribs. It then entered the heart, causing an open pneumothorax," he pauses, "Do you know what that is?" he asks Jack.

"Yes, an open sucking chest wound," Jack replies, "That's usually a fatal wound."

"It is," Dr Bogdan turns to look at Cristina. "We think," he pauses, then looks back at Jack. "We know that Cristina's blood caused the bleeding to ease. If that had not happened, then blood would have leaked into the pericardial sack, saturating it and killing your friend."

"I'm surprised you saved him."

"It is too soon to say that we have… saved him, but if we have, it will not be because of my actions, but that of Cristina. It is a miracle."

"A miracle?" Jack repeats.

"I do not know of another word to describe it; your friend should be dead," he says abruptly.

Jack looks across at Cristina.

"Thank you," he says, "Can I see him?"

"He is heavily sedated; there is nothing more we can do for him. We will monitor his progress tonight. If there is any more news, I will let you know."

Jack reaches out his hand and shakes the doctor's hand.

"Thank you," he says.

"That's okay," he replies, then turns to face Dr Schneider.

"I will speak with you tomorrow," he says.

"Well done Alex," Dr Schneider replies, shaking his hand.

The doctor then leaves the room.

Jack walks over to Cristina and hugs her, after a slight moment, she hugs him back.

"Thank you," he says, again.

"I just wish I could have saved Ivan, as well."

"I'm sorry," Jack says, looking directly into her eyes.

"I think we might have talked enough for today," Dr Schneider says. "A lot has happened; there's much for you to contemplate."

"That's true," Jack says.

"I remember when I was approached, brought here to Heaven's Gate. It's hard to believe such a place exists. All the questions you have, I had back then. I still have questions now. I'm not sure they will ever be answered. All we ask is that you consider our offer."

"I'll be staying as long as John is here,"

"Then use that time to consider your future. I will meet with you tomorrow, show you the facilities we have here."

"I would like you to meet my family," Cristina interrupts.

"You would?" Jack answers surprised, "Why?'

"They want to meet you."

"Sorin, this is Dr Carlisle," Cristina announces.

Jack holds out his hand. Cristina's brother glares at him.

"Hello, please, call me Jack," he says.

Sorin stands, motionless, his brow creased with tension. He's tall, broad-shouldered with an angular face and arched nose. He wears a blue and black plaid shirt and jeans. Jack feels awkward in the silence. They stare at each other. Then Jack turns to look at Cristina.

"Sorin!"

Jack looks to his right. An older man stands by the door to the kitchen. Sorin turns, slowly, to look at his father.

"Shake the man's hand," he says.

Sorin returns his gaze to Jack and holds out his hand. They shake.

"It's nice to meet you," Jack says.

Sorin lets go of his hand but doesn't answer. Jack looks across at the older man.

"This is my father, Stefan," Cristina says.

"Hello!" Jack calls out, striding over to him, his arm outstretched.

"His English is not very good," Cristina says.

Stefan shakes his hand. His aged face creasing, as a broad smile appears. Round silver-rimmed glasses are perched on his nose. His hair is grey but abundant on his head.

"Hello… nice to…. Meet you," He says, in broken English.

"Thank you for inviting me to your home," Jack says.

Stefan looks confusingly back at him. Jack then looks at Cristina. She repeats the message in Romanian to her father. He smiles then answers in Romanian.

"He says, you are welcome."

Stefan then quietly exits the room.

The house is small with, clean, whitewashed walls and a brown slate floor. In the centre of the room is a large black leather sofa, covered with a thick, multi-coloured blanket. A flat-screen TV is positioned in the corner of the room. It looks out of place, amongst the traditional furniture that lives within the four walls.

"Please sit down," Cristina says.

Jack follows her to the couch and sits down beside her. In front of them is an oak coffee table, with carved ornate legs and an oval laminated wood top. On it stands a silver picture frame, displaying a photograph of Ivan and Cristina. She is smiling, but Ivan stands there with his usual stern look. A small cranberry coloured glass sits next to the frame and within it, a single candle burns. Jack examines the photograph, then notices Sorin staring at him

"Is your brother okay with me being here?" He whispers, in Cristina's ear.

She looks over her shoulder at Sorin, then back at Jack.

"He will be fine," she replies.

Jack then stands and walks over to Sorin.

"I'm sorry I put your sister in danger. I did not know about….." he pauses, "this place, Heaven's Gate. I'm so sorry about Ivan. He was a good man. He looked after your sister well."

"He was a great man, a brave man," Sorin replies bluntly.

"Yes, he was," Jack agrees.

"Sorin," Cristina interjects, "He is my guest, our guest. What happened was not his fault; you cannot blame him."

Sorin continues to glare at Jack, then strolls away into the kitchen.

"Is everybody here going to treat me like your brother?" Jack asks.

"No," she replies, "We know the dangers beyond these walls. It is not your fault."

Jack wonders how true that is. Cristina's father then reappears. In one hand, he is holding a bottle of red wine and in the other, two glasses. Jack and Cristina take the glasses from him; he fills both glasses with wine.

"Is this a local wine?" he asks, noticing the bottle has no label.

"The men from our village often take trips to Jidvei. It's a small town about three hours away. have you heard of it?" she asks

"No, I haven't sorry," he replies.

"It is a famous wine area here in Romania. The men load a wagon with barrels of wine and bring them back to the village to distribute amongst us."

Stefan quickly shuffles away, back into the kitchen, returning with his glass, moments later. Cristina fills his glass.

"Cheers!" he says, smiling and raising his glass.

Jack and Cristina raise their glasses.

"Cheers!" they reply.

Stefan then says something to Cristina, in Romanian and returns to the kitchen.

"Dinner will be ready soon," she says.

"Have you always lived here?" Jack asks.

"Yes, for many years."

"It's lovely."

"Thank you."

Jack then gestures to the photo on the table.

"I'm sorry about Ivan."

"I know you are. I will not blame you. The men who attacked us, they are to blame; they are nothing to do with you. I have lived all my life knowing the dangers."

"When is his funeral?"

"Tomorrow."

"Tomorrow?" Jack replies, slightly surprised. "Do you think I could attend?"

"Yes."

"But if everybody feels like your brother? Maybe I shouldn't go?"

"You should be there, not everybody feels like Sorin. Ivan saved my life," she pauses, "that is the story I have told them, he will have a hero's funeral."

"And what have you told them about me? John?"

"Most people knew where I was going."

"To recruit another person to Heaven's Gate?"

"Yes."

"Is it always you….who goes?"

"No, there are others, but I made it my assignment."

"Your assignment?"

"Sorry, have I chosen the wrong word?" she asks.

"No, I suppose the word is correct, it just sounds so…"

"James Bond?" she smiles.

"Yeah, James Bond," Jack repeats.

"We are always nervous when someone new arrives—another person who finds out our secrets. But everyone knows the dilemma we are living through. We need help."

"I'm not sure I have the knowledge you require."

"As Dr Schneider explained, we do not know why this is happening to us. We hope you can help."

"And do you think I can?"

"You can try, that's all we ask," she replies.

Her father then calls from the kitchen.

"Dinner is ready," she says.

Jack follows Cristina into the kitchen. The room is small. A rustic, wooden, square table is stood in the centre of the room. A gingham red and white tablecloth covers its surface. The light shines through an open window, veiled by a translucent cream cloth. The room has a sink, a gas hob and oven. Reminiscent of a quaint country kitchen you might find in any Kent village back home. Cristina's father motions them to sit. Sorin is already seated; he has a beer bottle in his hand.

Jack takes the seat opposite Sorin, Cristina places herself between them. Cream earthenware bowls are placed before them. There's fresh bread, on a wooden board, in the centre of the table. Stefan carries a large, iron, cooking pot to the table. Placing it down onto the table, he lifts the lid. An enormous plume of steam is released, quickly disappearing into the air. Jack breathes in the aroma.

"It smells fantastic," he says, "What is it?"

"Papa?" she asks.

"Cartofi cu carne de porc," he replies.

"Sounds good," Jack says, smiling.

"A casserole of pork and potatoes, my father's favourite," Cristina declares, "and mine," she says to him.

He begins to fill each bowl with the stew, then sits down and raises his glass.

He says something in Romanian. Jack recognises the word, Ivan.

"We dedicate this meal to the memory of Ivan," she says.

Jack raises his glass, nervously. Cristina stretches across the table and tears the bread. Her father takes the bread from her and rips a piece off for himself. He offers the bread to Jack, he pulls it apart then passes the remains to Soren. Cautiously, he takes it from him. Stefan begins to talk in Romanian.

"What is he saying?" Jack asks.

"My father says, you are a guest in his home, a guest in his village and whatever has past does not rest on your shoulders. He says he is an old man and has seen evil in many forms, throughout his life. You are not responsible for the actions of others. We, our people, are good people, but we need help. If, what the superiors tell us is true? Then you are a man of integrity and a man with the knowledge to help us." Cristina stops, and her father continues to talk.

"He hopes your friend will survive. He knows the part he played in saving his daughters life. John is a hero."

Cristina's father looks at Jack, takes hold of his hand and begins to talk, staring intently into Jack's eyes. He then stops but continues his stare.

"He hopes with all his heart that you decide to stay and work with us. We need you." She says.

Jack pauses, looks directly at Stefan, then turns to look around the table. Sorin glares at him, then picks up his glass.

"Noroc!" he shouts.

"How was your day?" Dr Schneider

asks. Welcoming Jack into his office.

"It was fine. Cristina's brother wasn't so welcoming. I think he blames me."

The doctor pours a single malt whiskey into two glasses and hands one to Jack.

"Blames you… for what?"

"Ivan's death," Jack replies, taking a sip of his drink.

The doctor takes a seat on the leather couch.

"Please, sit down," he says, "You cannot take responsibility for that. We have people investigating his death. We will find out who they were."

"Am I still welcome here?" Jack says, sitting down beside the doctor.

"Yes, of course."

"How is John?"

"Sleeping. It has only been one day since his operation. It will take time for him to recover."

"You think he will?"

"The signs are good. But he is not out of danger yet. It was a serious injury."

"How did he survive it?"

"We have yet to find that out."

"What's going on here, doctor? What is this place?"

The doctor sits back and swirls his drink around his glass.

"The village has been here for hundreds of years. Heaven's Gate was established around 1880 by a doctor named Egon Heller. It was much smaller then but, the villagers needed somewhere to be treated in safety. It was becoming difficult to leave the walls at that time. Persecution was high. Wild tales of demons and monsters were spread amongst the inhabitants of Rasnov and the surrounding areas."

"Cristina mentioned a man called…."

"Ármin Vámbéry," Dr Schneider finishes Jack's sentence.

"Yes, she says, he was a friend of Bram Stoker's."

"Maybe? It was a long time ago."

"So, if they're not vampires, then what are they?"

"We do not know. We have made only small developments in understanding their metabolism."

"But they need blood to survive?'

"Yes, …and no. We have developed drugs that help, with the need for blood. It is not so crucial to their existence."

"That is why Cristina can travel without needing blood?"

"Yes, but only for a certain amount of time. Something in the blood is still required, what? We do not know. So regular blood transfusion's happen when required."

"Blood transfusions," Jack asks.

"Yes."

"Do you have enough blood for that to happen."

"Yes, we have a procedure."

"And what is that?"

"There are many avenues. Death is all around us."

"You use blood from dead bodies? How can that work?"

"It is another miracle that happens. They do not need fresh blood. It cannot be too mature, but, any blood, any type, will work in rejuvenating their organs."

"If that is true, then they are a remarkable race."

"It is true. You will see that for yourself."

"You mentioned the Romanian government, knowing about this and the U.K. Who else knows?"

"Most of the western world."

"How is this kept secret?"

"There are many more secrets than Heaven's Gate. We are just one of them."

"There are more settlements?"

"Yes. We have a duty to protect them, but they also conceal, within their bodies, the future of medicine. I am sure of this. We just need to discover ways of using their blood."

"To what? Cure cancer?"

"Maybe, we have, slowly, created drugs to stabilise heart conditions. Who knows what other discoveries we will make? With the right experts working together, we will unlock this mystery."

"You think I can?"

"Yes, with a great team working alongside you."

Jack pauses, contemplating the information. His phone vibrates in his pocket. He checks the screen. Grace is calling him. He lets it ring. It stops, then immediately starts ringing again. Grace again.

"Somebody wants to speak with you?" the doctor says.

"It's John's wife."

"Maybe you should answer it?"

Jack stares at the screen, then answers.

"Hi, Grace."

"Jack! What's happened? Where's John?" Grace shouts down the line.

"He's okay. He's just tired."

"Somethings happened? tell me what's happened?"

"Nothing's happened? he's fine," Jack replies, unconvincingly.

He looks over at Dr Schneider, who looks to be monitoring his response.

"Jack! I'm not stupid, where is he? I want to talk to him."

"Look, it's nothing, so don't worry. He's fine but, he had a fall."

"A fall?" She replies, concerned.

"I think the journey took it out of him, a bit, he stumbled and banged his head."

"Fell and banged his head? Really? Is that all you can think of?" she says, sarcastically. "Where is he? Is he ok?"

"He's got a slight concussion," Jack continues with the lie, "I'm not sure he's been taking his pills either, he seemed slightly confused, about where he was. He's been given some medication, to help him sleep. I'm sure he'll be back on his feet in a couple of days."

"A couple of days!"

"I'm here with him…."

"Where?" She interrupts, "Heaven's Gate?"

"Yes."

"And what have they said?"

"What have they said?" He repeats.

"About Johns condition, can they help him?"

"They're not sure, but, they have him here now. The fall was good in one way. It got him straight into Heaven's Gate. I didn't have to sneak him in."

"Is everything okay Jack?" she asks calmly.

"Yes, he's fine, don't worry, I'll look after him."

"And what have they told you?"

"About what?"

"About why you're there?"

"It's work."

"They've offered you a job?"

"More of a research position, I think?"

"And will you take it?"

"I'm not sure? Depends on John."

"John, why?"

"If they can help him? Then I'll stay, monitor his progress."

"I'm worried about him, Jack."

"I know you are, look, I'll call you tomorrow, let you know how he is."

"Okay, you better had."

"I will, bye Grace." Jack hangs up the phone.

Slowly, he turns his head towards Dr Schneider.

He raises his glass to Jack, saluting his endeavour.

The time is just before seven in the morning, Cristina and Jack are waiting, at the entrance to Heaven's gate, for Dr Schneider to join them. A hard frost has covered the ground, but the cobbled walkway is free from ice.

"Why is the funeral so early?" Jack asks while looking at his watch.

"The time is always decided the night before. It can change with the seasons, but is always before dawn," Cristina answers.

"Why?"

"It goes back many years. Even in death, we were persecuted. There used to be an ancient cemetery beyond the south wall. Anyone who died would be buried there. But time after time, their graves would be desecrated."

"Desecrated?"

"Their bodies dug up and stolen."

"By who? For what?" Jack asks.

"Stolen by the inhabitants of the surrounding villages. They would burn the bodies, use the ashes in medicines, in rituals, believing the living could use their souls. We had to change the way we disposed of the dead."

"How long as the crypt been here?"

"Hundreds of years. Our ancestors created the furnace to dispose of our dead with dignity."

"There's a furnace in there?" Jack says, surprised.

"Yes, it took many years to build. The crypt is our only way of making sure our friends and family could rest in peace."

"But why so early?"

"It was not enough to have a burial in secret. The crypt would be attacked during the service. A decision was made to hide the body until it was ready to be burned and the time not to be disclosed until the night before. It was always before dawn."

"Bloody hell, I'm sorry," Jack says.

"It is now a tradition that we hold dear in our hearts. We are happy in the knowledge the body is safe and beginning its journey to the next life."

"You believe in an afterlife?" Jack asks

"I know you don't. Scientists don't believe in the afterlife. But we and many others do." Cristina replies.

They both notice the doctor approaching.

"Good morning," he says, greeting them.

"Any news on John?" Jack asks immediately.

"He has had a quiet night. There is nothing more I can tell you."

"Can I see him?"

"Maybe, later?"

"Come, we must go," Cristina says, interrupting them.

She strides off into the morning darkness. Jack and Dr Schneider follow her.

"Has Cristina explained what will happen at the funeral?" The doctor asks.

"No."

"You have been chosen… to hold a candle."

"A candle?" Jack asks, wondering about the significance.

"It is an important role in the proceedings. It needs to be held by that of a stranger, so that the spirit of the dead may pass to the other side freely, without the burden of what has been."

"A stranger? But I knew him," Jack states.

"I don't think you did," Dr Schneider answers.

As they approach the crypt, Jack notices a queue of people slowly entering the building. They join the back of the line. The woman in front of them turns her head to see who is behind her. She cannot disguise her surprise.

"Hello," Jack says to her.

She just smiles, then turns away.

"Are you ok?" Cristina asks.

"Yes, are you?" he answers.

"This is a special moment. I loved him," she says.

Jack places his arm around her and rubs her back, comforting her.

They walk up to the small white door. Jack reads the sign above it. He knows its translation, Heaven's Gate. Two, tall, heavily built men stand either side of the entrance. They don't disguise their fascination with Jack. Their eyes following him, as he stoops and enters the crypt. Cristina leads him down a spiral, stone, staircase. He feels the warm air surrounding him, as he approaches the lower level. Beads of sweat appear on his brow. Cristina has a glance at Jack, making sure he's at ease, before entering the chamber.

The room is small, lit, only by candles. In the centre is a stone altar and on it an open casket. A group of women, at one end of the room, are singing a lament—all of them wearing identical black gowns. The heat in the room is almost unbearable. Jack wipes his brow and takes a moment to survey the room. A large stone oven is positioned at one end of the room. It crackles and hisses behind a plane steel arched door. Opposite him, a row of men, tall and muscular, stand upright, in a row, against the wall. They, too, are wearing black gowns. Hoods hang from their bowed heads, hiding their faces. Dr Schneider places a hand on Jack's back and softly pushes him forward through a crowd of maybe twenty people. They shuffle, slowly, to the front of the group. For the first time, Jack can see into the coffin. Ivan, beautifully presented, lies motionless, at peace.

"Jack," Cristina says.

Jack looks up from Ivan. An older woman stands before him holding a candle. She offers it to him, Jack looks at Cristina, confused.

"You must hold the candle," she says.

Jack pauses, for a moment, then takes the candle from the woman. She then threads her arm through Jacks and leads him to the end of the altar. She adjusts his position, moving him slowly, to stand facing the casket, looking down onto Ivan. Then takes hold of his hands and raises the candle to chest height.

The woman mutters something, that Jack doesn't understand, then leaves him there. Jack feels isolated, unsure of his situation. The women continue to sing, behind him. He looks across at the doctor and Cristina, hoping for some encouragement. Dr Schneider notices Jack's apprehension. He smiles then nods his head, gently.

The singing stops and the room falls into silence. Moments later, a man enters the room, dressed in a long white cloak. Jack assumes him to be the priest. He holds, in his hand, a tree branch. Slender, with a few young leaves growing along its length. The priest stands at the opposite end of the casket to Jack. He looks directly at him. Then begins to say something in Romanian. The flame flickers in Jack's hands. The congregation participates, joining him in verse. Jack stands silent, allowing the service to materialise around him. Two more, cloaked, men approach the priest, bow, then position themselves either side of the furnace door, taking hold of a handle each. The priest looks towards the two men raises his hands in the air and calls out. The two men, holding the furnace handles, pull open the two steel doors. The heat escapes, roaring, devouring the room. Four more, hooded, men approach the casket. The priest places the branch he is holding, into the coffin. Laying it onto the body of Ivan. Jack gazes at the open fire. Flames lick out, from the opening, the heat, now, becoming unbearable in the room. The four men take hold of the coffin and walk it to the oven door. The priest calls out, and the women behind Jack begin to sing again. The men place the casket at the opening to the furnace. Then, slowly and carefully, they glide the coffin into the blazing flames. Jack watches, in bewilderment, as it catches fire. The four men step away from the opening, and the steel doors are forced shut. The singing stops, one of the women leaves the congregation and shuffles towards Jack. In her hand, a small silver cup. She places it over the flickering candle in Jack's hands, extinguishing the flame. The priest turns to the room, holds out his arms and calls out. Everyone repeats his words. There is a moment of silence, then the priest turns and walks out of the room. People begin to follow him from the crypt. Jack looks across at Cristina. She has tears running down her cheeks. He stands there, waiting, for more instructions. Dr Schneider walks over to him,

"Well done," he says.

"For what?" Jack answers, "I did nothing."

"You did more than you think. Ivan is now on his journey to a new life. Everybody here saw him leave in peace. Come, now we must celebrate his life."

Dr Schneider takes Jack by the arm and walks him over to where Cristina waits, patiently.

"Are you alright?" He asks, noticing her red, glazed eyes.

"Yes," she says, calmly.

The priest, slowly, guides the congregation across the marketplace, to a house, just minutes from the crypt.

"We will now eat, drink and celebrate Ivan's life," Dr Schneider says to Jack. "This happens in your country?"

"Yes, it does," he replies.

The three of them enter the house. Cristina's father and brother are there to greet them. Stefan walks over, handing them each a glass of red wine. He then kisses his daughter, on the forehead and smiles.

The room has a similar feel and décor to Cristina's house. A table has been positioned against one wall and is laden with food. People start to gather around the table and begin to choose their food.

"Would you like some food?" Cristina asks Jack.

"It's a little early. I'm not hungry."

"This is not about you. This is all for Ivan. We must celebrate his life," she answers sternly.

"I didn't mean to offend you," he replies, sensing her frustration.

"The food must be eaten. It is tradition," the Dr interjects.

Handing Jack a plate. The two men make their way over to the food.

People bustle around the table, eager to fill their plates. Jack, nervously, chooses two cakes and a biscuit. Then leaves the table. The doctor joins him.

"Where is Cristina?" he asks, looking around the room.

"She is speaking with Ivan's mother," he replies, gesturing over to a corner of the room, where two women sit.

Both are dressed in black dresses; they don't look much older than Jack. Cristina is in an embrace with one of them. She says something to her. Then both women look across at Jack. Cristina beckons him over. He stands as if frozen to slate floor.

"Go," the doctor instructs him.

Nervously, he approaches the women.

"Hello," Jack holds out his hand.

Ivan's mother grasps Jack's hand with both of hers.

"Hello," she replies.

"You speak English?" he asks.

"Yes."

"I'm sorry about your son. He was a good man."

"He was a great man. He will be remembered as a soldier, who died for a great cause," she replies.

Jack smiles in agreement.

"I do not blame you," she says calmly, "I do not blame Cristina. Ivan devoted his life to Heaven's Gate, to Cristina. It was his way. His way to die."

Jack is surprised by her bluntness.

"He never left her side; he was a brave and courageous man," Jack says.

"I hear your friend was brave too?"

"John!" he replies, surprised.

"Yes, how is he?"

"I don't know?"

"But he survived?"

"Yes, well, he is alive right now. I think?"

"The doctors will look after him. I wish him well." She says.

"Thank you."

"And you?"

"Me?"

"What are you going to do?"

Jack doesn't know how to reply.

"We all know why you are here. We all know Cristina travelled a long way to find you…" she pauses, "Will you stay?"

"I don't know?" he replies, cautiously.

"I expect all of this…" she gestures around the room, "Has come as a shock to you."

"You could say that, yes."

"We are good people. You will have a good life here."

"I can see that."

"Do you have a family?" she asks.

"Yes, two daughters."

"And a wife?"

"No, divorced."

"Then, the decision lies with your children."

"And my friends."

"Friends can be found anywhere, but family, you have only one family."

"Maybe?"

She looks at him with an intensity in her face.

"I hope you stay."

"Well, thank you."

They are interrupted by an older man, who pushes his way past Jack and hugs Ivan's mother. He speaks to her in Romanian, animated in his movement.

"I'll leave you to your friends," Jack says, "It was lovely to meet you."

"It was nice to meet you," she replies.

Cristina and Jack, walk back over to Dr Schneider, who is talking with another man.

"She's a strong woman," Jack says to Cristina.

"She has to be; we all have to be."

"Who are all these people? Family?" Jack asks.

"Family, friends, people will come and go throughout the day, paying their respects."

Jack notices her expression change as she looks around the room. "Are you ok for a moment?" she asks

"Yes, why?"

"I just need to speak to someone." She replies, then leaves Jack.

He watches her walk across the room to a group of women. They embrace her as she arrives.

Jack places his drink down, onto a small table then takes a bite of one of the cakes.

"Do you like it?"

A man stands beside him. Jack swallows hard so that he can speak.

"Yes, it's lovely."

"It's called Kolachei. A sort of fruit bread that symbolises the sins of the dead," he says, then holds out his hand. "Hello, my name is David, David James."

"Hello, David…" Jack wipes his hand on his trousers, then shakes his hand, "m

My name is Jack, Jack Carlisle."

"I know who you are, Dr Carlisle. It's nice to meet you finally."

"You know who I am?" he ponders.

"I think everybody in this room, knows who you are."

"Do they? Is that a good thing…?" he pauses "Or a bad thing?"

"These are good people," David smiles, "They mean you no harm."

"I feel strange being here."

"It will take a while to adjust."

"Do you work here?"

"Yes."

"At Heaven's Gate?"

"Yes."

"Are you a doctor here."

"Yes."

"In what capacity?"

"The hospital does not operate in that way."

"What do you mean?"

"I have an area of expertise, but we work together as one."

"And how long have you worked here?"

"This is my seventh year."

"Was your interview similar to mine?"

"Maybe, not as dramatic though, but yes, similar."

"Were you shocked by what you found here."

"Of course, I didn't believe it could exist, this... Heaven's Gate...."

"And Cristina, her race."

"Well...That's the reason we are here. I'm not sure how much you already know, but what we have here is very complex. It will take time to fully understand why these people are, who they are."

"What do you know?" Jack asks,

David smiles.

"Right now, not enough."

"How has it been... adapting to living out here? Was, it worth giving up your life?"

"I wouldn't say I gave up my life. This is my life."

"Did your family come with you?"

"Yes, they have a good life here. Though the winters can be harsh."

"Hi David," Dr Schneider, joins them.

"Otto," he replies, shaking his hand.

"You've been introduced?" Dr Schneider asks David.

"Yes, we were just talking," he replies.

Cristina walks back to join them.

"Hi David," she says.

"Cristina!" He replies, then hugs her.

"How are you?" he asks, looking solemnly at her.

"I'm okay," she replies, unconvincingly.

"How was the funeral?"

"It was beautiful," she replies, a tear rolls down her cheek, "Jack held the candle."

"It was an honour to be there," Jack replies.

"It is all part of a long tradition. The spirt, of the deceased, has to have no obstructions on its way to the afterlife. A stranger holds a candle, to aid the spirit on its way."

"What was that, that the priest placed into the coffin?" Jack asks.

"It symbolises the tree of life. The passage from this world to the other."

"He has gone, but we will always remember him," Cristina states.

I open my eyes. I can't focus, my vision blurred. A beep echoes around me. My mouth is dry. I blink then take a deep breath; my chest feels tight. A pain engulfs me, streaming around my body. I clench my teeth together, waiting for the torture to subside. I hear myself cry out, then fade into a deep sleep.

"**Hi, Jack,** come in," Dr Schneider says. Then invites him into his office.

"You wanted to see me?" Jack asks.

"Yes."

"Is it about John? Is he ok?"

"I'm pleased to tell you that your friend opened his eyes."

"When?" Jack interrupts.

"This morning, when were at the funeral."

"Great! Can I see him?"

"He's sedated, but yes. I will take you to him now."

"Let's go," Jack says, excitedly.

"Before we go."

"Yes?"

"There have been several developments that I would like to share with you."

"What developments?" Jack answers suspiciously.

"John is recovering from his injury amazingly well, for reasons we do not understand. As you know, a knife wound to the chest is normally fatal."

"You think it was Cristina's blood?" Jack asks.

"It has to be the reason for his remarkable recovery. But we have tried before, to save lives, purely with blood and it has not worked."

"So why has it worked on John?"

"I wish I knew. From the tests, we've made so far. It appears that Johns blood reacted well to receiving Cristina's."

"And that's unusual?"

"Yes, very. John's blood has accepted Cristina's, without any negative side effects, well so far. Whereas Ivan reacted as we expected."

"He rejected it?"

"Yes."

"But, I injected John. With her blood. Cristina says she tried to get Ivan to drink her blood. Maybe if I had injected Ivan, he would be alive now?"

"If only it were that easy. There has been very little success in using their blood that way."

"Then what has happened?"

"We have taken samples of Johns blood. It is amazing what we have found. Cristina's blood cells have combined with John's, in a way we have never seen before."

"Combined." Jack repeats, confused. "Sorry I don't understand."

"We don't either… at this time. We can only assume that Johns body, John's blood, accepted Cristina's, in a similar way that a body might accept a new heart or a kidney."

"Similar to a transplant?"

"Yes, but the reasons why? We do not know?"

"So, what are you saying?"

"We know John has Motor Neurones Disease."

"Do you think that had something to do with it?"

"MND is a disease that very little is known about. It is difficult to treat, which makes our results even more interesting."

"You think the MND had something to do with it?"

"It is too soon to say, but it is an interesting development. We also took some samples of John's muscle tissue."

"You did what?" Jack asks, unsure whether he should be annoyed.

"He is fine, do not worry. The results were even more astounding."

"What results?"

"It appears that there has been some reconstruction of the muscle fibres."

"What! That can't be. He's only been here a day."

"I know it's quite amazing."

"Are you suggesting he could be cured… from his MND?"

"It is far too soon to say that. It is another exciting development. We will need to observe his recovery very closely."

"But that's great news."

"It is, but we cannot say he is cured. We do not know if he will fully recover from his injuries. He may have some side effects that take longer to appear. There are so many pieces of the puzzle yet to be put in place."

"But you will look after him."

"We will. It appears you have succeeded in admitting your friend to Heaven's Gate. We would like John to stay with us while we monitor his recovery."

"You would like him to stay… or he has to stay?" Jack asks.

"Both."

"I hope you won't use John as a bargaining tool to get me to stay."

"We wouldn't dream of it. I only hope that this discovery stimulates your interest, nothing more."

The two doctors observe each other across the room.

"Now, would you like to see your friend?" Dr Schneider says.

Jack follows the doctor down a long, whitewashed, stone corridor. He stops as they reach the top of a spiral staircase.

"Please, be careful, these steps can be quite dangerous," he says to Jack with a smile.

When they reach the bottom, Dr Schneider stops and turns to Jack.

"Welcome to Heaven's Gate," he says.

Jack looks on in amazement at the sight before his eyes. A large cavern opens up before him. Bright lights hang, suspended, from a network of metalwork, secured to the stone ceiling, illuminating the great hall.

"What is this?" Jack asks.

"An example of man's ability to work with natures beauty," the doctor replies.

Jack cannot believe his eyes, but the sound, familiar, unmistakable, is that of a working hospital. Nurses and doctors, busy themselves around him.

"Come, follow me," Dr Schneider says.

Jack advances through the open cavity. Either side of him, he can see more tunnels, leading off into the distance.

"Where do they lead?" he asks.

"To more wards," the doctor responds, calmly.

"This is amazing!" Jack states.

"I'm glad you think so. This is the main ward. Where most of our patients are treated."

Dr Schneider points to a large open cave to Jacks left, housing maybe thirty beds. Patients lay calmly, some of them sleeping, some are being examined. It all feels very familiar to Jack, and yet, remarkable. The doctor says hello to a nurse who passes by. Jack smiles at her. They continue to walk through the brightly lit underground chamber.

"How is this possible?"

"At one time, what you see here, were just caves — buried below the walls of the citadel. Who made them? Or why? Is unclear."

"Like a lot of things," Jack interjects.

"Yes, like a lot of things," the doctor repeats, with a sly smile.

"They were discovered by the Gepids, hundreds of years ago. Without these caves, Cristina's race would have been destroyed. They have kept them safe for many years, and we hope to continue that tradition."

"Is the air alright down here?" Jack asks.

"Yes, another wonder of Heaven's Gate. The air moves freely through the caves due to its design."

Jack looks at him, confused.

"I am not an engineer, so the concept is alien to me too. We converted the caves into this great hospital, many years ago. It did not look like this when I arrived. We have worked hard to achieve this."

The doctor then stops abruptly.

"Further down there," he gestures, "We have our research facility. I will show you around later."

Jack gazes into the long corridor ahead of him.

"But here are our isolation rooms."

"Isolation rooms?"

"Intensive care sounds better," he replies.

The two of them enter the ward through stainless steel swinging doors. The tunnel is smaller, maybe four meters in height and width. Glass windows run parallel, either side of the corridor. As they walk down the walkway, Jack looks into the rooms, every room occupied with a patient.

"It's busy down here."

"This is where we treat the villagers."

Jack stops and studies the patient beyond the glass divider. A man lies in a bed, his arm connected, by a tube, to a clear, sack of blood.

"Is he having a blood transfusion?"

The doctor stops and gazes through the window.

"Not exactly… but yes, you could say that. They need blood, that is one thing we know, without it, they die. Food and water alone are not enough."

"And do you have enough blood? It is a rare commodity back in England."

"We have a constant supply."

"From where?"

The doctor slowly turns to look at Jack.

"Wars are happening all over the world Dr Carlisle, dead bodies aren't hard to find."

"You're joking… right?" Jack looks at Dr Schneider.

"I wish I were, but we cannot prevent wars," he answers, then continues to walk on.

Jack looks again at the man, then tracks the doctor.

"Remember, your friend has had a serious injury," Dr Schneider says, as he stops, abruptly. Then turns to Jack and pushes open the large, white, door in front of him.

"Jack!" I call out as he enters the room.

"John!" Jack answers, hurriedly making his way towards me.

He takes hold of my hand and kisses my forehead.

"What's going on? Where am I?" I ask.

Jack looks around at Dr Schneider, then back at me.

"You've made it. You're in Heaven's Gate," he replies, smiling.

Printed in Great Britain
by Amazon

84357092R00192